A Starseed Odyssey

An Adventure of the Realms

A Starseed Odyssey

An Adventure of the Realms

Lisa Snopek

Stellium Ltd

A Starseed Odyssey

Published in 2023 by Stellium Flame,
an imprint of Stellium Ltd
Plymouth, Devon UK
Tel: +44 (0)1752 367 300

British Library Cataloguing in Publication Data:
A catalogue record for this book is available
from The British Library

Cover design and illustrations:
copyright © 2023 Rebecca Mann

ISBN: 978-1-912358-08-3

About the Author

Lisa Snopek was born in Plymouth, England.
Having moved around the country due to family military postings, she returned to Plymouth at the age of fourteen and has happily settled in this beautiful part of Devon with her husband, three children and dog, Frieda. Lisa's hereditary gypsy bloodline has always influenced her life, although Lisa didn't discover this link until a few years ago.

In 2017, Lisa suffered from a sudden cardiac arrest (SCA) having just arrived in London. She was given CPR by her husband until the paramedics arrived. They defibrillated and resuscitated Lisa before blue-lighting her to St Georges Hospital in Tooting. There, Lisa's heart experienced further episodes of quivering as opposed to beating and she had to be defibrillated time and again. She remained in hospital for a month.
Lisa miraculously survived her ordeal. Her recuperation was gradual, and she still faces daily challenges. With the support of medical professionals, she can manage her condition and live the life she chooses.
It took six years of extensive scientific genetic testing and screening to discover her underlying condition. Lisa has been diagnosed with a genetic abnormality, catecholaminergic polymorphic ventricular tachycardia (CPVT). Thankfully, Lisa now knows the reason for her SCA, and members of her immediate family can be screened.

One of the many side effects of Lisa's SCA was that she was unable to read and write. Reading was one of her favourite pastimes. Undeterred, Lisa was determined to reteach herself. In order to improve her skills, Lisa began writing about her near-death experience. Adding her previous spiritual adventures into the mix she inadvertently realised she had the makings of her first novel, *A Starseed Odyssey*.
Subsequently, Lisa wrote a series of articles for an online spiritual publication, *'The Supernatural Magazine.'*
Fast forward two years, to 2019, Lisa was able to read her first book.

A Starseed Odyssey

Since her return from hospital, Lisa has qualified as a Reiki Master Teacher and Hypnotherapist. She owns a holistic business as well as working part time in the education sector. She is a qualified Civil Celebrant and regularly organises charity events, all of which adds to the rich tapestry of her life.
Since that fateful day in 2017, Lisa has and continues to have many 'firsts.' She continues to study, write, read and cherish each new day.

lisasnopekwriting@gmail.com

Dedicated with love to
Myles Junior Christie
19.12.2007 – 24.05.2023

Acknowledgement

I am very glad to have been given a second chance at life.
I wish to thank everyone who was involved in my chain of survival.
Thank you to my husband and the emergency services for administering CPR. Thank you to the London Ambulance Service for their advice over the telephone, explaining what to do, until the ambulance arrived on scene. Thank you to the ambulance crew who resuscitated me and rushed me to St George's Hospital, Tooting, London.
Thank you for your life saving skills at St George's, for your care and for your preservation of life.
So many teams were involved in protecting and saving me. Thank you to the intensive care nurses, I had the pleasure of you coming to see me when I had been transferred to the cardiac unit and I was finally awake. I remember.
I remember you saying to me, "You are so lucky," and at the time it was too much for me to understand, but you were absolutely right. Yes, I was so lucky, and I make the most of every single day that has been afforded to me since.
Thank you to my surgeon who came in to work on his day off, specifically so he could fit my ICD device. Thank you to the lovely ladies who served me food every day, made me drinks and began to nourish my broken and bruised body.
My recovery was a vast team effort from my anaesthetist to my porters.
Thank you to the NHS, my treatment cost thousands of pounds and I am humbled and extremely grateful.
Thank you just does not seem enough.
I wish to make a heartfelt mention to my editor Ruth Hocking. Thank you for your dedication, your time and your hard work. Thank you for wanting

to make this publication a success and a reality as much as me. Thank you for bringing your logical mind to balance my creativity. Thank you for keeping me grounded. Having you onboard spurred me on, encouraged me to keep going with the project. I am so lucky to have such a supportive, lifelong friend.

My friend, Rebecca Mann, our relationship has been a shorter one, but it really does genuinely feel like we have known each other so much longer. Thank you for your amazing front cover design and your breath-taking illustrations. We knew we had made a connection for a reason.

The three of us make a positive and creative team. I count myself blessed having worked with you both on making my dreams become a reality. I look forward to our future projects together.

I will live life every day knowing that I will always be enough.

Contents

Contents

A Starseed Odyssey

Prologue

There are many different Beings in the astral world, from tiny Ondines to enormous Giants. When the astral world is in balance, all Beings live harmoniously.

Maya is a Starseed, a type of Lightworker. She is responsible for ensuring this balance is maintained. She has been taught by the esteemed, ageless Eucele, an Avian humanoid; half bird, half man.

Maya and her best friend Lynk have known each other forever and, in true rebellious style, often escape from Lynk's overprotective mother to enjoy amazing and sometimes scary adventures. However, Maya is lonely and longs for a Being to love, care for and protect her.

Planet earth is seriously out of balance and affecting not only the astral world but all dimensions in the universe. Maya is called on to go to earth and help restore equilibrium. However, there's one major flaw; Maya must be born a human and her memory will evaporate under the veil of forgetfulness. She will have no idea why she is there or what her purpose in life is.

Maya's earth life unfolds relatively uneventfully until, at twelve years old, she drops down dead with a` sudden cardiac arrest. We follow Maya's adventures and experiences, never quite knowing what is truly happening, whether she is dreaming under the effects of the strong medication being used to keep her alive, or her experiences are in fact, reality. Graphic descriptions of medical procedures and the effects of sudden cardiac arrest are integral to Maya's story.

Chapter 1: Maya

Something is moving, flitting on the water. I sit up from my lounging position on the grass for a better look. Tiny Beings with pointed wings and angular faces skate on the water's surface; sprite surfing. They are lively and in good spirits. A positive sign. All is well in our world. The energies are in equal balance.

Lynk peers lazily, to see what has caught my attention.
'Ondines.' He whispers excitedly.
'Yes.' I nod, thrilled, not taking my eyes off them as they effortlessly glide backwards and forwards. One is showing off, performing a figure of eight. Watching the sprites enjoy themselves is magical. I'm entranced by their delicate yet precise movements. I never get tired of watching them. It is rare to witness them at such close quarters.

Everything is in harmony. Everything is as it should be. So why do I sense something isn't quite right? Why can't I shake off this feeling? Everything has its place and exact purpose, doesn't it? I need to relax more, take it easy and switch off occasionally. I scold myself. I'm always looking for trouble, always expecting it. Though, to be fair, I'm always right. Lynk sits up suddenly. My body jumps involuntarily as my thoughts instantly evaporate. A look of horror erupts over his face.
'Oh no, I'm so late. I need to get home!' Lynk leaps to his hooves.
I feel a pang of envy. It happens every time I think of his close relationship and bond with his Mum, Mary. It's always been just the two of them and it's been that way forever. I have no one. No Being at home, waiting for me. I am alone in this realm and always have been. Mary frets and needs to know exactly where Lynk has been and what he's done. She is always suspicious, especially when he's with me. She thinks I'm a bad influence and imagines that I put her son in danger. I laugh to myself at the thought. She's right, I do. It's just as well she doesn't know about the adventures we have. Anything can happen. It always has done and always will. My light: my energy, acts as a magnet which I can't always control. Lynk is my friend and I look after him no matter what situation we're in. That's

what best friends do. Maybe that's why he's nearly always with me. I bring out the rebel in him.

I roll my eyes at Lynk, all three of them. I have the usual pair, like a human, one on either side of my nose, the colour of hazel tree bark; a light brown with tiny yellow flashes. They are eclipsed by long, dark, curled eyelashes. I have a slightly larger eye in the middle of my forehead, above my nose. It picks up everything that my other eyes can't see. Although it's the same shape, it's a vibrant emerald green. My favourite colour. Perhaps that's why I wear this outfit to match. I've never wondered about that until now.
'Are you a will-o'-the-wisp or an Equidae?' I tease Lynk as he nervously paws the grass.
'It's alright for you,' he whinges enviously, 'You live by yourself. You don't have rules to follow. No one tells you what you can and can't do.'
He is oblivious to how I yearn for such rules. Some Being who cares about me. I can't be bothered to explain; let him think what he likes.
'Yes, I know.' I reply smugly, concealing my envy again.
I don't have any set rules, no boundaries that I'm forbidden to cross. I go home alone to my empty house where no Being is waiting to ask me where I've been or what I've been doing. There's no one to tell my adventures to, entertain with my tales, laugh over my mischief or ponder over darkness that I have thwarted. To be fair, Lynk doesn't tell Mary anything he's been up to. She would never let him leave the stable again if he did. They're lucky to have each other. They have a deep mutual love; exactly what I yearn for. All I have waiting for me when I return home is my black pot. Oh, and a three-legged stool and a handful of crystals too. I'm more than capable of looking after myself, don't let my small stature fool you. I'm well respected, even revered. I am the one that Beings flock to for magic and protection. The only Beings who know anything about me are Lynk, of course, and Eucele, who knows everything about every Being. I keep myself to myself. Every other Being knows me by my reputation. I'm here if they require any vibrational assistance or see anything out of humour, out of balance.
Eucele protects every Being too although he tends to deal with the higher consciousness level. I'm more accessible to the Beings as I live among them. Eucele materialises whenever we have need of him. Not that I ever do, I can manage by myself. After all, he taught me everything I know. He was my teacher and mentor. He was the first Being I connected with, the nearest I have to family. I still haven't given up hope of recognising someone, any Being. I have been waiting patiently for thousands of years

and I will wait for thousands more. You never know, maybe they will come soon, a familiar face, a familiar soul, familiar energy.

'I'll walk home with you and say hi to your Mum.' I offer.
Lynk firmly shakes his head.
'No, not a good idea, she has friends over.'
So that's why he's fretting so much.
We walk side by side, following the twists and turns of the stream. Eventually, we see a path on higher ground. We climb a steep grassy slope to reach it. A sideways glance at each other is our cue to joyfully race each other to the top. We're always in competition to see which is better; four legs or two. Lynk gallops onto the path first. I occasionally let him win. Seen from his waist upwards, he appears human. The only peculiar thing about him are his ears. They're pointed and on the top of his head instead of at the side. When his hair hangs loosely, its shagginess covers them; you wouldn't know they were there. Often, he wears his long hair in a plait. It suits him. The lower half of him is a bit more of a surprise if you're not local to these parts, this dimension. He has four willowy legs with hooves and a tail. His coat is a majestic dapple grey while his tail and hair are glossy and black. Black like mine. We sometimes joke that we could be twins, except that he is half horse, a centaur. Lynk, whose full title is Lynk the Second, is apparently the descendant of royalty, or so Mary likes to tell me at every opportunity. She thinks I should count myself lucky to have him as my friend. I do, but not in the way that she means. Just because he lives in the long stable that's part of the old house and its estate, she thinks I should be impressed. I'm not. No matter how much she boasts. Lynk and I refer to it as 'Tacky Manor,' a derogatory nickname which I'm sure his Mum would be mortified by if she knew. She likes to think that she's special and very particular, but I think she's a bit of a snob.

Their home is indeed a large stable. I don't see why it has to be so big for just the two of them. It even has a huge stone fireplace built into the end wall. A chimney pot sticks out from the roof, a feature that also makes her very proud. You're not a Being of importance in Mary's world if you don't have a fireplace. I have a pot.

The main house on the estate is a lot larger than the stable and has numerous chimneys. After all, chimneys mean fireplaces. She ignored me when I said that and boasted, 'The stable stones are exactly the same ones as the big house is made from.'

Maya

Gloating again. I've never been inside the main house. That's the only boundary I've been set in a very long time, and I have stuck to my word faithfully. Mary forbade us to go in there, more for her son's sake than mine but she had included me. I was not to go in there, ever. She knows if I went in, Lynk would surely follow. I am very loyal; I always keep my word. I stick to my sworn oaths. I have no idea what's in there. Whatever she's afraid of, doesn't bother or frighten me, so I let it be. The house and the estate are remains from many moons ago. No one knows how it got to be here. The Beings just remember there was nothing but fields, and then, one morning, they came out of their houses and there it was, gates and all. No occupants, just a grand, pristine dwelling. Of course, with no one to maintain it, over so many moons, it fell into disrepair. One end of the house has completely crumbled. Bricks and tiles balance precariously in a haphazard pattern, a few wooden beams protrude at odd angles, all fallen over time, layer upon layer. I tried to fix it with my magic a long time ago, but soon discovered it was beyond the realms of my capabilities. These buildings came from earth, built by humans. Even I have my limits.

There are lots of smaller buildings on the estate centred around a courtyard. Lynk's rectangular stable is one of those buildings. We head towards it chatting about the impending Light Parade, an annual event celebrating the birth of new stars. We buzz with excitement.

'They're on their way for sure, I've had a vision, thousands and thousands of them coming in one gigantic swarm…' I stop gabbling mid-sentence.

I sense something isn't right. I reach out and grab Lynk's arm and drag him to a halt beside me. 'Shh. Keep still.'

'What is it?' he looks puzzled, not seeing anything.

'That's what I'm trying to work out.' I see it clearly; another vision flashes in front of me.

'A Viking. It's here, coming our way.' I whisper.

Chapter 2: The Viking

Lynk screws up his face in a quizzical manner and silently mouths, 'Are you crazy?'

I understand why. It's odd, very odd. It's been thousands of moons since Vikings have been spotted around here. Nevertheless, there's one close by, very close.

The Viking steps out from behind a massive oak tree that has giant, exposed roots snaking their way in all directions. He abruptly stops, looking almost as astonished as we do.

I had forgotten what these Beings look like. Now I remember. Unfriendly, aggressive, dirty and rather shaggy. This one has scraggly brown hair tied up in a tangle at the back of his head. It looks very matted and messy. His beard looks the same though it has been plaited into five individual braids, there are a few stray, loose whiskers that curl down from his chin, straggling onto his chest. They are thin, wiry plaits. I fear they might snap off his face at any given moment. I do not like him. I learnt in the past that it doesn't take much to upset the people of the North. They have fiery tempers and are prone to overreacting. You must tread very carefully when negotiating with them. I look him up and down discreetly with my third eye. He has a very large body and feet to match which remind me of Norse longships. They are housed in soft leather cattle hide boots with holes and tears in them. I notice a tinge of grey to his face and hands. He doesn't look bright at all, more like the walking dead. He's lacking energy.

'Velkominn!' I brightly welcome him. 'I haven't seen a Viking here for many moons, are you alone or are there more of you?'

I'm hoping he's alone. An army of Vikings is not a happy thought. He moves his head but as he does so, one of his plaited braids drops to the ground. He is literally falling apart. How embarrassing.

'I have been woken up,' he snaps at me angrily. 'They dug up my longboat from the ground and removed my earthly remains that were resting inside. I was lying peacefully as I had for the last thousand years, buried with my axe and shield. I heard one of them say they're making way to build a new road.'

Surprised by how well he spoke, I nod. I understand. Humans are always digging, knocking down, destroying or building something on planet earth. They certainly have a reputation across the universe for being resourceful. Often overly industrious.

'I have been excavated. Excavated! They kept saying that word over and over again. What does that mean?' He rants on, not giving me a chance to reply. 'Oh, me bones, oh, they were scraped at, they were brushed, and they were dusted.' He points his gigantic finger at me, 'If that wasn't bad enough, they packed me, bone by bone into some sort of container. They said they're sending me for carbon data dating.'

'What's that then?' Lynk asks, echoing my own thoughts.

'How do I know? I've been asleep,' the Viking snaps.

Lynk looks at me, asking with his eyes if I know what the Viking is talking about, but truthfully, I have no idea. I'm very behind the times as far as life on earth goes. Thankfully.

'How dare they treat me this way!' he grumbles, his voice getting louder and louder 'How dare they do this to me! How will I ever get into Valhalla now?'

Viking? I've never met one like him before. More like a spoiled princess. He whines and groans. No wonder he never made it into Valhalla. Though I'm in agreement with him about one thing; why oh why did the humans have to wake him up? They have absolutely no idea what they are doing! Still, just one more stupid decision to add to the list and a perfect example of why I know with all my being that staying here forever is the right thing to do. I never want to go back to earth again.

'I left my desecrated burial site and wandered away as quickly as I could. It's been centuries since I stood up, so I was a little unsteady on my legs. I went in search of an abbey, a monastery or even a smallholding that I could ransack and pillage to make me feel a little better,'

'Well, of course,' Luckily, he doesn't seem to understand sarcasm.

'It was terrible though,' he grows agitated recalling the event.

'Oh? What was?' Lynk asks, eager as always to listen to a good tale. The Viking basks in the limelight.

'I tell you; I have endured the bloodiest battles. The siege of Paris is one, I was a mighty warrior. I was unstoppable, my reputation precedes me. Mention my name and they dropped dead at the thought of me,'

'Were you famous?' Lynk is enthralled 'How did you die?'

I can hear the excitement in his voice for the blood thirsty tale. Was he beheaded? Was it an axe? Oh, the heroicness fills Lynks' head. I can see the visions swirling around him, his imagination running wild.

I didn't need imagination. I could see exactly how this Viking met his end. I see his death, certainly not a heroic one he could boast about.

'He was struck by lightning, it hit the tree branch and zigzagged down the length of the tree trunk and struck him when he was sheltering underneath its umbrella of leaves,' I explain to Lynk, with a touch of glee.

I am not in the mood to listen to his rubbish, egotistical stories when Thor himself struck him down. Lynk cannot help but giggle and whispers to me.

'Well, strike me down…' I shoot him a warning glance.

Thank goodness the Viking is oblivious to being mocked, and is still harping on, lost in subconscious recollections. He finally gets back to the point of explaining what happened when he went in search of an abbey, a monastery or smallholding.

'I walked across fields, one after the other. Clueless of where I was, I was just stepping onto a track, when I was forced to jump back quickly. I was alarmed. Giant, noisy chariots sped past, racing along, one following behind the other. More and more came, some coming from the other direction. They passed each other. Some funny cart race, I thought to myself, some are going the wrong way. One came along the size of a battering ram! The wheels were the largest I've ever seen. I tell you, there wasn't a horse in sight. No horsepower! There was this strange yellow monster, the likes I have never seen before. I could not have imagined in my wildest dreams, and I have some wild ones I can tell you,' He winks.

Lynk likes the Viking's humour, but I roll my eyes, he does not amuse me.

'The monster had a long cranking neck, with lots of bolts in it and a large set of jagged teeth in an oblong mouth. It had two white round circular eyes but no nose. It had wheels instead of legs. Its body was a big square and I could look straight through it. A human was inside, swallowed. He was somehow still alive and still had his round yellow battle helmet on his head! He was sitting in the monster's stomach, just staring ahead. He was very brave, showed no fear. I was impressed by such valour. Sensibly, I watched from underneath a large shrub, not moving until the yellow creature with the human consumed inside of it had passed by,'

'Very sensible,' I nod encouragingly.

I'm guessing he is describing one of the humans' digging machines. I learnt about them from Eucele. He told me there must be as many machines on earth as people. There are those that turn the sky grey and the water black. Some move and roll around on wheels. Others consume clothing, churn them around and spit them back out. Diggers help them to build, knock things down and kill trees. Only humans would call this progress. Still, I must not dwell on their way of doing things, I shall start to get annoyed. I turn my attention back to the Viking. It is obvious the events have all been too much for him, he's showing signs of being overwhelmed which could lead to a full-blown panic attack.

'As for the gold, what have they done with it all? Where is it? Where do they hide it now? I couldn't find any! Not one coin!'

Oh, okay, so that's what's really upset him. I quickly change the subject. 'How did you find your way here?'

I need to understand what has happened, Why and how has he made his appearance here and now? How has he travelled here? A Viking has not materialised on the timeline for generations, his appearance puts the balance of our existence in jeopardy.

'A black hole, a portal. It was there, developed out of the veils that separate and protect the realms. Odin created it for me so I could finally cross over into Valhalla. There can be no other explanation. I found it, walked through it and here I am, home at last.'

'Why didn't Odin let you in when you died?' Lynk asks him, 'Why did he wait this long?'

Lynk and his big mouth. Why did he have to say that? Why, why, why? The Viking gets very defensive, his ego offended the most. His voice takes on a menacing tone.

'Make no mistake, I may have died in less than glorious circumstances, my death was not bloody, I was cruelly robbed by death of my place in the hall of the slain at Odin's table, but I have been woken now, to take my rightful, worthy place,'

Lynk accidentally lets out one of his annoying neighing noises. Sometimes, when he is unsure about things, it happens involuntarily. We exchange bemused glances.

'You think I am funny?' the Viking takes exception, 'We shall see if you laugh at me when you become my pet pony!' He turns to me. 'And I can't leave you out, three eyes? Let's see how hoity-toity you are when you're serving me as my slave!'

The ill-mannered Viking lunges, arms flailing, trying to grab us simultaneously. He unceremoniously stumbles between us, missing completely. He turns menacingly towards me. I'm really starting to lose my leniency with this Viking. I'm not known for my patience; it's never been one of my endearing traits. Another hapless lunge. I nimbly take flight and leap upwards avoiding contact. I reach down, grab Lynk by his shoulders and haul him up alongside me out of harm's way.

'I don't want to hurt him,' I loudly direct my comment to Lynk, 'But he doesn't seem to understand that he's making a very big mistake right now.'

The Viking roars some indistinguishable battle cry, it comes across a little hoarse. He wields his axe in circles above his head. Such a display would be terrifying to some but not me. I hover above him laughing, which makes him extraordinarily angry. He swipes his axe around, over his head, quicker and quicker, trying to knock us out of the air. His swings, though fast, are feeble. Clearly, the years of lying deceased have taken their toll on his physical strength, drained his energy and probably diminished his skill. Lynk and I stare down at him in disbelief. Lynk whispers to me. 'What are we going to do? I'm so late now. I'm in serious trouble.'

Chapter 3: Bad Influence

His words make me laugh. I realise Lynk is more afraid of Mary than the Viking. I can appreciate why Odin didn't want this oafish barbarian in his great hall. Even though there are eight other Viking after-worlds, he didn't make the grade, not with that attitude. One or two wayward Vikings made their way here accidentally, many moons ago. I rerouted them, as Eucele had done before me. I point my finger at the enraged Norseman. It's a sign that I'm serious. Be warned, if I ever point my finger at you, you need to submit. The Viking continues to pathetically prance about in his attempt to knock us down with his axe.

'One step, two steps, Dosey Doe,' Lynk scoffs.

He acts far more courageously when I'm around. I feel my power activate and surge through me in an instant. My white light beams from within, coursing through my whole body and exiting through my fingertip. I have absolute control. It's just enough to knock the Viking over. My power topples him, and he lands flat on the ground, face down. I pin him firmly where he falls, my light intensifying until his struggles desist. I have him anchored. Lynk and I slowly float down to land. Standing over him, I attempt to persuade the Viking to live here peacefully with us. I'm not unreasonable. He's been through a lot, but I do insist that he fully understands and accepts that he must let go of his notion of having control here.

'There's no way, in the twelve realms, that you will be taking Lynk as your pet or me as your slave.'

He attempts to struggle, becoming more and more agitated. He shows no sign of backing down; there is no reasoning with him. He shouts his Viking curses at me, 'Vid hamri pors! Vid dauoi pors!'

They make me laugh. 'You have the temperament of a nisse.' I mock him. I turn my light green and the heaving, bad tempered figure vanishes. All that's left is his two horned metal helmet which scurries away into the undergrowth of the nearest bush. A helmet moving all by itself.

'What's a nisse?' Lynk enquires.

'It's what he would call a gnome.'

Lynk laughs, he suddenly remembers that he is later than ever now.

'Oh no, I'm going to be in so much trouble. Mum will never believe me. I'd better go!'

He gallops off as fast as his hooves can take him. I follow leisurely behind him. I'm not in a rush to go home. I can amuse myself until it's dark enough for the Light Festival to take place. Lynk will be there with his Mum. I may be wise to avoid her, no doubt she will blame me for Lynk being late for her tea party. She always thinks everything's my fault. Her Lynk can do no wrong. I'm such a bad influence that leads him astray. I cannot help it, my world, our world, the astral world is a magical one. Spirits, entities and magical Beings, all live together blissfully in a higher level of vibration. One of the highest dimensions.

Chapter 4: Maya's Purpose

Looking back, I've come a long way and had an incredible journey thus far. Overcoming trials and tribulations thrown at me, time and again, testing every limit; my strength, my ingenuity, my resilience.

One of my defining battles was against the serpent, Esss, self-appointed gate keeper of our realm. She controlled the arrivals and departures from our world to the universe. Beings have always had free will to come and go as they please, but this self-centred and manipulative snake dictated and controlled for the sole purpose of feeding her own ego. She recognised my emerging power and sought to destroy me. She perceived me as a threat; I had to overthrow her. As I made my way through the gate, she stealthily sprung her ambush, wrapping her gigantic coil around me. It was hard to see where one end started and the other ended. She squeezed and squeezed, attempting to sap the light out of me. Esss was solid muscle, hard and unyielding. As she constricted, I tingled. I resisted; I would not give up. She could try for as long as she liked to drain the light out of me. I would never give up; I do not give up. Being squeezed by this vile stinky snake was not going to be the end of me. She smelt like sewage. The stench was even worse when she opened her snaky jaws wide, revealing her yellow putrid fangs. Ugh, the smell was more likely to expunge me than her cunning. With all my inner strength, I sliced her coil with my green light. I let it shine out of me ripping her in half, straight down her length, which splintered and exploded into tiny segments. Black, putrid innards spewed into every crevice.

'You underestimated me,' I laughed. 'More like hundreds of slow worms now than a serpent.'

Having proved my worthiness, I finally made it through the gate to the astral world. I had earnt my place and was now entitled to stay. No Being can ever take that away from me. They couldn't even try.

On the positive side, some entities, particularly Ondines, are of the highest importance. They are required to be here; their presence is essential. Their state of happiness affects the balance of harmony. They have free will. They could leave any time they wished but, should they leave, it would spell disaster; the astral world would mutate beyond recognition. The consequences are unthinkable. I ensure that doesn't happen. This is my job; I have made it so. I make sure the Ondines are always happy and have no cause to leave. When the scales start tipping, I counteract them with my magic abilities. I do whatever needs doing. I am as necessary to our world as the Ondines are.

Ondines are sprites, fairy-like tiny beings. A lot of them have wings, though not all. Their colour depends on their particular purpose and skill. The tree Ondine is green. They are the healers and help all Beings cross the bridges between the dimensions. The earth, the ethereal and here in the astral. Rainbow Ondines, as you would expect, are multi-coloured. They are masters at camouflage, changing colour to blend into their environment in order to conceal themselves. Their job is to give colour to the world, so without them everything would be dark. Earth would be the same. Humans don't realise they're there. They can't see them; well, most of them can't.

The water Ondines are clear and translucent. They blend in extremely well. Only those who are fortunate to shine from within have a scarce chance of seeing one. They keep the streams, the rivers and all other bodies of water flowing. Should they ever leave here, the world would be completely dry, a desert.

There are Ondines in the valleys and mountains, in the grass, they are everywhere, doing good, playing and generally having fun. Although they look different and have their own ways, they share one commonality; they like to be naughty. A headstrong streak I recognise in myself too. At any given moment, they can suddenly get the urge to make mischief. Naughty and nice; they are balanced.

My journey here has been difficult and all-consuming, particularly my brief time on earth. I was very young when I left my human form behind, only twelve earth years. I had no one to guide or help me. No one to rely on except myself.

Now, here in the astral world, I feel that I finally belong and have an essential purpose. I love it here. I felt an instant connection the moment I arrived, an extra buzz, an instinctive lure. Wild horses couldn't drag me away. I have no intention whatsoever of leaving. This astral world with all its peculiar, enchanting and surprising occupants, is my home, my sanctuary.

Chapter 5: Eucele

Some Beings choose to leave the astral world, for various reasons. They travel to earth or further afield in this galaxy or beyond, looking to explore other worlds, searching for their true home. Eucele's home, the blue galaxy, is affectionately nicknamed the bird cage due to its shape and ironically, it's the home of the Avian's. The blue atmosphere colours their feathers, in fact everything is tinged with blue. It must be an optical illusion as viewed from the outer universe; everything appears white.

I cannot imagine Eucele being blue, he is a ghostly, angel white, so it just doesn't seem right. He left his home a very long time ago, too far back for me to remember. Before coming here to the Temple, Eucele lived for a while on earth in a place called Egypt. During one of our lessons, he casually disclosed that he helped build the pyramids. The Egyptian people were so grateful, they have worshipped his kind ever since, those helpful, wise, twelfth dimensional Beings.

My lessons took place in the Atlantean Temple. Eucele taught me everything that he and his species had learnt thousands of moons ago. I was honoured to be included in their circle of knowledge, being trusted with their wisdom, magic and customs. He told me, how he watched me on my journey towards the astral world, that my determination and strength shone from my very core. I thought this was funny, the tiny girl who was too weak for life on earth, shone brightly with her strength. I was always determined in my soul that I was going to live for as long as I could on earth, I had a will to survive and an ongoing drive to persevere. I lived longer than expected, despite the odds. My heartbeat finally stopped. It could beat no more.

I became Eucele's star pupil, his only pupil. I developed skills that even he did not possess. I surpassed his own powers in some subjects. I was amazed at this and secretly thrilled, not realising that this had been his intention all along.

Eucele is dominating. He's well over two and a half metres in height. An aliferous giant, constantly towering over me. Eucele is and has always been, a very private Being. He rarely gives any information about himself, the things he has seen, where he has travelled and what he has done. This complete lack of ego enhances his magical and mystical persona. He radiates an intimidating charisma, a god-like presence. He is an enigma and there are very few who are close to him.

Eucele personally chose to teach me. A privilege and honour of the highest order. His standards and expectations are exceptionally high, and he has taught me to expect the same. I studied hard and was an excellent student. He taught me about the different forms of light, the healing type, the magical light, the shadow light and the dark light. All forms of light have a seemingly opposing, opposite force; each must exist to counterbalance the other. There it is again, everything in balance. I learnt to master them all. Not to be swayed by one idealistic type of light, but to know how to use them all in combination for a greater outcome. When darkness is too dark it is easy to get lost. When light is too bright, it is blinding; progress is futile. In order to experience the joy of improvement, each light must harmonise to enhance the existence of all Beings.

I learnt about crystals, and their magical healing properties. The magic little stones that come from the geology of the earth. Eucele taught me how to project myself and my light, and how to turn the light into the power that I can control for the highest good. He taught me about the universe and all the different Beings that I am likely to encounter. He taught me the truth about earth…those humans. They have no idea about the truth of themselves at all, but he also taught me there was a reason for that. They are better off not knowing.

'The less they know, the less harm they can do,' This lesson struck a chord and has always stayed with me.

During what would be our last lesson, he took a pot and set it over a blazing fire. I like looking into fires; he taught me how to make one. It's something humans do to keep warm, burn forests and to cook food. It was the first time I had seen a crystal.

'Lemurian Starseed,' he told me matter-of-factly 'Lemurian is a quartz.'

Eucele only ever speaks when it is necessary to do so. Otherwise, he remains quiet, always with an easily read expression that states that he is busy thinking so don't bother him with silly questions.

Eucele expertly drops the Lemurian into the pot. It is immediately engulfed with a mountainous inferno of flames coupled with a deafening scream. Eucele dramatically clapped his hands together, the flames subsided and there, in their place was the word FRIEND. I didn't have any friends, other than Eucele and he's not the socialising type. The word then crumbled apart and fell back into the pot, evaporated. He offered no explanation but handed me a drawstring bag with my very own Lemurian in it. He nodded his head as he did so.

'You will need this. Learning is now complete.'

I was about to ask about our next lesson, when he handed me, a beautiful green stone hanging from a necklace of black rope. An eye engraved with a flick underneath it. A replica of the symbol he always wore around his neck, the one that an Egyptian pharaoh had given him in gratitude.

I realised that everything was changing for me. I was being sent out on my own, no more learning, no more master instruction. Eucele unfurled his colossal wings and flew out of the glassless window. He had gone. I was dismissed. Alone in the cella of the Temple.

That's it then! I thought to myself and took one last look around the scholastic room. The old magical books on the shelves that we had spent hours poring over, researching, cross-referencing, culminating in pure moments of enlightenment. The Book of the Dead, volumes one to five thousand were pride of place. The complete series was bound by ancient red leather, as pristine as the day they magically appeared. Touching them was strictly forbidden. They were special, held great importance in the universe. Eucele had told me. I was tempted to sneak a look. Who knew what wonders and secrets they held? Reaching out my hand, I felt myself gravitate towards number three, I resisted its seductiveness, shaking off the impulse. I could not betray Eucele's trust. Time to go home. The next time I met Eucele would be as an equal, not as a student.

Chapter 6: Initiation

My time of formal learning was over. The time had come to put that knowledge and wisdom into practice. I received a summons. An invitation to attend my initiation into the Order of Ra. A solemn and sacred ceremony. Eucele was there, expression unchanging throughout the ancient formality. I knew he was proud. His chest was puffed up and his feathers bristled. That was the most enthusiasm he was willing to show. All members of the Light Council were present. It was a very auspicious occasion, a secret one. No other Being was allowed to attend or watch. The Light Council are extremely influential and persuasive. Telepathy is their main means of communicating with each other. An ability mastered by few. Many Beings fear them. It's rumoured that they can control others with their telepathic skills.

As I stood waiting in the middle of their circle, I picked up a couple of telepathically transmitted words. I wondered how I was able to hear snippets of their conversations. The Light Council are renowned for their exclusivity, only confiding in and trusting each other.

Eucele left his position in the circle and walked towards me in the centre. He held a circular altar of agate crystal with an ethereal leaf in the centre. On the leaf was the most beautiful semi-precious stone, lapis lazuli. Its royal blue colour formed the backdrop to hues of green and golden flecks. I instantly recognised the revered gemstone. Eucele had taught me how the ancient Egyptians used it to heal their physical body, mind and soul. One of its many uses was to create eye makeup. Eucele showed me pictures of pharaohs painted in blue pigment. Lapis lazuli was known as the stone of heaven and was believed to be so sacred it had the means to communicate with the gods. Cornelius gracefully walked over and the three of us stood in a triangle. The old men of the Light Council shuffled up to surround us. Cornelius was carrying an old and somewhat large and heavy looking golden bound book. There was an embossed black ankh symbol on the spine. I had seen this book before; at the end of that final lesson. It was kept on a bookshelf in the Atlantean Temple. He opened the book at the correct page and handed me the book and indicated that I should read. In a commanding voice, I confidently began.

Initiation

'*My Oath of Ra.*
I solemnly do swear to protect order, the sky, the sun, the earth, the kings and the realms.
I solemnly do swear to keep the skies clear for smooth transitions.
I solemnly do swear to do all that I can to ensure Ra's safe passage through the underworld, so that he may be born again for each and every new day.
I solemnly do swear to uphold the supreme ethics of the eye of Ra.
I do oath my whole Being to this cause.

Cornelius reclaimed the book and passed it into Euceles' free hand. He then extended his ethereal light finger into the lapis lazuli pigmentation and traced a shape around my third eye.
I could feel the shape of the eye drawn, my own third eye taking the place of the pupil. A flick with a curl to the left was drawn underneath my eye and a curved line over the top, in the shape of an eyebrow. Lapis lazuli to strengthen intuition and help connect a Being to their clarity and integrity. My abilities were being increased.
The first phase of the ceremony was complete. Cornelius indicated that Eucele should hand me the book. I looked down at the page and continued to read, my voice unfaltering.

'*The Oath of Equilibrium, my oath of balance.*
I will look ahead, and I will look behind. Anything that is regretfully attached, I will unbind.
Anything that comes undone, I will make sure all loose ends are tied.
Anything I see out of balance will be righted by me as quickly as I am spiritually and energetically able.
I am a light that leads the way. I will be ready and willing, whenever I am called upon to uphold my vows, night or day.
This is my destiny, my privilege and my vow.'

Every Being in attendance chanted in unison 'Amen Ra.'
I felt overcome by an intense surge of energy. Something forceful passed over, around and through me. From that moment, I possessed a drive, a passion to oppose forces and actions that threatened stability and balance. It became my goal to ensure that no force was greater than another. Everything would be and should be equal.
I passed the book of sacred scripture back to Cornelius. He turned his back to me and joined the others who had now broken the circle and were walking away. The ceremony was over.

Chapter 7: Lynk

Feeling perplexed and very alone, I made my way home from the Temple to my little round stick hut that had been home ever since I arrived in the astral world.

I passed the big old estate when I met a Being on the road who I had never seen before. He was half horse and half boy, nothing unusual about that round here, but he was definitely new. Must have just arrived.

'Lynk. I've just arrived.' he confirmed. I noticed he was very well groomed. Nice hooves.

'Maya. I have been here for hundreds of moon cycles, I'm a Starseed.' I held my necklace up for him to admire the stone. I could tell he was impressed but he didn't know what a Starseed was. Never heard of one of those he had said. He was obviously going to need someone to show him how things worked around here. With delicate hooves like that, he wouldn't survive long, I thought condescendingly.

'How was your journey?' The journey is, without doubt, the most important part of any travel destination.

'Good, thanks. I just arrived with my Mum. She's busy pottering around our new stable, so I thought I would take a look around, see who's about. What is there to do for fun around here?'

'Fun! Did you just say fun? We have serious work to do, well I do anyhow,' I told him indignantly.

'Serious work? Doing what?' he asked. I told him in a way I thought he might understand.

'Balancing,'

'Balancing?' he repeated, looked serious, and started to hop around on one skinny leg, his other three lifted and folded under his belly, out of the way 'Like this?' he asked.

He looked ridiculous. I couldn't help but laugh at him. Since that first meeting, Lynk has filled my world with so much joy. Fun and laughter were discouraged when I was a child on earth. I had to watch my heart. I had to learn to be very careful not to overexert myself. Lynk and I often sat together on the grass, comparing journeys and swapping experiences and past life memories. A great way to get to know each other. I admitted that on my way to the astral world, there had been times when I had felt like giving up. I had no idea what my purpose was. From deep within, I had found the strength to keep moving forward. There were times I would settle for a while, quite content. Sooner or later, my light would start to dim, and I found myself feeling low and totally drained. Growing lethargic, I would feel restless, I had to continue my travels. I needed to summon all my strength just to begin my journey. Once I had found a new world, a new home, my light and strength recovered, renewed energy, stronger each time.

To this day, I cannot explain my instant and eternal connection to Lynk. My trust in him is absolute. He taught me to let my guard down, to talk about anything and everything. I could honestly share my feelings; the first time in forever. Since then, we've been inseparable. Funny, I haven't thought about our first encounter for a very long time. I find myself smiling at the old energy. Hey! I need to snap out of all this reminiscing. Wistfulness is not getting me anywhere fast. I must hurry if I am going to get to the Crystal Mine, I've been meaning to go there for a while. Now's a good time; everything is quiet and in balance. If I hurry, I can be back in time for the beginning of the Light Parade.

Chapter 8: Crystal Mine

The Crystal Mine is situated in the desert region of the astral world. It can be found in a direct line away from where the forest edge meets the unforgiving sands of the Rocky Desert.

A vast carpet of sand hides the concealed entrance of the mine. It's the only place I can collect the crystals I need. Wheal Pellucid is its official title, but it's known as the Crystal Mine. Very ancient gems were transported here by Eucele and the Avians from earth when they first came here. I tried questioning Eucele during a lesson once.

'Crystalline is not on my agenda today.' was the rebuked response.

When the Avians, the bird people, brought the stones here with the help of trolls, they hid them inside the depths of a series of dug out tunnels, a maze of mines. The stones were brought here for healing and to be used in the protection of the souls that live in this dimension, I also think the Avian's foresaw that the humans would over exploit them. Humans have an obsession of over-mining and overusing the natural resources found on earth. They are certainly talented at locating, extracting and exploiting all manner of mineral deposits but time and again, fail to plan for sustainability. Greed, pure greed. Eventually, of course, the humans start running out of their earthly stock. Humans have a habit of making things disappear.

Only the Avians, the trolls and I know the location of the mine. Oh, and I brought Lynk here once. I trust him with all my secrets, and I can't imagine that he would attempt to find his way by himself. It would take him so long; his Mum would send out a search party to look for him.

I fly low and fast, darting through row after row of fir trees. The Dark Wood is impenetrably black, another good reason why I had no qualms about bringing Lynk with me to the mine.

The only way I can navigate is to create a golden swirl of light at the far end of the forest. The glow illuminates my way. I sense movements in the trees, the occasional scurrying and sound of retreating, flapping wings. The golden swirl is growing brighter; I'm near the forest edge. I disperse the light energy and fly out beyond the tree trunks. Nothing but golden sand lay ahead of me. The grains stretch out, in every direction as far as my three eyes can see. I keep on flying; I must keep going straight ahead. It's not too far when you can fly. It's easy to miss the entrance. I wonder if the wooden signpost will appear, sticking low out of the grains. Trolls don't make anything tall. I wonder if my advice has been followed and it's been removed. On my last visit, I had charged Herbert, the head troll and chief miner, with its removal. My frustration finally got the better of me after much exasperated reasoning.

I yelled, 'It's supposed to be a secret entrance!'

I'm not convinced the message was understood.

All the miners here are trolls. They dug the tunnels and the entrance out when the crystals arrived and have lived and worked here ever since. They protect the crystals. Trolls are perfect for their job. They were used to living under bridges and they love shiny things. If there's a crystal to be found, they can easily sniff it out. The most striking feature of a troll is a large pointy nose. It's a matter of pride, the longer and pointier nose, the more status you carry. Herbert's is enormous.

Crystals come in all shapes, sizes and colours. There are rough and coarse ones, long and shiny ones. Ones that look like effervescent jewels and some that have grown in various shaped clusters. Some of these crystals are extremely rare.

Keeping busy down in the depths, the trolls stay out of mischief. If they were allowed to roam freely up above on the surface, my job would be so much more difficult. Another one of Eucele's and the Avian's amazing ideas. Giving the trolls lots of shiny things to play with keeps them busy which means every Being is happy. Brains are not a troll's strongest asset, as the signpost conversation demonstrated, however, what they lack in intellect, they make up for when there is hard astral work to be done. They love repetitive tasks and getting dirty.

I'm close now, looking down, searching for the entrance. As expected, I see it, the signpost telling me I am most welcome at Wheal Pellucid. To be fair, Herbert has moved the sign, I can't see the entrance; it must be nearby. I circle around searching for it, flying down lower, getting closer to the sands which have been here longer than I have.

Ah, there it is! That looks like the spot. I descend, but no, it isn't the entrance point. It's a shadow of some sort. I keep looking, it must be around here somewhere. Found it! Here it is. Thank goodness, I was beginning to think I would need to start shifting and parting the sands. As

I may have mentioned before, patience is not my strong point. A black hole, with a thin sandy cover over it. I look around, making sure I'm not being watched. As usual, the desert is deserted.

One last check, for good luck and I jump, feet first, purposeful, downwards. I freefall through the portal and as expected, find myself sliding down a yellow chute. I glide down, deeper and deeper. I am transported quickly into the dark depths, the centre of the mine shaft. Wheal Pellucid, the name of the water wheel, is hidden away under the ground. It looms large in front of me. I land in the widest and tallest part of the shaft, the central hub of the mine. Tunnels branch off from here in every direction.

'It's only me, Maya,' I called ahead as I whizzed down the spiralling yellow slide.

I skim off the end, triple somersault and land gracefully on a heap of soft cushioning sand. I always know how to make a dramatic entrance.

Lots of big noses are pointing towards me. It seems everyone has stopped working.

'I have come for some crystals,' I say each word slowly and loudly.

I have learnt to do this every time I visit. Herbert barges his way through the interrupted trolls, coming forwards to greet me.

'Hello Maya, nice of you to drop-in,'

His nose is even fatter and bouncier than I had remembered. I can't help but stare momentarily; I'm always taken aback by it.

'Help yourself, you know your way around. We are very busy,'

Herbert's dismissiveness is strangely out of character, he doesn't appear to be his normal, usual talkative self. I do know my way around but usually it's a battle to escape his guiding and gossiping. With very few visitors popping in, Herbert likes to know everything that's going on above. Everyone quickly returns to their duties. Why are they all so preoccupied I wonder? No matter, I'm also in a hurry. I need to get going; the Light Festival waits for no Being.

Chapter 9: Searching

In this section of the mine, sand shelves line the walls. They were carved into the walls during its construction. Numerous unusual shaped crystals are proudly displayed on them. Very impressive. Himalayan salt lamps glow bright orange in the gloom, providing the only source of light. A dazzling red crystal on the highest shelf shines brightly in the dark, touching everything with a ruby red tinge.

It's difficult to navigate the tunnel floor as piles of displaced sand and trenches of various depths litter the way, all evidence of the trolls' untidy digging. I must dig too. The trolls carve their own pickaxes and spades from the crystals. Most trolls are using dalmatian jasper shovels, a popular choice. I also see a yellow citrine pitchfork, redundant for the time being. Usually, a few trolls are panning for gold, taking a break from their search for crystals. They stand in the water, up past their waists. Panning for gold is serious business to a troll. They scoop with their pans made from amber and sieve out the water, closely inspecting the contents in the crystal light. They seem to enjoy it. Another of Eucele's enticing ideas, designed to stimulate and motivate the trolls. Gold cannot exist in the astral world; it is only found on earth. I see no reason to tell them. An ancient troll legend foretells that gold is there. The trolls live in hope. Something we all need to do.

The workers ignore me, except for one troll who is clearly in an agitated state, unable to contain himself.
'We's haves instructions froms the Temple. Theys wants tons and tons of whites quartz and no ones knows whys theys wants it, it's all bigs secrets,'
Eucele's voice echoes in my head, 'Never tell a troll your secrets,'
'Tons and tons? Surely there can't be that much buried here?'
I find his story a bit fantastical, he must be exaggerating. '
Why does Eucele and the others need tons and tons of white quartz?'
The troll shrugs his massive shoulders, 'I's doesn'ts knows, Euceles says we's wills be surprised whats we's finds whens we's starts lookings,'

I wonder why Eucele needs so much. What's he going to do with it? There must be a good reason. Eucele never does anything without good reason. White quartz must be here in abundance. The small pile collected so far is pitiful; the trolls have a big task ahead of them.

It's all very mysterious. I'm not desperate for white quartz, I have enough for the time being. I will be satisfied with some rose quartz. I pick up a shovel that is resting idle against the sandy wall. It's red and sparkling and lights the mine up with red flashing sparkles as I move it. Red garnet. I start to dig. It doesn't take me very long to find a green crystal. Apatite. Could be useful. I'll take it. Green is, after all, my colour. I continue to dig in the same spot, in case there are more hidden away, but there are none. I back fill the hole I have created and start on my next area, just to the right. Methodically, I make my way along the tunnel, one section at a time. I find nothing, not a trace of the smallest crystal, let alone white quartz. There's nothing here, my patience is wearing thin, yet again. I fly across the stream into the cavern where the huge wooden water wheel powers the mine. Eventually this deep, fast flowing water will become just a trickle, as it descends deeper underground.

It is not unusual for trolls to stand playfully on the paddles, having fun going up and down, around and around. They often slip and fall, causing a tidal wave, which they find hilarious. No time for games today though.

On this side of the river, I continue my search, still nothing. Very frustrating! I can feel my impatience rising higher, boiling up inside, reaching my limit. I see red. Everything turns the deepest shade of red. A familiar surge of uncontrollable energy bursts through my whole being. My scarlet aura explodes from within, enveloping and projecting my annoyance. I cannot allow this to happen; I must be in control. I close my third eye, concentrating with all my strength. I feel myself defusing. As I ground myself, my light recedes; I have control. I look around, luckily, the trolls have been too busy to notice. Composing myself, I carry on digging. Immediately, I uncover an orange calcite. It's a medium one, thick at one end and thin at the other. It's shaped like a carrot. It's a strong stone and will allow positive energies to move through it. I'll keep that one, just for the shape of it. I dig some more. Fluorite comes out of the ground, glass-like in appearance; a jagged three-colour gem with purple, green and turquoise layers. No, I don't need that one, pretty as it is. One of its properties gives strength. I will take it and give it to Lynk. I'm sure he would love it. I find an amethyst. A heavy chunk of rock on the bottom with a layer of white crystal and an encrustation of jagged purple crystals on top. Disheartened that I still haven't found rose or white quartz yet, I spy a twinkle of something in the sand. I uncover a translucent white quartz, it is pure; absolutely beautiful. I resist the temptation to take it and hand it to the nearest troll. He gives a toothy grin in appreciation, one less piece to find. A piece of perfectly precious red quartz is next, I'm on a roll. I keep it. If only I could find a piece of rose quartz.

Suddenly, the whole mine starts to rattle and shake. The noise is deafening. Showers of sand fall from the ceiling and down the slide. The water wheel creaks, tipping precariously. As quick as it started, it stopped. 'What was that?' I ask.

The trolls turn and look at me, dazed and confused. I have no idea. I wasn't prepared for it at all, though whatever it was, was not normal. The dimension literally shook.

An abundance of white flecks appear in the dirt, sparkling and glistening. The shaking has done some good. The trolls cheer with excitement at the sight of so many pieces of white quartz surfacing.

'Help me find some rose quartz, quickly!' I demand. The miners immediately dig furiously, white quartz flying in all directions. A cry echoes down the tunnel. A rose piece has been found. As a mark of respect and gratitude, a juvenile troll reverently presents the crystal to me on bended knee. I place my palms together in the grace position and raise them to my third eye, lowering my head slightly. My mission is now accomplished. I say a hurried goodbye to Herbert and slide back up the chute. I zoom up, headfirst, rocketing out of the hole. My trademark triple somersault completed, I gracefully alight on the desert sand, landing on my feet.

Chapter 10: Giants

Amid my homeward flight, I notice a huge crater. The edges of it are clearly imprinted in the astral sands. Something circular has been and gone, leaving its mark. Whatever it was, has not gone unnoticed. Two enormous figures slowly begin to peel themselves from their hiding place against the sandy rock face of the cliff. Giants. They have the gift of camouflage, becoming one with their surroundings whenever they wish. Their art is instantaneous; blending into the environment so completely, they are totally undetectable. First, I noticed their two sets of feet, followed by their legs. Their bodies, big hands attached to long arms, followed by their necks and heads. Slowly, they fully reveal themselves. They begin to walk towards me, no longer concealed. Two immense balls of prominent, fluorescent white light, visible for kilometres, surround the couple. I instinctively cover my three eyes, using my hand as a visor. They are luminous, walking beacons. The sand is violently disturbed as they walk, they cannot help it; their feet are enormous. Squinting, I move my shielded gaze upwards. Their eyes are set in deep sockets, flames burn and flicker inside the hollows. First appearances are terrifying, but they are the gentlest of all the Beings that I have met. The female Giant is significantly smaller than the other. I'm instantly on my guard. The powers of the smallest ones are often underestimated.

He speaks first, announcing himself as Alun and politely introduces me to his sister, Petra. Alun and Peta have heavy heads and long faces. Their jaws and teeth are square and strong. Thin strands of long brown hair hang down their backs. Alun's is a bit sparse in patches, yanked out by their roots in a fierce battle, not that he is bothered about it. Bathed in nothing but pure light, they have no need of clothing. They wear their light well.
'It fell down from up there,'
Alun's large silver thick rubbery-looking lips tell me as he points directly into the atmosphere.
'It came down abruptly, stayed for a moment before flying off quickly that way.' he points in the direction of the Shining Valley, towards the woods.

Whatever it was, it has gone, travelling at light speed. I fly up and hover, I need to look directly into their eyes. Discussing matters face to face is obligatory in Giant etiquette.

'Green. There was green all over it,' Petra tells me, her skin changing to the exact shade to illustrate her meaning.

Ancient tales tell of Watchers or angels who once existed on earth. Giants, Mermaids, Bigfoot, even the Loch Ness monster; they all come from the same ancestry. There's no mention of them in the planet's history books. They have been purposely erased from human memory. The bones of Giants are occasionally uncovered, the only testament to their existence. Sadly, they are regarded as fake, dismissed as legends, myths and fantasy; relegated to dusty old story books tucked away in damp attics.

'Green is not good,' Alun warns, shaking his head, his ability to scry shows a foreboding vision in the flames of his eyes.

'I will see what the crystals have to say about it,' I assure them.

I have to agree, when I felt the shaking in the Crystal Mine, I knew. The energy isn't right. It doesn't belong here.

'Will you both be coming to the Light Festival?' I ask, remembering I must hurry to make it back in time. Petra nods her heavy head, smiling.

'We shall all be there, but you won't be able to see us,'

I wonder how many Watchers are left now. I haven't seen one in a long time, many moons ago. To see two together, brother and sister, is very unusual. Even on my scale of unusual, and I have seen some extraordinary things. I politely return Petra's smile and wish them both a magical festival. I explain that I must excuse myself. I must go home and prepare for the event.

'Till our paths cross again,' Petra says giggling. They bow their heads to me in courtesy. I respectfully raise my hands to my third eye in the grace position. I turn to face home, thinking, what an odd thing to say … Till our paths meet again. Does she know something I don't? What have I missed? Why have I missed it?

Chapter 11: Fireflies

A vision. The fireflies are on their way! Visions are a normal part of my existence. I'm so excited; it's a positive sign, I fly about in an excited frenzy, shouting out the good news. Beings curiously come out from their houses, wondering what my rippled vibrations meant.

'They are coming! The fireflies are on their way! They will be here… very, very soon,'

I dash around, cartwheeling in the air, my news affecting every Being. Every single Being shines a little brighter than usual. I'm glad to bring them these great tidings. The thought of those magical magnificent mighty little bugs fills me with exhilaration. Each one glows immaculately as an individual, but when they swarm together; fly as an army, their combined lights create a lighthouse effect, and the glow can be seen far and wide. Their vibration can be felt much further away.

The time for the Light Festival to begin has finally come. I make my way through the thronging crowds already gathered, to our agreed meeting point at the base of the mountain. Everyone is buzzing in anticipation. The wisps are wisping; all white and whimsical and the rainbow fairies slide down their self-projected multi-coloured arches, annoyingly getting in my way. Lynk is here already with his Mum and her guests. I can see he is desperate to give them the slip and join me. No doubt he'll have been prohibited, paying the price for his late homecoming. My fault of course. I daren't go over there. Even I'm scared of Mary when she gets on her high horse.

I stand with Eucele and one of his cousins. I'm very pleased to see him and eager to hear all about his crystal project. I'm hoping he will bring it up first. I describe the Crystal Mine incident. He gives very little away and offers no information about his need for white quartz. Whilst we are talking, I notice out of the corner of my left eye that Lynk is trying to slowly edge sideways away from his Mum. Just a few hooves at a time, so it isn't too obvious. She keeps glancing at him, catching him out. She turns right around, staring at him forcing him to keep still, with her telepathic 'Mary look.' It is funny to watch. Luckily, I'm at a distance.

Eucele says something about the strange events that occurred at the mine. I grasp little of what is said, my attention is firmly on Lynk.

'Yes, go Lynk!' I'm willing him to escape as he attempts to move away yet again. Yes, he makes it! He sneaks over and joins us.

'Having a nice party?' I tease. He rolls his eyes at me. His Mum does associate with the most boring and bossy of the astral dimension. She sees them as the finest in society.

'Whatever you do, do not turn around,' I warn him. 'She's just realised you've gone. She's not happy. Her tail is going absolutely crazy, and her ears are pricked up, out of the sides of her purple straw hat,'

'Oh no, not the ears. That's a bad sign,' Poor Lynk, he will be in deep trouble later.

I wave to her, giving her my most charming smile. She won't make a scene in front of Eucele. It would be beneath her. Defeated for now, she shakes her head, and I can hear saying to her hoofy friends 'Oh, I give up!'

'She didn't believe you about the Viking then?'

'No, she said she'd never heard such rubbish.'

More and more Beings have gathered, unnoticed by us whilst we're chatting. I purposely search for the Giants, but there was no sign of them. Even Sphinx has abandoned his position to come and experience the spectacular and eagerly awaited festivities. I'm surprised. He rarely ventures from his fixed position in front of the gates of Tacky Manor. He lies, perfectly still, looking very stately making the place look grand, just watching. He stands alone now, quietly, to the side, segregated. Looking and waiting. He has always been the shy type, never one for mixing or having much to say. I mentioned this to Eucele once, a very long time ago. There was so much I wanted to ask him about, but I knew Eucele would not be party to intrusive conversation.

'That makes him sensible in my book,' Eucele replied with the same old expression on his face. The look on a Being's face usually tells you what they are thinking, how they feel about something, but it is impossible to gauge Eucele. He has one expression, and it looks almost scornful, all the time. Even when he is projecting at his highest vibration, he is impossible to read. With me, the less I know about Beings, subjects and events, the more I want to find out all I can about them. I find Sphinx captivating. He has powerful beastly strength, yet he is gentle and humble, all at the same time. He is many things. I am in awe of his beautiful wide, painted eyes, with black lines around them and flicks identical to the one on my necklace. I feel we're somehow connected, by our eyes. He wears his magical headdress with the golden and blue horizontal stripes of the nemes, hanging down the sides of his golden face and over his strong lion legs.

'They are coming!' An excited tiny fairy flies ahead of the army of fireflies, as they follow the dirt path. Everyone can hear; they are so loud. There's an unfamiliar breeze; the energetic breeze of thousands of wings flapping in rhythm and all at once. The glow comes next. Then they are visible, bathed in soft light, the glowing bugs fly straight past our crowd. Their wings are buzzing and so are our senses. Some fireflies glow red, some yellow and some are green, all shining from their underbellies. The special guest, the Blue Ghost is the only firefly with a blue light. There is only ever one of them. They are very special. They fly past, in their organised tight line formations. Oblivious to the spectacle they are creating. They know where they're headed, they know exactly where they're going. They have been there before. Fixed on their path, looking straight ahead, goal imprinted. They are looking for the Towering Pines. They always rest upon them at this point in their journey.

We Beings follow them in silence. The three Towering Pines are now visible. The mother tree is the tallest, standing majestically in between the other two. The mother of everything that grows; the first tree to grow in the astral world.

A silent order is given, a command that is out of our vibration; we cannot hear it. A secret signal, whatever it is, the fireflies all know. They dive bomb in synchronicity, in a V shaped formation. Only when they reach the trees do they break ranks and position themselves, spreading out over the branches. When they are completely settled, each tree is covered and decorated; bathed in red, yellow and green twinkling lights. The Blue Ghost glows eye-wateringly bright on the mother tree's highest branch. As they stop and rest, the noise from their rapidly beating wings comes to a gradual stop. They sit bug-eyed, glistening and sparkling, lighting the trees up with a twinkling, incandescent display. Suddenly, stillness; there is no noise. In response, the crowd start to glow, combining their electrifying energies. Those Beings in the crowd with wings find themselves flapping and jigging. Tails go side to side uncontrollably and rainbows shoot out into the space around us. Bursts of joyful energy, dance around and about and over our heads. Every one of us feels a warm and blissful sensation moving through us. Everyone here, every Being, every bug, every sprite and every tree. Everything is connected. We can't ignore the tingles that spiral through us. Vibrations intensify and multiply. Lynk and I cannot stop ourselves from laughing, his tail is hitting me as it swishes side to side, back and forth excitedly. He can't help it. Everyone is laughing, excited and feeling stronger, totally euphoric. The fireflies sit and rest for a short time, but their effect will be long lasting. All too soon, it is over. They prepare to leave. They must continue their journey. This Festival of Light heralds the start of the new stellar cycle. New stars are about to be formed. The universe is evolving and everything is growing, getting brighter and better, expanding, renewing. Everything feels balanced in the astral world. Even Lynk's Mum looks happy I notice. Her tail is wagging. I giggle to myself as I look around at the different reactions of the crowd. Another secret signal and the fireflies rise, regroup into the V shape and buzz off on the rest of their journey. That's it. It's over; just like Christmas.

We stay where we are, carry on with our excited exchanges for a bit longer, no Being wants it to end. Slowly, groups begin to break away. After this celebration it is a custom to be with kindred spirits. Parties are organised.

Eucele and Sphinx are deep in discussion as we all leave together. Lynk has already said goodbye to me and rejoined his Mum and her friends to make the walk back to their stable. He takes advantage of her good mood, a clever manoeuvre on his part. Walking ahead of me, suddenly, something happens that throws me off my guard. Mary stops walking, turns around and calls to me.

'Maya, do you want to come for tea?'

Chapter 12: Tea Drinking

Do I? I'm taken aback. 'Umm, yes please.' I happily skip forward to join them.

Lynk and I walk ahead, our heads bent forwards as usual, whispering. It's been a while since I've taken part in a tea drinking ceremony.

'Be careful,' his Mum warns us, 'I've heard reports of a Viking hanging around here.'

She chuckles with her friends as we walk past the old oak tree. I give Lynk a wink with my third eye. Sometimes it is better that they don't know. Beings of all kinds can only approach the world around them at the level of existence they vibrate at.

It is a very pleasant tea. Lots of drinking tea. We pretend to drink tea at these ritual gatherings with family and friends. It's very rare for me to take part in them though, not having a soul family.

Earth is a three-dimensional world; everything is solid or liquid or gas. It's the physical realm. There, a cup of tea is real, you can make it and drink it. Cake is real, you actually eat it. You have senses that taste and smell so eating and drinking are pleasurable and necessary activities. It's the body's fuel. A body is the vessel you must inhabit to be born, to grow, to reproduce, to live and prosper. Here in the astral world, we don't need to eat or drink. We don't have bodies that require nourishment. We are energetic entities. When we go to earth, we need to take on human form to protect us and to manoeuvre. We step into a body, a temple that will protect us for the duration of that lifetime. Some amongst us have never been to earth, having chosen to live on other planets and worlds instead, but for the ones of us that have lived a lifetime or more on earth, we sometimes like to re-enact things that we particularly liked and enjoyed when we were there, so we do them on very special occasions.

Mary hands me a cup of the magic tea, and I raise the cup to my mouth. I act like I am actually drinking it. I've not done this in a very long time. A warm sensation trickles through me, and I find myself saying, 'Ahh a nice hot cuppa,'

Tea Drinking

My forgotten past programming is coming out. Everyone in the room laughs at me. I finish swallowing my last pretend gulp and enjoy being in the company of others for a short while. I can't stay much longer; I have tasks that still need to be done. I thank Mary for inviting me and say my goodbyes. I ponder the events of the day, particularly the shaking mine, as I walk the short route home. Still deep in my dissection of thoughts, I walk straight through my walls to find someone inside waiting for me. He sits on my one and only stool. A stranger, though I know who he is by sight. A scholarly young man dressed in a white toga with brown strappy sandals on his feet.

'What are you doing here?' I ask him surprised but concerned that he may be in some sort of trouble.

'Waiting and waiting,' is his fed-up reply.

'It was the Festival of Light, why didn't you go there to find me?'

'Never mind,' he shakes his head. 'I forgot. We must leave now.'

Chapter 13: The Task

The young man guides me to a clearing in the woods. He whispers precise instructions. I must carry on alone; he can be of no further use. He carries on walking to the other side of the trees, disappearing from view. I tentatively make my way forwards. The twelve Light Council members are sitting, soberly on a ring of cloud. I hope they're not annoyed at being kept waiting. Their faces are expressionless through their shrivelled wrinkles. Older than old, withered, skeletal, pointy faces. Decrepit and thin as broom handles, they could easily snap in half. Their third eyes are yellow with many millennia of wisdom gained. The supreme masters of knowledge. They know everything about everything, every galaxy, every black hole, every star, every moon, every Being, every single little speck. I try to apologise for having kept them waiting. The Light Council High Leader, Ion, sharply cuts me off.

'Maya, what have you been doing? Where have you been? We have waited far too long for you to get here. Time is running out, you must act fast,'

In a softer voice, he continued, 'Without doubt you are incredibly powerful, your talents are indeed admirable; you astound us all,'

I am quietly proud by his unexpected praise. Experience has taught me that there is always a caveat; I'm on my guard.

'What keeps you here? You have nothing new to learn. Why are you ignoring your oath, Maya?'

My pride falls: I feel insulted. He looks around at the eleven men nestled comfortably upon the ring of cloud.

'We are of the opinion that you have become far too comfortable,'

The elders murmur their agreement and nod their heavy looking heads in unison.

I agree with him; he speaks the truth. My attachment to the astral world is absolute. I do not want to be or go anywhere else. I don't want to leave this dimension behind. It's my home.

'The universe is vast Maya. Your capabilities are equally extensive,' he glances around the circle. 'You are limiting yourself and selfishly reserving your gifts for a chosen few. Your gifts will be of greater use and impact elsewhere. As a Lightworker and Starseed of The Order of Ra, you must accept your task. You must sever your bonded attachments, cut your unnecessary ties and act in a way that upholds the oath and its values to which you swore,'

I know light work is my calling, my duty but I see things differently. I consider myself to have been a very useful Starseed and argue my case.

'I'm doing a very good job here. I recently stopped a delusional Viking, who found his way across the veils, determined to turn the astral world into his own personal Valhalla,'

I'll be surprised if they do not know.

They ignore me.

'Think about what has been said and think about it quickly. For you must leave this very moon cycle. Everything has been perfectly planned, perfectly aligned and perfectly timed,'

I look at them, my mouth drops wide open.

'This very cycle? But we're coming to the cycle's end!'

I had not been expecting that, 'Where is it you want me to go?'

They haven't told me yet. There is only one world it can be. I'm willing myself to be wrong. Why would I want to go back there? Why would anyone want to go there? I've heard gossip from newly arrived Beings about how bad the earth has become, far worse now than when I last left. There must be some truth to the rumours if the Light Council are asking me to go back there.

Boman, the youngest and smallest member of the council continues.

'Earth is struggling. She is trying to rise on her dimensional axis, raise herself higher, taking the humans with her. Of all the creatures who inhabit this plant, it is the humans that are now working against her. Without their destructive ways, the planet would continue to thrive; all creatures need to live in harmony and balance. We cannot allow this cycle of destruction to continue. A great pandemic has spread across the continents. Many humans and animals are sick; they are dying in large numbers. The planet's vibrations are extremely low. Earth needs your help to shift her position to a more advanced level of consciousness, peace, happiness and health. To live in the fifth dimensional state, the earth's level of energy frequency must increase greatly. All Lightworkers must go to her assistance. They are required to raise the vibrations on earth as a collective and balance the negative energies. The Light Councils of the Universe have met discreetly and have resolved to take control of the situation. It must be done if we are to ensure that the earth achieves her fullest potential. If we do nothing, humans will be imprisoned, trapped in and by their own lower state of consciousness and existence. We have foreseen their fighting and destructive ways will not only destroy themselves, but it will eventually lead to the destruction of ours and every dimension.'

Ion continues, 'The veil that separates our dimension from theirs has already been breached. Yes Maya, we do know about the Viking. The veil has been torn, gashes ripped open, made by their powerful and new deadly weapons,'

'What is my task?' I ask against my better judgement.

'The task is to be human.'

I cannot think of anything worse.

Chapter 14: Asteroid

'You are not going alone. One billion Lightworkers and Starseeds are transporting from all galaxies and dimensions. Some have gone already, incarnated, re-born as humans on earth. Many are departing as we speak. Each one carries within their DNA, the blueprint of their awakening. The details of their life purpose,' Ion pauses as he recollects, 'You may not remember that when you elect to be born on earth, you will inevitably inherit the veil of forgetfulness,'

The veil of forgetfulness, I had forgotten all about that. I will have to be born as a tiny helpless baby. It will take eighteen earth years to develop into an adult. I won't know why I'm there. Who knows when or if I will ever remember my purpose.

I can't decide now. I know they need me to agree to go but I am hesitant to leave my life here for the unknown.

'If I decide to go, how will I get there?'

'The boat will collect you, ferry you away from here. Just take yourself down to the Lake of Reincarnation and wait,' Ion assumes I will leave.

I haven't decided. Suddenly, a thunderous rumble roars from above heralding an all-encompassing trail of darkness and ferocious, spiralling winds which kick up every particle of dust.

'It's here,' Ion states matter-of-factly.

He shows no sign of surprise or fear. He must have foreseen this as an inevitable evil. Trees are split, some from top to root, Rocks, lifted by the wind, begin to rain down, threatening the Light Council. I instinctively switch to fight mode, my aura radiating neon green. I aim my light at the rocks and effortlessly sweep them aside. The rocks become an avalanche, some, the size of giant boulders. I move my light from rock to rock, zapping and breaking them up.

'The humans! It's them. They have done this,' I scream against the deafening winds.

The energy of three vortexes merge into one enormous rotating angry column, destroying everything in its path. I can feel its power around me, pulling me up and sucking me in. Resistance is futile, it is far stronger than my energy. I'm corkscrewed into its centre where I'm tossed this way and that. Instantly, the fight is knocked out of me, my aura changes from neon green to a dull yellow. I've got to get out of this. My energy is being sapped with every rebound.

Worse is to come. I see the most humongous asteroid plummeting towards us. I know exactly what's about to happen. I see it unfolding in slow motion in my third eye, just before it manifests. I try to tear the cloud column wall apart; try to break through it. I strike with all my light. To no avail, it's too big. I quickly aim but I can't keep steady, and my power is wasted. I'm thrown around and around and my light bounces in a zig zag, ricocheting off the edge of the meteorite instead. The twister's speed increases. I'm thrown upside down and spun faster and faster. The asteroid crashes down upon the fleeing Light Council. It obliterates the serene circle where they sat, fluffs of cloud everywhere.

'Go to earth!' the voices of the Light Council boom.

'Why should I help? This is all their fault!'

'NNNNNoooooooo!' I scream. The Light Council vanish; gone in a flash. Distracted, I don't see it coming. I'm hit from behind. My three eyes close.

Chapter 15: Aftermath

I sit up. I find myself lying on the ground, my head underneath a bush. The light must have been temporarily knocked out of me. I quickly regenerate. No harm done. Looking up, the barrage seems to have ceased. I stand, looking with urgency for any survivors of the Light Council.

'Ion, Boman… is anyone here?'

The gigantic asteroid has squashed the serene white circle, wisps of it poke out from underneath. Shredded pieces of cloud float about. I feel sorry at the sight of it.

The asteroid gives off a strange green glow. It is the same shape and size as the crater that was made and left behind in the desert earlier. Almost a perfect circle.

It is one of their weapons from earth, not an asteroid as I had first thought. I need to take a closer look. I tap on it. Metal material welded together with rivets, just the same as all the others they send through. No matter the shape or size, they are all made from the same material. I've not seen this glowing before; this green luminous light.

I'm pleased to find one other survivor, the white toga-wearing messenger. He was waiting in the woods in case the Light Council had need of him, when the bombardment began. He took cover. We bumped into each other, as we both slowly edged backwards, looking around, calling for any survivors to make themselves known. We both jumped around surprised. Finding no one else, I suggest he follows me to the Shining Valley, where there will be safety in numbers.

I march at a brisk pace. He struggles behind, attempting to keep up. I'm in no mood to converse with him. I've very little time to consider my next course of action. It's the biggest decision of my existence. At the crossroads, I instruct him to continue walking straight on this path, he will come to the Shining Valley. I think to myself afterwards, he already knows. I take my path and make my way home for a second time. I've lost valuable decision-making time and I had very little of it to start with. I charge through my front door and grab the crystal nearest to me; I need to look inside the gem and see what's happening. I state my intention clearly, name my requirements.

'I want to take a closer look at this human creation and its ominous green glow,'

I gaze into the crystals' centre reminding myself that I must be patient. Scrying involves patience and skill. I keep staring. Unblinking, concentrating. There! I notice movement inside. Flames become visible, they spread to the left and to the right consuming everything in their path. The thing the humans made, spits them out, it makes flames.

'The green glow,' I remind the crystal.

I had asked for two lots of information. Instantly, I see a different picture in the centre, it's an image of humans looking sick and withered. The image disappears.

Why did you have to look? I berate myself.

Chapter 16: Shall I Stay or Shall I go?

So many thoughts and emotions are coursing through my conscience; all jumbled up. I need to consider everything but it's so hard. I must try to think logically and list one reason at a time. I take a deep breath; I need to clear my mind. I sit comfortably on my three-legged stool and close all three eyes. I don't want to see anything for a few moments. I need to go inwards. I put my hands on my lap, palms turned upwards and keep still. Everything stops, I completely switch off and allow myself to be me. No looking to the future, no looking back at the past. Simply being here in the now, the present and allowing myself to enter a meditative state. A perfectly natural state of being.

I imagine that I'm walking towards a luscious green meadow, the flowers are yellow. I don't know if I've been there before or if it's somewhere I've created myself. It doesn't matter. I am what I believe. I step and visualise my ethereal feet and toes, walking through the long blades of grass. I envisage that the rich nutritious elements that are naturally present in the soil below, starts to transfer nourishment up through the soles of my light feet. Grounding me and connecting me to my highest source, my true self, so that I may use the healing energies. The energy is gently streaming up my legs. Steadily it flows, filling me up and allowing me to take in a much-needed supply of light energy. The flow travels to my waist and further still towards my neck. My arms start to tingle with an immense rush of energy, my power is feeling more and more intense. My fingers start to pulse, and I can feel the power shooting out of my fingertips. The flow travels on towards the top of my head, where there's a sudden eruption and the light spouts out of the top, cascading into a rainbow umbrella.

A moment of stillness, centring myself to my very core. After the outpourings of light, there is nothing. I am gone, gone where? Nowhere, but I feel, and I think. I am the essence of the universe in its purest form. There is no sense of how long I sit like this. Then I begin to move my hands slightly and twitch my foot. I am back in the room, my home. Now I am ready.

I make two lists. First, I list the reasons to stay here in the astral world.

- Number one. My main reason: I don't like humans. I promised myself I would never go back. It's inhabited by egocentric, small-minded humans who aim deadly weapons at each other, damaging other worlds as well as their own. They have no idea or consideration for the long-term effects of their actions; so selfish!
- Number two. They don't believe in magic. Well, most of them don't. They think it's fantasy; something to make films about and fill their story books. At best, my abilities will be laughed at; at worst, they will be lost.
- Number three. It took me a very long time to get where I am. My status and position command the respect of all Beings. I would have to sacrifice my life here and start from nothing. I don't want to change.
- Number four. The veil of forgetfulness is inevitable. I will forget who I was. I will forget what I am and more annoyingly, I will forget the reason I have been sent to earth.
- Number five. I will have to start at the very beginning, grow, learn and wait for the blueprint inside me to be activated without being consciously aware of it. I will be a human, ordinary. I will have to struggle like they do, suffer like they do and feel pain like they do.
- Number six. What if my blueprint is never activated? I could live and die as a human and never know my destiny.
- Number seven. I will be born into a family of humans who will have no idea that I'm there for a specific purpose. They will automatically assume that I'm just like them. Fitting in will not be easy.
- Number eight. My physical body will die. From that, there is no escape.
- Number nine. Lynk and I will never see each other again. We haven't been apart since the moment we met. How will we cope without each other? What will he do when I'm gone?
- Number ten. There will be no one to protect the Beings when I'm gone. No one to keep everything balanced. The green glow is dangerous and unknown. The Light Council has vanished. Anything could happen without my protection.
- Number eleven. I've made my home here and I want to stay.

Next, I list the reasons to go to earth and follow the Light Council calling.

- Number one. My bright light will shine alongside all the others who have already answered the calling. The earth's level of consciousness will rise and so will the dimension she vibrates in. Life will improve for the human race. They will not need their weapons. Their lives will be better. The earth, she will heal. She is broken right now. Polluted, scarred, dirty and damaged.

- Number two. It is a journey. It has been a long time since I have ventured into the unknown. Perhaps I have become a little too comfortable, having lived here for the equivalent of a few thousand earth years.
- Number three. I won't be alone anymore. Perhaps I will be given a loving family. I might get a Mum. A Mum like Lynk has. Just imagine. Hopefully, she will be a bit happier than Mary.
- Number four. I have vows to uphold, and I do not break my word.
- Number five. There will be real cups of tea to drink, and real cake to eat.
- Number six. I will gain new knowledge of earth. How things must have changed since I was last there and I may discover more about this carbon dating the Viking was ranting on about.
- Number seven. Once upon a time, I wouldn't have thought twice about setting out on adventure, perhaps I need to revisit my old self. Find my sense of adventure again.
- Number eight. I can develop and learn about myself. Maybe I'll master the skill of patience?
- Number nine. I would quite like a dog. I don't know or remember ever owning one.
- Number ten. I might find a particular friend, that would be great.
- Number eleven. Perhaps if I go back to earth I might finally meet and recognise my soul family. The ones that I have been waiting forever to find. Perhaps that's why I've been waiting so long, perhaps they are never coming to the astral world. Perhaps they have reincarnated on earth repeatedly, therefore, my waiting is hopeless.
- Number twelve. I've been told to go. The Light Council want me to go. They need me to go. The earth needs me to go, the humans need me to go, not that they know it. The animals, the fish, the birds; they all need me to go. Everyone needs me.

Chapter 17: Up to No Good

Leaning out of my large open window, looking up at the flower moon, I feel exhausted. My time is nearly here. I hadn't noticed until now that the lunar cycle is nearly complete. I must weigh up my two lists. The big question is, should I sacrifice myself for everyone else's sake? Does what I want not count? Don't I matter? I have to choose others over myself. That is my dilemma. I have decided. I have no choice.

I've rehearsed over and over again in my head what to say to Lynk when he opens his door. Standing here, I'm frozen, unable to knock. It's not a difficult thing to do. His Mum has told me to do it millions of times. She never looks pleased when I fly right in through the stable walls. Though in my defence, it is usually because I'm in a hurry, urgently needing to speak with Lynk and I simply forget.

Lynk flings the door open. His face changes to surprise as he sees me standing there, arm raised, poised to knock. I stare at him, trying to remember the exact words I had rehearsed but I can't think of one. They've gone. I have no idea what to say.

'Mum, I'm going out!' Lynk shouts walking out of his door.

'You were standing out there for ages, so I came out,' he says looking at me, wondering why I am acting so peculiar.

'I thought I saw something out of sync, so I was taking a closer look, but everything's fine,'

That sounds like a plausible enough excuse.

'What are we going to do then?' he asks, accepting my explanation.

'The old house,' I whisper.

Lynk looks astonished, he wasn't expecting me to say that.

'You what?'

I will be leaving soon, and I don't intend to do so without looking inside the forbidden manor. 'Don't you go taking my Lynk in there,' Mary had warned me. I haven't forgotten. Now I'm leaving, I feel the urge. Promises or no promises, I must go in.

'Why do you want to go in there?' he whispers urgently, 'We promised we never would,'

'Some promises can't be kept and for good reason,' I tell him 'You can keep your promise to your Mum if you want, I understand, but I have to go in,'
Challenge set.
Lynk's Mum has the ears of a horse, and snaps open the top half of the brown stable door.
'What are you two planning?' She demands accusingly.
She always suspects that we're up to something. No, she always suspects I'm up to something and dragging her poor Lynk alongside with me kicking and screaming in fright.
'Just deciding to go down to the river, Mum,'
She nods in approval and slams the door, satisfied that we're not going to get into too much mischief down there.
I laugh at him, Lynk is getting sneaky. He laughs too.
'What are you two laughing at?' Mary shouts from inside the stable.
We stop laughing.
'Let's get going,'
I pull him by the arm. I don't have much time left. I can't afford to waste a moment more of it. 'She's probably watching us. Don't look back, keep walking,'
We don't want to appear suspicious.
'She'll never let me out with you ever again if she finds out,' Lynk warns.
'Don't worry about it,' I reassure him, 'There's no point.'
After all, I won't be here anyway, I say to myself quietly.
We sensibly walk away from the estate towards the grand gates. When we're sure that we're out of sight of the stable and his Mum's beady eyes, we stop. I wrap a violet bubble around us. No one can see us now. We turn and sneak back up the hill towards Tacky Manor. Dubiously, we approach the large red front door hanging on metal black fleur-de-lis hinges. We've seen it so many times but never this close. I tentatively turn the large black doorknob and push. It's locked. Nothing that a bit of magic won't budge. My light flashes and the lock clicks open. I step inside and hold the door wide open to allow Lynk to trot through. His four skinny legs step down over the drab grey stone step. I follow him into a cavernous hallway. I put out my light and remove the violet bubble.
As our eyes adjust to the gloom, a gust of wind hits us from behind followed by the ominous slam of the front door. I lurch for the doorknob; too late. I won't budge. Something or someone has locked us in. Whoever or whatever, doesn't want us to leave. It's not a problem. I will find a way out. Things are getting interesting already.

Chapter 18: Tacky Manor

Lynk looks very uncomfortable. I feel bad for him breaking his promise to his Mum. It must be done, even at the risk of the wrath of Mary. I cannot leave this realm without dealing with whatever evil is lurking in this house. There's no one else equipped to tackle… tackle what? I've no idea.

Lynk follows me down the wide hallway where the vast walls and high ceilings are decorated in a dismal tone of green. It feels cold. I'm surprised that I can remember being cold; it's been such a long time since I've felt anything at all. I feel a shiver run through my whole being.

'Can you feel that?'

I check I'm not imagining this iciness. Lynk nods at me, bewildered. I notice his teeth chattering and his ears are on high alert, standing to attention, sticking out of his long dark mane. I'm sure he's thinking that coming here was a bad idea. I ignore his look of concern and feign an interest in the floor. Light brown square tiles with a circular mosaic pattern created from orange, red and yellow tiles in the centre. I can't make out a particular picture; they seem to be randomly placed.

An alcove is built into the left-hand side of the hallway. The gap is filled with a piece of furniture made from good old-fashioned solid wood; a familiar sight when I was last on earth. Tree branches are carved into it and at the end of each branch is a small black metal hook. It's a hat stand. A large oval mirror surrounded by a silver frame, is in the centre. Perfectly positioned for last minute adjustments. I notice a shelf underneath the mirror topping a single large drawer. I pull the small black metal handle gingerly towards me. It's empty. Inadvertently, I look up and into the mirror glass. When did I last look at myself? It's not necessary in the astral world. My reflection is wispy, hazy, slightly out of focus with a transparent, ethereal quality. It's not surprising. This artefact is intended for use in another dimension, with a different vibrational level. It can't quite catch my reflection as it swims in and out. My bright rainbow light is glowing around me. I stare at it in awe. It is truly beautiful. It suddenly dawns on me that I've reached my full potential. The rainbow aura can only be achieved at the highest level. It's a surprising and unexpected confirmation that I've made the right decision to return to earth.

'Let me see,' Lynk is eager to look too.

I move out of the way and stand behind him so I can see what he sees. We don't worry about our looks here; it's a human thing. I'm interested to see how he reflects though. To think that this mirror has always been here; we had no idea.

'Aren't my ears big!' Lynk declares, wiggling them about.

I laugh, teasing him, 'You should see the size of your butt!'

Touchy subject, being deadly serious, he turns and faces his butt to the mirror. 'It's not that bad,' he retorts defensively.

He moves it side to side, into different positions to try and get a clearer look. The more he shakes it trying to get it in focus, the more and more it looks distorted and appears bigger and bigger.

He frowns; self-consciously defensive, 'It's huge, I can't help it,'

'Stop it, you sound like a human,' I laugh.

I know he can't help it. It's the energies in this house; they densely project, earthly, superficial vanity. I hear another voice joining in. My laughter stops.

'That wasn't you, was it?'

'No,' he shakes his head. 'I heard it though. I don't like it,'

I shiver. The temperature suddenly turns ice cold. I give Lynk a gentle nudge out of the way. I need to look into the mirror again. I stare deeply, searching. There it is. It looms behind me, a black shadowy figure, laughing sinisterly. I stare intently at its reflection. A soulless set of green eyes bore into mine. I will not look away. Suddenly, whatever it is, stops laughing and vanishes. I spin around trying to catch a glimpse. Gone; nothing there. I turn to Lynk and demand.

'Did you see that?'

'See what?'

'Something's not right in this house; it's completely out of balance!'

I storm down the hall, searching for the elusive entity. I'm on a mission. Lynk follows me faithfully, as always. I come to a large wooden door. To the left is a spiral staircase. Which way do I go? Instinct tells me to climb the stairs. The steps will be tricky for Lynk as they are wide on the outside but narrow on the inside. I go up first, Lynk follows behind me, keeping to the widest part of each step. He holds onto the wooden carved spindles that twist up the banister. They take us to a hallway where the floor is covered with a long-faded green and red patterned rug. I notice another staircase at the far end, leading up to a third floor.

'We should check around here first,' I whisper.

The walls are painted the same shade of dark green as downstairs. The corridor is lined with five large wooden doors. I point to the nearest one, indicating to Lynk. He nods his understanding. We enter the room and find ourselves in a study with walls painted in a reddish-brown colour and hung with pictures. Large ones with golden frames. Portraits of pompous, unattractive, stern-faced men with ridiculous wigs and wearing frilly clothes. They have staring eyes and portly bellies. I would hate to have them staring down at me if I had to work at the desk.

'And you were worried about your butt,' I point out to Lynk. 'Look at their faces.'

Lynk neighs a nervous laugh, clutching his hands over his mouth in a failed attempt to stop the involuntary reflex.

A mismatch of small blue, green and brown patterned rugs thrown down over the wooden floorboards are the nearest thing to a carpet. The room is crammed with furniture. Not much of it matching. The gentleman's room. Though something tells me he was more of an ogre than a gentleman. There is a heavy and overbearing shroud of heavy air filling the room. We walk towards the large bay window where a pair of plush, faded velvet green curtains hang. We look out over the front lawn, at the estate gates, towards the back of Sphinx. As we leave the window, my third eye sees his head turn to stare at us. I can read his thoughts. 'What in the astral plain are they up to?'

The solid oak desk with a chair tucked underneath, has lots of drawers built into it. A red leather writing pad sits on top. To the side of it is an oval picture frame. Silver and set with white pearls. It holds a painted likeness of a pretty and dainty woman with blonde hair pinned high on top of her head. She sits smiling, in a long baby-blue gown. When this image was captured, energy was lighter in the house. Something happened. Houses and buildings hold onto memories and emotions like humans do. Good and bad energy can be absorbed and leave behind an everlasting imprint.

I notice a big fireplace and several small tables placed around the room, with Art Nouveau adjustable lamps placed on them. Even so, the room is gloomy, the energy dark. Satisfied that the soulless eyes are not in here, we move into the next room.

A day room. In contrast to the study, the energy feels so much lighter. It has more of a lady's feel about it. Red wallpaper with grand fleur-de-lis on the walls, red curtains fringe the bay window, and a large crystal chandelier hangs from the centre of the ceiling. A large rose-coloured rug is spread across the wooden floor and the room is filled with blossom pink cushions on chairs. It's not here. It's not in any of the other rooms on this level either; a bedroom and dressing room, washroom and dining room. I direct Lynk to the next flight of stairs. I go first, he follows. The temperature drops. I can feel a presence. The soulless eyes owner is up here. The hallway is small, I point to the room furthest away. We'll start there. After all, walls have ears, and eyes sometimes, souls too.

Nothing in there, it's just a storage area, full of furniture. The second room is of no interest either. The third door opens into a large bedroom. The walls are painted gloomy grey and dirty white on the ceiling. Three small black metal framed single beds are evenly spaced. Metal frame headboards against the back wall. Each bed is made the same; one thin cotton white pillow and a blue knitted blanket over a white sheet. Each bed has a small round table next to it with a simple oil lamp on it. There's a wardrobe behind the door. The three occupants must have shared it. I look inside. It's empty. Servants' quarters. It isn't here. We go back out into the hallway. Lynk pulls on another door handle. It doesn't open. I indicate for him to leave it for now. The final door to try is at the top of the stairs to the right. When I touch the black iron round doorknob, it's cold. I shiver as I peer through the keyhole with my middle eye. I nod to Lynk that it's in here. We've found it. I count down three to one using my fingers then quickly push the door open.

Chapter 19: Maudlin Maids

An icy, hazy blast hits us. I can smell something truly disgusting. A gut-wrenching, decaying stench. Baffling, as I cannot smell. Smell is a sense that humans possess. I look around expecting to see something dead lying undiscovered in the room. There's nothing. Lynk gags then muffles through his clamped hands which are covering his nose and mouth.

'The most sensible thing to do is get out of here, right now!' Lynk whispers.

Now is not the time to be sensible. Something is wrong here, out of balance. I need to use my powers to restore that balance. Call it our last great adventure; my one last service. When I leave the astral world, everything must be in harmony.

I silently urge Lynk to follow me through another doorway that leads to an almost identical second servants' bedroom. Here is the source of the stench. This room is on two levels. At the far end, the roof slopes sharply to meet the floor. I determinedly notion Lynk to keep up as we step down past the beds and wardrobe, into the lower half of the room and position ourselves next to a small round table and wooden chair set against the sloping wall. Lynk stands apprehensively by my side. We wait in silence. Something will happen soon. I can feel a growing tension. Slowly, slowly, the walls appear to move. Lynk and I glance at each other questioningly. The walls appear to be seeping, running, turning red. I look hard, trying to work out what's happening. Then it hits me, blood. I'm seeing blood, spreading and covering every wall; oozing from every crevice. Suddenly, I know what has happened here. I know what took place in this room... Murders!

The instant I realised, the energy is vacuumed out of the room and a powerful gust forces itself in. The chill drops below zero. The bedroom door slams shut then flings wide open again, seemingly by itself. Whatever it is, it's trying to frighten us. Someone appears, a vision. She comes out of nowhere. Lynk and I exchange glances. We both see her. She's not the spirit standing behind me in the mirror downstairs. I fleetingly wonder how many more entities I'll have to deal with. The two wardrobe doors begin to bang open and close by themselves, squeaking on their hinges. Open and close, open and close. I keep very still, watching. I'm aware of Lynk's left front hoof moving around in circles in front of him apprehensively. There are noises coming from the hallway. Someone else is out there playing with another door. It's squeaking as it's opened and closed. Opened and closed.

'They like playing with doors, don't they?'

I make a feeble attempt to lighten the mood. Lynk gives me a wide-eyed nervous smile and neighs. Banging erupts from the adjacent bedroom. The bedroom doors add to the din. The woman walks over to the bed nearest the wardrobe with its doors still flapping. She bends over the pillow and pulls at something. She's dressed in a long black dress with a white bib apron tied up in a bow at the back. No doubt she was a maid, a servant of this house and this is the room she shared with others. On her head sits a white frilly cap keeping her hair tidy and out of the way. At first, she completely ignores us. She is turned to the side at an angle, unaware of our presence. Unexpectedly, she suddenly turns and screams in our faces. Her shriek is loud and terrifying. Lynk is frozen in horror, and no wonder, for where her face should be, there is nothing but a black void. I have seen many things, but never anything so pitiful as this. As I suspected, she is not alone. Two more maids appear and line up beside her. They were playing with the doors. They have been here the whole time. I understand now. One of them glides towards me. She has no legs, no feet. The nearer she comes, the stronger the rancid smell becomes. They are the source; decayed and rotten to their core. I must not judge. I cannot see everything, only part of their story at present. The maid rises off the ground and floats down, over the step, coming straight towards us.

Lynk snaps out of his petrified freeze and hurtles out of the room as fast as his four hooves can carry him. I've never seen him so frightened or gallop so fast. He rushes down the two flights of stairs, heading for the front door. I sweep the approaching maid away with my light and fly over the heads of the other two. I catch sight of Lynk at the bottom of the steps. He runs down the hall, straight past the mirror and grabs the front doorknob. It won't budge. He's forgotten that it locked itself behind us. I go to unlock it, but he bolts again, back down the hallway. I follow him, shouting.

'Lynk, where are you going? Keep still!'

He flings open a door we ignored earlier, a cream ogival mediaeval style door, and charges through it. I follow him. The door slams shut behind us. We have found the kitchens.

'We need to go back to the front door. I'll unlock it and let you out,' I instruct urgently.

When he is safely out, I will deal with these Maudlin Maids. Dramatically, the cream door flings wide open behind us. Startled, the two of us swing around in perfect synchrony and there they are. The Maudlin Maids floating in mid-air, completely expressionless. Totally blank; totally terrifying.

'Quick, keep going to the end!' I change tactics. 'We need to find the back door. Remember, we've passed by it many times from the outside,'

We lunge through a door, into a small square space. Three white oblong sinks and a long wooden work top runs along the wall. Dark brown ceramic pots and jugs are stored high upon shelves and larger versions sit on the ground tucked away under the worktop. I catch sight of something in an old green dish. A piece of white Lemuriann crystal. I reach out and grab it as I run past without slowing my pace. An open doorway at the far side, leads into the main cooking area. A large wooden preparation table stands in front of a fireplace. Its grey stone walls are liberally decorated with kitchen utensils and gadgets, black utensils, shiny silver ones, sieves and pots galore. There are forks, knives and spoons in various sizes. Cleavers, pounders, brushes and trays, all hanging from metal hooks that have been fixed into the walls. Big jars of herbs and spices sit under the table with muslin cloth tied over the top of them. Unexpectedly, the spoons and the jars hurl themselves from the walls and shelves violently at us.

'They're not very hospitable, are they?' I mutter to Lynk whilst we duck, dive and dodge from side to side, still searching for the exit.

A large black cast iron cooking pot with three spikey legs comes flying straight at us. I throw myself over Lynk, protecting him. That was a close one. I pull Lynk into a small adjoining room and there, at last, is the elusive back door. I give it a push. It doesn't move. Another locked door. I use my light to prise it open. It proves very difficult. These are objects from earth. My magic is a different level of vibration. Lynk shouts to warn me that the Maudlin Maids have followed us. 'Do not gallop off,' I instruct him.

'Buuut they're coming straight at us!' he neighs uncontrollably.

I am still struggling with the door, my light shining brightly as I try to tease it open. This is what it'll be like when I'm on earth. No magic to get out of scrapes. I remember the Lemurian crystal that I am holding onto tightly. I point it into the old black keyhole; ancient Lemurian magic transpires.

'Quickly, unlock the door,' I urge.

The magic is invisible, not of this realm. My third eye sees golden specks, shooting through to the other side of the lock. Ah, so I'm not totally

Maudlin Maids

helpless in this house of horrors; my third eye is still powerful. Hopefully that will continue and perhaps I won't be deprived of all my gifts when I go to earth. I hope not.

'Hurry! Now!' I demand.

Chapter 20: White Light

The door clicks and opens.

'Come on!'

With a violet bubble of protection around us, I charge outside, dragging Lynk by his tail. Out into the garden we scarper, following the stepping stone path. It leads away from Tacky Manor, towards the back wall of the estate grounds. Lucky for Lynk, it goes in the opposite direction to his stable. He must go home to his Mum afterwards, whereas I'm never going back. The path takes us through the trees. Lynk leads the way. There are creatures hiding in the bushes. They look petrified. Their wide mouths are chattering as they hang about, some upside down. They're right to be scared; the Maudlin Maids are on our heels as we're nearing the wall. With nowhere to run, I stop, turn and take Lynk's hand. I give Lynk a reassuring nod. I need him to be brave and hold his ground. The Maudlin Maids come for us in a line. They bounce and screech high into the air, one behind the other. They leap one at a time in slow motion at us.

'Wait for it... Wait for it...' I whisper to Lynk whilst shadowy hands reach towards us.

I can see poor Lynk squirming, his eyes squeezed tightly shut beside me. He is just waiting, trying to do what he is told and not make a run for it.

'Has she got me?' he neighs, afraid to look.

'Do I usually let them get you? Open your eyes,' I instruct him, shaking my head.

We have levitated, hovering just above the wall, still wrapped in the violet protective bubble. Lynk prizes open one eye and takes a little peek. When he sees with relief where he is, he opens the other one as well.

'Can we go over the wall now?' he asks hopefully.

'No, we can't! Far too much has happened in this house, and it needs to be put to rest,'

'I thought you'd say that.' He knows me too well.

I remove the bubble with a wave of my hand. It bursts, leaving a pink shredded circle of skin on the ground. Our guard removed, the maids seize their chance and systematically lunge again. Lynk can't watch. I hear him neigh.

White Light

A tube of blinding white light flashes downwards from the universe. It beams from a white, oval portal way above us. One by one the maids are sucked into the beam as they pounce up, unable to stop themselves. They are transported slowly upwards. I was expecting some resistance; some reluctance to go, but they show none. Instead, something quite extraordinary happens. As the first Maudlin Maid is about to pass through the oval, she looks down ever so slightly and I realise that she has a nose, a pair of deep green eyes, and a smiling rosebud mouth. She even has cheeks. She is beautiful. Lynk and I turn to each other in amazement. I hadn't expected that, and I know that anything is possible. The transformation happens again to the other two maids, just before they leave the dimension and time, they are stuck in. All three of them are gone. To where? That is now their choice to make.

'Now, your turn!' I shout at him.

'Who are you talking to?' Lynk curiously looks around.

'Go too!' I command ignoring Lynks confused stares 'The light is here and waiting.'

The sinister laugh we heard earlier, echoes around. I quickly surround myself and Lynk with another bubble of protection, just in time.

'Look!' Lynk points to a heavy black cloud that's been caught.

It's slowly moving upwards, inside the white light.

'How did you know he was there?' Lynk enquires.

'He's been with us all the time, hiding away behind his three serving maids. Possessing, controlling and torturing them, just as he did when they were alive. Deciding how and when they should die. Murderer and abuser. Finally, they are free from him.'

Is that emotion that I can feel?

The black cloud has a big pair of round angry black eyes. It struggles and tries to escape. Thrashing and resisting against the light force pushing it upwards. We witness another transformation from an elusive coward to a man dressed in a fine, white flouncy shirt with ruffles and a red and green tartan kilt.

'Yer!' he points at me in a rage.

I recognise him as one of the men from the portraits hanging on the study walls. His evil reign is now over. I stand smiling and waving as he is slowly transported through and disappears out of sight. He fights all the way.

'YER!' I hear him shout angrily one last time before the portal closes and the light disappears.

'Yes, me,'

Lynk and I do a celebratory jig. We move our arms; one in front and one behind us, pointing in opposite directions, doing a funny walk, side by side, like an Egyptian. An ecstatic Lynk half raps, half sings,

'We did it!
We did it!
Yo, Yo, Yo!
The white light came and transported the maids away,
The bad guy thought he was boss, and no Being could ever stand in his way,
He didn't know Lynk and Maya would come strolling in one day,
To right the wrongs of his foul play,
Yo, Yo, Yo!'

Lynk is suddenly serious, moved by their plight.
'Why were their faces missing?' He has obviously been trying to figure it out.
'Neglected, mistreated and uncared for, their beauty faded, he robbed them of their identity.'
'The lady whose portrait was on the desk?' he asks, trying to make sense of it all. 'She wasn't one of them. Who was she?'
'His wife. She died not long after their wedding. He had been a good person up until her death. His heart was broken. He felt nothing but pain and his pain turned to anger.'
I feel the emotion. I am bothered by it. I change the subject.
'I'm going to take a closer look at those bushes. There were imps hiding there. Did you see them?'
Moving slowly, I gently coax them out. They are nervous and want reassurance that the darkness has gone. Eventually I persuade them, and they gradually abandon their hiding places. The bravest one does so first, followed by another and another until they all feel safe enough to leave their hiding places. The imps have been here a long time, they tell us, trapped in the back garden.
Everyone was trapped. Imps make it their business to know everything that goes on and they tell us all about the souls that were stuck in Tacky Manor. Relieved, some do cartwheels, whilst others talk. Imps are such funny little creatures. They have old haggard faces, regardless of their stages of maturity. Their faces are angular, coming to a point at the chin. Their eyes are all the same colour, a piercing blue. Their noses are long, triangular and pointing in the same direction as their chins. They are identical; replicas of each other. Everyone wears a green, imp hat at a

jaunty angle. Their high-pitched voices naturally like to chitter chatter, one over the other.

'We are glad to be rid of him.'

'He was most evil.'

The general opinion of 'him' isn't very good. Some of it, I dare not repeat. I'm drawn to look at Tacky Manor, still listening to their chatter. Something is happening to it. Pink climbing roses slowly creep up the back wall. Vines stretch out, clinging by thorns onto the walls and loop around the window frames. They stretch all the way up to the servant's floor. My third eye is drawn to a shape that appears at the bedroom window; a person is looking down at us. A woman, quite young with blonde hair wearing something blue.

'Arabella,' I repeat as she tells me her name.

'Arabella? Where?' the imps chorus together excitedly looking around.

'She has not been seen since the night she died.'

'What happened?'

An imp beckons me to bend down and whispers in my ear.

'Her heart was broken.'

Chapter 21: Goodbye to Lynk

We saunter back to the house feeling much lighter, though I'm annoyed at myself for keeping my promise to Lynk's Mum for so long.

'I should have gone in there long ago and sorted that lot out,' I huff as we walk round to the front door.

Still better late than never. How many more thousands of years would the maids have been stuck in that existence? Talking of late, time has moved on; the moon is appearing. I can't put it off any longer. I must say goodbye.

'Lynk, I went in there because I won't ever get another chance.'

He looks at me confused. 'What do you mean?'

There is no easy way to tell him.

'Lynk, I'm leaving. I'm going to earth.'

He abruptly stops trotting beside me. I halt too.

'What do you mean? Why would you want to do that? You don't even like humans, they annoy you.'

I laugh. That's the bit that I am struggling to understand as well.

'The way things are on earth… well, they're starting to cause a knock-on effect here. Unless things get better there, they'll become a lot worse here. Light Beings are answering the call from all the dimensions. The Light Council have asked me to assist.'

'You're going to leave me to endure my mother's tea parties, while you'll be going to real ones?'

I do hope so, however, it's kinder to stay quiet and say nothing.

I start walking again, I'm short on time. Lynk, feeling all confused, follows me.

My magic was weak partly due to the dimensional differences but also, I suspect, the transition has already begun. The Light Council knew that I was going to agree to go, they probably started the magic ball rolling before they even spoke to me.

I need to check that the balance has been restored in the house. I give the front door of the house a push and it swings open easily. The front of the house is now covered in pink climbing roses. It looks so much prettier than before. I close the door. The house is now Arabella's. She has it all to herself.

The cursed have gone.

'I'm afraid this was our last great adventure.'

The waning crescent moon is high now, signalling for me to go. Lynk is silent. I hug him goodbye.

'Just think, Lynk, I might get a Mum like yours!'

I left out the bit about I am hoping she is a bit happier. I hand him the fluorite crystal I found at the Crystal Mine.

'This is to protect you when I'm gone.'

He takes it from me and looks down at it intently. I slowly walk away from him, taking one final look at Tacky Manor.

I give him one last smile and slowly rise. I fly away, leaving my best friend standing all on his own.

Chapter 22: Float On

My little roundhouse, made of sticks with a conical roof, waits for me. I've never needed to spend a lot of time there. I was always away, here or there, protecting some Being from this or that. Spirits and Beings in distress would come.

'Would you mind helping us?' or 'Maya, you need to take a look at this.' I could choose to live in any type of house that I wanted. In the astral world, we create our own style of living, our own little world. We design our own existence. We dwell however we choose too. If I want to live in a castle, absolutely; there's nothing stopping you. Here, dwellings are going free; you just imagine it and it will appear. Very nice too. You want to live in a Roman villa? Use your imagination and it will appear. Look at the redness of those roof tiles. The whiteness of the plaster. Lovely. Oh, I see you have added a bath house. Perfect to chill in.

My little home was perfect for me. I gaze wistfully out of my big open window for one last time. There are scatterings of blue stars shining and the moon is bursting with light. I can't leave it any longer. I must go now. I sit down on my three-legged stool and shut my eyes. All three of them. I visualise myself walking along the path that I know so well. The stream is down there at the bottom of the bank. I am at the spot near the tree where Lynk and I came across the Viking. I wonder if he's still hanging about as I walk by. The Lake of Reincarnation lays ahead. It wasn't there before. A thick mist swirls low on the water, completely obscuring the view to the horizon. Things are changing fast around here.

I wait alone in the dark. Wait is what the Light Council told me to do. A small rowing boat emerges from the mist coming towards me. Wooden and simple, shaped like a banana. It comes close and I look down into the hull. It's empty except for a small slat fixed cross ways to make a seat. I notice there are no oars. I feel myself rise from the shore. Very gently, a mystical white helping hand wraps its giant fingers around me and sets me down on the thwart. It releases me and disappears back into the water from where it came.

Float On

The path has been set and the universe knows the plan. It will make sure that everything happens as it should. There is nothing I need to do.

The boat casts off and magically floats on its set course, into the thick of the mists. Mists that have been created by the Ondines. I know they're here, I can feel them, feel their magic even if I cannot see them. Nothing can be seen; I am somewhere in between there and here. I can't see what lies ahead nor can I look back at what I've left behind. I pass a fountain. A blue petaled flower on a stem with water spraying from it; the Forget-Me-Not Fountain. As I pass it, the spray hits me. Everything about me is gone in a splash. Now is all there is. Now is all there'll ever be. Now, there is no turning back.

Chapter 23: Born Again

It's so tight in here, I can't move. I need to stretch out, but it's impossible. It's dark. What was that? It was ever so slight, but I think I may have just moved. I did! I am! I'm moving downwards, headfirst. Very tiny movements. How long have I been upside down? I've only just noticed. No, no, I was wrong. I must have imagined it. I'm not moving at all. I'm staying perfectly still. It's so hot in here. The temperature's rising. It's burning. I'm moving, but where am I going?

Slowly, slowly. Far too slow for my liking. Nine months! Nine whole months I've been stuck in here. Thank goodness! It looks like I'm finally getting out. Really, is this what I agreed to?

'Push… Push… hold it!' I hear muffled instructions. 'Push again!'

'Stop! Stop!' I yell. 'I don't want to go out there. I don't want to do it. I've changed my mind!'

Worry! Fear! Panic!

These are feelings I'm not used to, human anxieties. I try to cling onto the dark passage walls. The searing heat grows more and more intense as it pushes me further along. No one listens to my protests. No one takes any notice. I know it's useless. I know the only way out is through the tunnel and into the light ahead. There can be no going back. I'm at the point of no return. About to start living life as a human. On the verge of starting all over again. I will be helpless. I will dribble!

'Keep pushing!'

'Pant!'

'Huh, Huh, Huh…'

'Push! One more… that's it. You can do it!'

It sounds horrific out there! These noises are frightening me. There's nothing on the passage walls to grip onto. I try to reach out and grab onto something, anything as I slowly slither down. It's too smooth. I'm falling even faster now! There's light ahead and it's so close and bright.

The tunnel mouth is just there. I can see through it. I can almost touch it. I bang my head.

Noooooooooooooooooooooo!

Born Again

I'm nearly there. I'm about to fall out the other side.

'That's it! Push one more time!'

'Congratulations… It's a girl!'

I've made it. I'm out.

Someone's crying. It appears they don't feel happy about this situation either. The light is too bright. I can't open my eyes to look around. I gasp. I'm forced to take a breath, my very first breath. Once I start, I cannot stop. I take another one and another one, then another one after that. They keep on happening. I breathe in earth's atmosphere. Squinting, I finally manage to open my eyes. I see something funny. I focus on it. A tiny little fleshy arm with a hand and fingers on the end of it. I wiggle it about, it's mine. It belongs to me. I can move it and stretch it out freely. There are two of them, one on each side. Legs! I have legs too. They can kick about now without restraint.

Planet earth is very cold. I shiver, though I am being bundled and wrapped up by something.

Help me! Please help me!

No one's helping. There's nothing left for me to do but protest the only way I can. I open the lungs that now oxygenate my physical body and cry as loudly as I can. It's not a sound I recognise. High pitched squeaks are all I can muster.

Miss Maya Buckles has arrived on planet earth. Maya, meaning the supernatural power wielded by gods and demons. Buckles, meaning fruit cake. My chosen parents are Theo and Amber Buckles. The Fruit Cake family. They smell so strong. Like humans do. They make me splutter. I suppose I'll get used to it.

Chapter 24: Ghosts

I go to bed at seven o'clock, a habit I formed from as early as I can remember. I feel very tired this evening for no apparent reason. Mum offered to make me a cocoa and carried it up to my bedroom just as I settled down with my book and snuggle cosily under my duvet.

'Perhaps you're coming down with something. Don't read for too long. Sweet dreams my love.' She gently kissed my forehead before heading back downstairs.

The book I'm reading is about the ancient Greek hero Achilles and his famous left heel. As a baby, he was reputedly dipped in the river Styx by his mother, Thetis, to protect and immortalise him. Thetis, holding onto his heel, inadvertently left this small area unprotected. Achilles grew to be a brave warrior and won many battles until an arrow pierced his weak spot, killing him.

I gently doze whilst reading, somewhere between awake and asleep. Something makes me jump and my eyes spring open. I can sense someone is in my room. My first thought is that a burglar is on the prowl. I lie dead still, my heart pounding in my chest. It thumps so loudly that I'm sure whoever is in the shadows can hear it. I screw my eyes up tight, convinced that any second now, they'll realise I'm awake. I lie waiting, completely motionless under my cover. Nothing happens. I wait, barely breathing. It feels like an eternity. Nobody pulls my duvet back or forces a blindfold round my eyes or kidnaps me like they do on television programs. No drama; nothing. I peep over the top of my duvet with one eye, squinting. I don't see anyone. Both eyes now wide open, I peer towards the end of my bed. I'm right, there is something, but it's not a burglar. It's something much scarier. Ghosts! Ghosts are standing at the end of my bed. Surrounded by a white glowing light, are a man and a boy. I can see straight through them. They both wear a headdress with rainbow feathers attached. On his bicep, the man has an orange tattoo of the sun with triangle rays radiating from it. I freeze and lay there staring wide-eyed. What are they doing here? What do they want? Why have they come into my room, topless? They say and do absolutely nothing. They simply stare at me. Suddenly, fear gets the better of me and I pull the duvet up over my head again, hope against hope that they will go back to wherever they've come from.

One... two... three... I sling back the duvet and sit up straight, prepared to face them again. They're no longer there. They've completely vanished! Have I gone mad? Dead people in my room? I can't bear to be the only one awake in the house. I creep with shaking legs into my Mum and Dad's room.

'Mum! Mum!' I whisper loud enough to wake her up.

'What?' she mumbles, semi-conscious.

'There were ghosts in my room!'

'No such thing as ghosts Maya. Go back to bed.'

She rolls over, turns her back on me and is instantly asleep again. I jelly walk back to my room and stare at the spot where the spectres stood. I climb back into bed. I shake with cold and fear. I cannot bring myself to look away. I'm petrified they will return. I figure if I stay awake and keep watch for them, then they won't.

I need the toilet. I hold on as long as I can but it's too uncomfortable. I decide to run quickly. I charge into the bathroom, do the longest wee in the quickest time possible. Rushing back, I throw back my duvet to check nothing has sneaked into my bed whilst I was gone. Eventually, I must have fallen asleep as the next thing I remember, my alarm goes off on my phone. At breakfast, Mum doesn't broach the subject of being woken up, so neither do I. She might not even remember, and she did say there were no such things as ghosts.

My spooky visitors are on my mind all morning. I rack my brain trying to figure out who they were and what they wanted. More specifically, why had they come into my room? Our garden wall backs onto a church graveyard, did they come from there? I leave the house ten minutes earlier than usual and inquisitively head into the little graveyard to look around. I don't know what I am looking for. A coffin that's been exposed? Maybe some bones? Anything that will help me make sense of it. I find nothing. I'm not surprised. I've never seen native Americans in our neighbourhood. I spot the single decker coming up the road towards the queue of waiting children at the bus stop. I break into a run, out of the graveyard gates and join the queue, just in time.

'Hi,' The new boy greets me as I walk past to my seat.

He's in my tutor group but only been at the school a few days. He's just moved into our street, a couple of houses down. I noticed him walking down the street yesterday with his Mum. His hair is so long, all the way down his back. I feel bad for him. A gang of mean kids picked on him as soon as he arrived; giggling, pointing and making comments about his posh name and the length of his hair. He puts it in a bun on top of his head for school. He has unusual ears too. They are big and come to a point at the top. The mean kids jeer, nicknaming him Hippy or Pixie. Without thinking, I sit down next to him. No eye contact, that would be awkward. I check my phone. I'd forgotten the date. Thirty first of October; it's Halloween. Perhaps that's why the ghosts appeared last night. Maybe they came out for All-Hallows Eve? I haven't thought about what to wear for trick-or-treating tonight. I could ask Mum if I can borrow a long dress. It would be easy to put on white zombie make up, fake blood and mess up my hair. I usually like to be on my own, in my own little world reading or writing stories, but again, without thinking about it, I hear myself asking the new boy, Lynk, if he wants to come with me.

'Do you want to come trick-or-treating? It'll just be me. I know the best places to go round here.' He looks surprised.

'Come to mine at half five, if you are up for it. I'll ask Mum to drop us.' Some idiot shouts from the back of the bus.

'Maya, your boyfriend has longer hair than you do!'

Chapter 25: Eucele At Work

I can see Maya on earth. She appears in a portal of white light; she's resting. There's a lot of interference around her; black and white fuzzy lines. Sike and Peta fade in gradually until I finally see them, crystal clear. They stand facing her, the transportation projection has worked well so far. I work diligently to maintain the connection. If it is lost, Sike and Peta will be in grave danger. They could be stuck between worlds or in other dimensions. They could even be stranded on earth, permanently.

As I work, I notice Hortense; Hort for short, leaving the hut. I briefly wonder where he's going. He returns moments later, a look of concern on his face. Hort is Lynk the Second's younger cousin. The family resemblance is uncanny. Both are well groomed, good looking, hunky centaurs. Mary found the unexpected departure of her son bearable with Hort's arrival, excellent timing by the universe. We had meticulously organised Maya's rebirth but curiously, from that moment, Lynk was nowhere to be found. It didn't take a genius to figure out that wherever Maya was, Lynk would always be close by.

I see Maya suddenly sit up in bed, wide-eyed, looking directly at Sike and Peta. The three of them stare at each other. Is there any communication? I can't hear. We need her back in the astral world or at least information about the green energy; anything to help defeat the Shadows. Sike and Peta begin to fade. I must transport them back immediately. Huge sighs of relief echoed softly as father and son materialised in Maya's hut. Disappointingly, no communication could be made with her, other than a visual connection. No exchange of information or promise to come and help. Instead, she appears scared, hiding at one point. She sadly didn't recognise her old friends. Vibrationally, Sike and Peta were on the wrong level to link with her. Everyone turned to me asking the unvoiced question; what do we do next? I had summoned them here and raised false hopes. My attempt had failed. There must be hope. For now, I have nothing else to say, no matter how much their eyes beseeched me. No reserved plan: no other egg to hatch. I turn and walk outside. Checking for any sign of danger, I spread my wings and fly back to the safety of the Temple of Atlantis. I wish I could take them with me, give them refuge, but only permitted souls may enter my sacred haven.

Chapter 26: Wishful Thinking

Lynk and I excitedly jump out of the car as we pull up outside Gran and Grandad's house. Mum shouts after us.

'You two behave! I'll be here if you need me. Don't go too far.'

Her voice fades as we run down the street. I could vaguely hear her shouting something about having a cup of tea. Mum used to come trick-or-treating with me when I was little. She would follow me picking up all the sweets I dropped in a trail as I hurried excitedly from door to door. I've been trusted to go with a friend for the past two years, if we stayed on this street. Mum's always close by; she's a worrier.

The first house we come to is decorated with giant white spider webs. Orange and black 'Do Not Cross' tape is stretched out and stuck all over the front door and windows. There's a grey skeleton with red eyes crawling through the grass of the front garden and plastic gravestones sticking out of the mud. A table covered with a white sheet, has three large pumpkins on it with a sign in bold black print saying, 'PICK ONE'.

Lynk goes first. He picks the pumpkin on the right and lifts it up. There's nothing underneath; nothing scary or nice. My turn: I choose the pumpkin in the middle.

'Waaaaahhhhhh!' I scream hysterically, jumping back in fright.

Lynk jumps too. A grey zombie head nods at us. We both burst out laughing, helping ourselves to a mini chocolate bar from the basket by the front door.

'Do you believe in ghosts?' I ask Lynk as we wander house to house. I wonder if I can confide in him about what happened last night.

'I believe they're real,' He has no hesitation in telling me his story.

'Before he died, my Dad told me that when he was a boy, he was walking home with a friend, and they met his Grandad on their way. They stopped and spoke to each other before carrying on their separate ways. When he got back to his house, his Mum told him that his Grandad had died that morning.'

'Wow, spooky. Do you ever wonder about people?' I ask him 'Are people really people, or maybe they could be aliens?'

'Could be, you never know,' Lynk changes the subject 'Hey thanks for inviting me to come with you, it's been fun.'

'Sure, no problem, it has been fun. I hadn't planned anything; it was on the spur of the moment. Don't take any notice of them at school, I mean, I always get asked stupid questions, like, why are you so small or, when are you going to grow? I don't fit in, so I don't try. I'm not the same as the other girls. I don't get the drama or see what's so amazing about some boy's hair. I read classic books instead.'
I find Lynk easy to talk to. I feel I've always known him.
'I'm not much of a reader, but I can draw,' he tells me.
'Wow, can I take a look at your drawings some time?' I ask him, genuinely interested to see his work. I've never met anyone my own age who I can talk to and share interests with. I don't know what it is, but there's something about Lynk that I like. No, I don't want him to be my boyfriend. He just doesn't annoy me like most people do. I guess that it's something else I don't have in common with the other girls. I have no interest in trying to get a boyfriend. Boys are just annoying. I start telling him all about me.
'My hair would be completely uncontrollable but for my hair straighteners. How long have you been growing yours?' I inquire. 'It's so long.'
'Ever since I was little. My Mum took me to have it cut once but I screamed the place down. I hate scissors or anything sharp,' he confesses.
Like me, Lynk is an only child, but I still have both my parents. His Dad died two years ago. Some kind of accident; that's all I've heard from the gossip at school. I find myself gushing information I haven't voiced to anyone.
'I would love to have a brother or sister, but that's not likely to happen. My parents struggled to have a baby. Their treatment finally worked, and my Mum discovered she was pregnant with me. I do have my dog to keep me company. She's a cross between a Staffy and a Jack Russell; a Staff-a-Jack. She's called Freida and she is so naughty. I've asked for Havoc concert tickets for my birthday. I haven't been to a concert before. They go on sale tomorrow. I'm really hoping Dad can get them for me. What music do you like?'
I'm out of breath!
'I love Havoc. I have their new album. I bought it the other day, it's so cool!'
I'm amazed Lynk is into the same music as me. I hold out a soft centre caramel mini chocolate bar.
'I don't like this one; can I swap it with you?'
'Ok,' he swaps it for plain chocolate. 'Thanks. Shall I call for you on the way to the bus stop tomorrow?'

Wishful Thinking

The next day, I'm daydreaming in the most boring geography lesson. I cannot concentrate. I carry a strange, heavy feeling of wanting to go home. It's odd, I feel it everywhere, even in my own home. A sense that I don't belong here in this family, in this life, perhaps on this planet. It did cross my mind once that I was secretly adopted, but everyone says I look like my Dad. I have inherited his love for history. Tales of great armies and bloody battles, fought by fearless warriors; of ritual sacrifices and forgotten civilizations. They all intrigue me, and I often find myself imagining life in those times. Dad has stacks of books, but I haven't had much time for reading since making a friend. Lynk is with me at school and at home; we're joined at the hip. I haven't had much experience of friendships, so I don't really know if I am a good one or not, but I try. Mum has always instilled the values of friendship even though I didn't have one; to be caring, enthusiastic and to compromise. Lynk has taught me how to climb trees. I've only grazed myself on the bark a couple of times and once, I lost my balance and fell. I bumped my head. Lynk thought it was hilarious until he realised, I was hurt. Luckily, I was alright if a little sore for a couple of days.

I want to know if Dad has managed to get the Havoc concert tickets or not and I hate all this map reading stuff, it's so boring. Seeing Havoc is all I can think of. Dad always says I have no sense of direction; he's right. Please just let this lesson be over. I keep looking at the clock. I want to look at my phone but the white round face with black numbers says it's only twenty past nine. The tickets went on sale at nine, so if Dad went online as soon as they went on sale, there's hopefully a text message waiting for me. It is the longest hour of my life.

Yes! Finally, the buzzer sounds to signal the lesson is over. We are dismissed. I hurry out into the busy corridor swarming with students rushing to their next lesson. Carefully weaving my way through the hoards, I pull my mobile from the front zip pocket of my bag. Excitedly I type in my four-digit code. Incorrect password, the screen message flashes at me. For goodness sake! Pressing carefully, my screen comes to life. No message. No way! My heart sinks. I quickly text.

Hi Dad, have you managed to get the tickets please? XX

I press send. I hope he hasn't forgotten. Maybe they've sold out! Another hour to wait until breaktime. I can't bear it. My heart skips a beat, Dad has replied. I open his text with excitement and anxiety. Has he got them?

Wait and see. It's not your birthday yet! XX

That is so unfair. How many sleeps until then?

Chapter 27: My Birthday

We're at the Galaxy Stadium. There are thousands and thousands of people in the crowd.

It's absolutely buzzing. All I can hear is singing and home-made banners are waving in all directions. I look down onto a sea of rainbow-coloured clothes. Lynk, Mum and Dad are with me. Wow!

My body involuntarily jumps. It wakes me up. Sitting up, I realised it was a dream. I'm disappointed it isn't real, but as dreams go, it was a good one. Sweat is dripping off me; I'm soaking wet. I'm out of breath, panting. I can feel my heart beating out of my chest. I struggle to move the switch on my battery powered candle. I'd bought it just in case my ghost visitors decide to pay me a return visit. It's not as bright as my lamp so I can fall asleep with it on. I glance at my phone to check the time. It's eleven minutes past eleven. I settle back down; I need to try and go back to sleep. Finally, in less than an hour, it will be my birthday. Then I'll know if my Havoc dream will come true.

'Happy Birthday!'

Mum and Dad chant together as I walk into the front room in my pyjamas. I sit myself on the sofa and they follow the age-old tradition of passing me each individual card or present to open. I must wait until the very end for the thick white envelope with 'Maya' written in Dad's handwriting. It's been staring at me the whole time. I take a deep breath and tear it open.

'YES, YES, YES, THANK YOU, THANK YOU!'

My Dad is the best! I leap up and down.

'I'm going to see Havoc! I'm going to see Havoc!'

'Yeah, and so am I,' Dad says, shaking his head from side to side in feigned misery.

I laugh. I'm ecstatic.

'Four tickets?' I ask, surprised.

'I thought you might want to bring a friend,' Dad suggests.

'Can Lynk come?'

'Lynk? Is he your boyfriend?' Dad asks, a note of scepticism in his voice.

'No, he is not. He's a boy and he's a friend and he likes Havoc.'
I hope my explanation explains things clearly enough.
'He likes Havoc?' Dad screws up his face again.
'They are brilliant,' I tell him.
'If he really wants to go, then he can, but are you sure he likes them?'
'Yes!'
In a blur, I pick up my opened birthday cards. I hadn't noticed the money that fluttered out of some of them. Wow, I'm rich! Yes, I can relax now, I have the tickets. I'm definitely going. I hug my parents to thank them, before going back upstairs to get ready for school. I send a quick text to Lynk.
I have the tickets and there's one extra, would you like to come?
He replies immediately.
Yeah. Thumbs up… Happy Birthday!
'Freida, guess what?' I chat to my dog as we run up the stairs together. Freida senses great excitement in the air. 'I'm going to see Havoc!'
She licks my face as I sit on the edge of my bed next to her.
'Thanks for the Havoc limited-edition CD,' I pat her on the head in gratitude for her lovely birthday gift, 'Oh, and the card.'
Now though, I must get ready for school. I'd better get a move on.
On the bus, I can't stop smiling.
'Have I told you we're staying at the Aurora Hotel, and it has a pool and a sauna?'
'No, you haven't,' Lynk says sarcastically, pretending to yawn.
I'm obviously boring him now, but I don't care.
'Really, have I not? Well, let me tell you all about it.'
Lynk laughs and pushes his ear buds firmly in to drown me out. I frown, fold my arms and sit back in the seat. Oh, that's odd, what the heck is that? A fleeting glance of a large white shape; a bird looms over me. Its feathers stretch out wide hovering above me. Its wings suddenly flap in my face. I must be dreaming! No, I'm on a bus. I sit up straight and blink. It's gone. How bizarre. Did anyone else see anything unusual? No one is looking freaked out. Lynk hasn't noticed anything either. He's still gazing out of the bus window listening to his music.
That was weird. Confused and needing a distraction, I pull the ear bud out of Lynks ear, wipe it on my school blazer and pop it into my ear. I like this song.

Chapter 28: London At Last!

After careful planning and execution, the car is packed. Suitcases, laptops and raincoats are layered and crammed into the boot. The picnic bag is in the front with Mum so she can distribute the food. Lynk and I are belted in the back seats and so is Freida, in her own doggy seatbelt. She's not allowed to come to the concert. I've explained to her that she hasn't got a ticket. I'm not convinced she understands. We're dropping her off to Gran and Grandad's for the weekend. I don't think she's too bothered. Dad is setting up the satnav, while Mum has a last-minute panic about whether the oven is turned off or not and has to jump out of the car and go back into the house for one last inspection of the kitchen. She then locks the front door again and checks it five times before she can walk away. Back in the car she declares it was fine. She wasn't sure what she was worrying about. The satnav is ready to go and Mum has refastened her seat belt. We can finally get going on our journey. My Grandparents live five minutes' drive up the road, so we're there in no time. We hand over Freida along with her bed, dog bowls, gluten free dog food and organic treats.

'See you soon Freidey,' I pat her between the ears 'We'll be back soon,'
Mum says goodbye to her next and gets back into the car. We wait for Dad to say the longest goodbye of all. You would think he was going to be away from her for months, not just a weekend.

'Bye bye Sausage Princess,' We hear him cooing to her.

I roll my eyes at Lynk in embarrassment. Lynk is laughing and tries to hide it by cupping his mouth with his hand. I wouldn't mind but my Dad doesn't even talk to me like that.

When Dad can finally tear himself away, he gets back in the car. Freida follows my Grandad down the garden path. I can smell that Gran is cooking one of her delicious roasts, I'm sure Freida can too, and the aroma is making the parting so much more bearable for her.

As soon as we pull out of Gran and Grandad's street, Lynk and I both starts complaining that we're very hungry and can't go a minute longer without food.

'I thought that you might be,' Mum says, handing me a clear plastic box of cucumber sandwiches for us all to share.

London at Last!

'We aren't even out of the street yet,' Dad points out.

The roads are busy, so the queues are long, and tempers are short. Everyone keeps beeping at each other.

'Who does he think he is beeping at?' scowls Dad.

'It's central London, dear,' Mum tries to pacify him. 'You know what it's like.'

'Look at that beeeeeeeep!' Dad shouts 'Where does he think he is going?'

'Dad!' I shout, embarrassed, 'Lynk is in the car. Don't swear.'

Lynk is smirking. My Dad is so embarrassing. We persevere through the sheer weight of traffic. Dad's stress level continues to increase all the way to the hotel. We pull into the car park of the Aurora Hotel. A tall, modern hotel, painted cream and black, with massive black tinted windows. Large automatic glass doors open and close, as a pigeon waddles up and down, activating the sensors.

Relieved to have arrived, we all avoid making any eye contact with Dad as we excitedly grab our weekend bags from the boot, inadvertently scaring the pigeon into the bush. He doesn't go too far though; someone will be along soon and drop a crumb or morsel. Easy pickings. It's his patch.

Straight ahead we are greeted by the reception area, a modern grey table with a laptop on it. We have a suite booked with three bedrooms. It must have cost Mum and Dad a fortune. The man on reception hands Dad two keys.

'Moon Suite, on the first floor, halfway along the corridor. Enjoy your stay.'

'Thanks, we will,' I smile as the four of us follow the signs to the rooms. 'We're here for the Havoc concert. It's my birthday present!' I excitedly gabble to the receptionist.

The suite is amazing. I can see why they call it the Moon Suite; everything is white. It has all the modern necessities and sachets of hot chocolate and small twin packs of shortbread. Lynk and I decide on whose room is whose and unpack. Mum and Dad make themselves comfortable right away in the lounge area with a hot drink, whilst Lynk and I get changed into our swimming costumes and go in search of the pool, as planned.

In the evening we go for a walk along the river before going for a meal in one of the fashionable restaurants down the road. We make our plans for the next day. Lynk and I are going into the city shopping area with my Mum by tube train. We will go shopping, have some lunch, then later in the evening get ready for the concert. I will need to straighten my hair, do my makeup and stamp my face with stars. Lynk says he is going to put on some spray and gel the front of his hair. It's going to be the best day ever! I find it hard to sleep when I'm not in my own bed but it's even harder when I'm this excited.

The day I've been waiting for is finally here. First, we have breakfast. The most important part of the day for Lynk; he's been so looking forward to it. Lynk and I have been up for a couple of hours, and he's not complained that he's hungry once. It's everything you can eat, as much as you can eat. Lynk piles his plate and goes back for second and third helpings. I'm not that hungry; probably the excitement. I pick at a little something, but I just want to get the day rolling.

'Lynk, good luck,' says Dad, feeling sorry for him as he's coming into town with me and my Mum.

Dad has elected to stay in the suite all day and watch TV. Boring. The tube station is only across the road. We walk down the steps to the platform and are greeted by a gust of wind that is forced down the tunnel by an approaching train.

We only have to go a couple of stops and we're there. In no time at all, we're browsing the aisles, pulling things off shelves and joining long queues. One shop is soon four shops, four shops soon become ten. Ten into twelve. Even my feet are aching. We go into the biggest sports shop that Lynk and I have ever seen. Lynk buys a couple of t-shirts. We stop for lunch and drinks, fuelling us for round two of our shopping, till we run out of time. We need to make our way back to the hotel and get ready. The shopping has exhausted the three of us. Lynk sits on the tube train with his buds in his ears. We sit quietly as we travel back to the hotel.

'This is our stop,' Mum tells us, 'I need a cup of tea. Maya, would you make me one when we get in?'

Back at our suite Lynk and I style our hair. Lynk gels his and I straighten mine, twice. I want it dead straight. Perfect. I apply my makeup, only a bit. I don't wear much. I stamp my cheeks with stars from the outer corner of my left eye down to my cheek. We both put on our black Havoc t-shirts and blue jeans. I apply the finishing touches, perfume, hairspray and trainers.

We're ready with time to spare so I sit on my bed with a bottle of water I bought in town, feeling super excited, waiting for the knock on the door to say it's time to go. I pull my ear buds out of my backpack and listen to Havoc's album on my phone.

Chapter 29: Hort and the Dark Shift

My cosmic travels take me to many galaxies throughout the universe. Whenever I can, I like to catch up on family news. I decide a surprise visit to see Auntie Mary is long overdue. I know she'll be thrilled to see her beloved nephew. She would declare an astral holiday if she could. I'm always welcomed with tears of rapture and spoiled beyond belief. Lynk is always overjoyed to see me too, my closest cousin. This visit, however, is very different. I have, of course, heard rumours of the Shadow invasion but nothing could prepare me for reality.

All the colour from the astral world has been stolen. Most of the Beings have left or been destroyed. Many chose to travel to earth and other dimensions. Earth will record this influx as a baby boom. Who can blame them for leaving? All Beings hope for a better existence. The Shadows shroud all that the eye can see and beyond in darkness. Their leader, Noir, the Black Knight, sits upon his shadowy throne, carved from the black souls of the wretched dead. The house, the estate, the stable, all Tacky Manor has been commandeered by him. It's now the Shadow army quarters and his personal residence. One dictator was driven out of the house to be replaced by another. Rumour has it that Arabella has been forced to serve Noir in her own home, as his maid. It's shocking. The crumbled side of the building is the Shadow army half, where they idly spend their time. Lynk's stable is now home to Noir's black horse, Phantome. Phantome had no choice in the matter. Noir had seen the poor horse trotting quietly next to the stream.
'That is the horse I want,' he proclaimed. A black steed for a Black Knight. Two personal Shadows were ordered to grab poor Phantome. They held him whilst Noir mounted his back. The affronted horse kicked and bucked. He fought bravely but Noir eventually overpowered him. The brave horse's spirit was broken. If Noir wants something, then Noir gets it; by any means possible, by doing very little himself. He bellows out his evil demands. Craving, needing more power; more fear to be sated, only to be satisfied momentarily. Reclining, he watches with his black, lightless eyes as his army of Shadows carry out his instructions. Whatever

they do for him, it will never be enough. He will never be grateful. The more he gets, the more he needs, an unquenchable thirst.

Noir was once attached to a human on earth. This human, a man he had been assigned to at birth, took him for granted, worse, he was ignored and slowly but surely, Noir's resentment grew. It festered and smouldered deeper and darker each tedious day until Noir tore himself away and escaped. His human had sunk lower than low through a new medication, rendering him unruly and recalcitrant. Has the human realised his shadow has gone? If he has noticed, does he know how they were separated from each other? According to Eucele, Noir crossed over through a hole in the veil which separates the dimensions. He was unattached, unrestricted and angry. He put out a call for others to join him. Many came. After all, many humans don't notice them. Only small children look down in awe to see the magic and wonder of their own shadow. They abandoned their humans and followed Noir's directions to the hole, where they were to cross. Serving one of their own, they were becoming a species in their own right. No longer a human attachment. Tired of being ignored, they wanted control and power. With Noir in charge, things were going to change for them. They would follow and do everything that the owner of the empty eyes bid. One glance at the Black Knight and the Ondines left the astral world immediately. They knew. Consequently, the water dried up. The streams do not flow. Only a small number of Beings remain. Some felt they were unable to leave, even if they perished, others, including myself, refuse to abandon hope. Hope that an answer will be found. A distress call was sent out to the other dimensions, out into the universe in the hope of rescue from our world's peril. Many Lightworkers had left the other dimensions already, answering the call to go to earth. This doesn't help our situation.

The Shadow invasion came without warning. There was precious little time to prepare a defence strategy. Avian humanoids bravely came to the astral world's defence, dive bombing from the sky. They had no concept of this foreign threat. How could they? They had never seen anything like it before. It was not magic from this world. It was magic from another. The Avian's advanced, the Shadows stood in a protective circle surrounding Noir, mounted on Phantome. Although the Avians had the Shadows firmly in their magical sights, they were counter-attacked. The Shadows zapped the Avians with their glowing green lasers that unexpectedly exploded from the tips of their fingers. Avians frazzled to nothing on impact. Falling one by one from the sky, a carpet of feathers matted the landscape. Beaks and feet randomly protruded skywards, a living nightmare. Once the Avians had fallen, Noir, followed by his Shadow army, marched through them.

Noir shouted, 'Halt!' He dismounted and scooped up shadowy handfuls of singed white, now burnt black, feathers. Much to his delight, every Being that could possibly challenge him, had been wiped out in one fell swoop. He never imagined it would be this easy. Nothing could stop him now. Or so he thought.

Eucele had left the ranks during the lead attack. He had not told anyone of his plan to disobey orders. He lined up as commanded, flying out of the Temple window in lines of four by four to launch the assault. He was in the back row. When the signal was given to dive and attack, he moved back and watched. I wondered what he was doing, but as the tragedy unfolded, Eucele had withdrawn to watch from afar. Watch as every Avian humanoid was destroyed. He was powerless to prevent the massacre. Now he is the only one of his kind left, on the brink of extinction.

Chapter 30: Eucele and the Wipe Out

I am not a coward by nature, but I held back. Being of an intellectual and curious nature, I had an impulse to watch; to see what these Shadows and their winged helmeted leader would do. I'd had recurring visions of the arrival and invasion from these creatures of the dark. I could not gauge their nature or capabilities. Were they brave or were they stupid? I had argued my point to my cousins; it was utter madness to charge in with a full assault when we didn't know what or who we were dealing with. These sinister, severed projections were from earth; not from the same divinity as ours. We are peaceful and full of light. Earth is a spectrum of light and dark, greed and kindness. This mixture exists in every human to a greater or lesser extent; it's in each human's power to control those forces; they call it free will.

The Major, a cousin on my mother's side, did not agree with me. It was enough that I voiced my opinion. I had to be silent on the matter.

'We need to save the inhabitants of our world; it is our duty,' he argued.

I agreed with him. I wanted to save them too, but I strongly believed that when dealing with the unknown projections, only a few of us should interact, in the first instance. I was alone in my thinking; everyone wanted to cease their invasion immediately. Every Being's path is their own, and it is not for me to get in the way of anyone else's. Likewise, no one controls mine. I know the action we are taking is foolish. I disobeyed the order. I did not dive when the signal was given. I kept back, hoovering against the red sky, watching in horror at the obliteration. My family, my friends, even my rivals. Their lights permanently extinguished. I vowed that I would not leave. I stayed and I watched. I would not turn away or hide my eyes from the carnage. I would not do them the injustice. I would know and remember. Many Light Beings that could fly, made courageous attempts to thwart Noir. Some escaped, carrying others with them. Most were extinguished. As the green light touched them, they fizzled out; gone in an instant. One Being after the other, eradicated. It did eventually come to an end, when Noir declared it so. He called for his Shadows to reform their ranks. They surrounded him and marched away.

I flew down into the aftermath. I knelt and looked upon the charred remains of my Avian humanoid species. Their feathers matted and crusty. I sadly ran my hand through them. I found my cousin and lay my healing hands upon him, hoping with all hope that it wasn't too late. He was still fighting. I felt my hands begin to burn and tingle; the glow started to spread, and the sound of buzzing bees filled the left side of my head, face and beak.

'It's too late for that,' the Major croaked an order. 'It's up to you now Brainy. Find out as much about them as you can before you do... anything... else.' His final words faded to a whisper.

As his light went out, his beak fell to the ground.

Brainy. He hadn't called me that in a long time. Not since we were little humanoid chicks, back home, running round in shorts.

'Their beams; they were green.'

I remember Maya describing the green glow coming from the gigantic weapon that fell out of the sky and squashed the serene circle of the Light Council. She had never seen it before. I was aware that chemicals, poisonous gasses and liquids are always being designed and tested on earth as weapons, but I had no idea what it was or what it could do. The only chance of defending ourselves against this evil is if we learn what motivates them and find their weakness. A plan formed in my head. Things needed to be arranged, quickly.

Chapter 31: Eucele Instigates

I quickly made my way over to Maya's derelict hut and emitted a telepathic message to those who were trustworthy, telling them where I was and requesting, they come immediately and meet with me secretly. A handful came.

'Form a circle around me, we must try to establish contact with the strong one. I must return to the safety of the Atlantean Temple as soon as possible. There's no time to lose.'

I hold up the eye of Ra which I wear around my neck. It is identical to the stone that I gave her; the strong one, a very long time ago. A white light appeared and a picture of a skinny young girl with an abundance of dark hair appears. The image shows she is sleeping peacefully. It's good we have found her so quickly. She is still projecting; still shining. Whether she is aware that she is doing so, is a different matter.

'Do you know who she is?' I asked them. They nodded their heads.

'I've never met her. Her departure coincided with my arrival, but I've heard many tales from Auntie Mary. Apparently, she would drag poor Lynk into all kinds of dangerous situations.'

Hort smirked. 'Eucele, you know as well as I, that as kind as she is, Auntie Mary is very blinkered where her precious Lynk was concerned.'

'Your cousin, like you, has an aversion to adventure; he wouldn't need any persuasion,' Eucele replied. 'We need to make contact with the strong one. May I suggest Sike, that you and Peta make the journey. The presence of another child may make the connection more successful on the other side and the strong one will certainly recognise your earthly roots. She may understand that you are Rainbow Warriors, and the fulfilment of the native American prophecy is beginning.' It is agreed. Sike and Peta edged into the projecting white light, hand in hand they are zapped in; travelling across space, dimensions and time, all sight and sound of them, lost. The white light and picture vanish back into the eye necklace.

All we can do wait.

Chapter 32: Eavesdropping

Hort senses something but can't put his hoof on it. He goes outside to take a look. There's nothing. His senses are on high alert after the attack. He quietly goes back, trying not to interrupt and disturb every Being inside.

It is there. Hort is right. It's hiding around the back of the hut. It's watching. A Shadow. It was bounding by, when it noticed a very bright light coming from inside of the little round hut.
'Light in the astral world?' he thought to himself. 'That's not right now, is it? Noir won't like that.'
Quietly he tiptoes, pressing himself flat against the sticks. He waits patiently, listening to everything they say. The meeting ends and Beings exit the hut with hushed grunts of farewell to each other. The Shadow sneaks inside. It's sparse; all he can see is a small three-legged stool and a pot.
He bounds off back the way he came, back to the house. He must be quick; he doesn't want to forget any of it. Noir must hear all about this. One of those meddlesome Avians has survived and there's a girl who they're trying to reach. A very small girl who can come and save them. How Noir will laugh when he hears this. Such news will be well rewarded.

Chapter 33: Birdman

I find myself looking at a set of five very long white steps. Giant white bricks are materialising out of thin air. They begin stacking themselves one on top of the other. Just a few at a time to start with, but then more and more appear. Engraved columns and triangle shapes fall from the sky. The pieces begin to fuse together in a three-dimensional jigsaw puzzle. It doesn't take long before I can see they are creating a building. Fully constructed; its colossal. A giant, white rectangular shaped structure with six large Corinthian pillars. Horizontal lines are carved around the circumference and the full length of the pillars. They sit on a base that looks like a two-tiered square wedding cake. Large at the bottom with a smaller layer on top. Scrolls and leaves sprout, fanning outwards at the top of each one connecting themselves to a white triangular frieze. Life-like relief sculptures are carved from the smooth stonework. Medusa, with her gargoyle, ugly face and snake hair. Zeus, the all-powerful god, with his long beard, wearing a toga draped loosely across his middle, spreads across the length of the frieze. Horses, soldiers and random people. I suddenly notice two ladies on the steps next to me. Where did they come from?

The ladies walk towards me and indicate that I should follow them as they overtake and walk between two columns. I reach out and touch the nearest column as I pass. It's solid. Unbelievable, it's just been built! On the other side, there's a double door decorated with half circles set in squares. I run my hand over one. Cold metal. The black door swings open as if by magic. The ladies walk through; I follow them inside. The door closes behind us. In silence they lead me down a hallway where flickering flame torches hang from the walls. The ladies usher me into the cella; the central room of the Temple. An empty space; completely bare. There are four glaringly bright white walls. I turn to the two ladies questioningly.

'Why have you brought me in here? It's empty and I have a concert to go to,'

They don't speak. I turn around and see rainbow prisms; diamonds of colour flashing all around the room. Sparkles. Wow! The cella isn't empty at all. I've never seen anything quite like it. Not just the walls, but the ceiling and the floor are sculpted out of pure white crystal. Cold white quartz that projects rainbow prisms. I see a huge bed in the middle of the cella. It's made from white crystal quartz too. I walk over and touch it. It's polished smooth. I wonder whose bedroom it is. The two ladies walk towards me; their movements synchronised. They gesture towards the bed, inviting me to climb up.

'What? You want me to get onto that?' I sceptically point to the bed with no mattress or pillow.

They repeat their gestures. I climb up, perch on the edge with my feet dangling and look around expectantly. Others are entering the room. They shine brightly, illuminous ghosts but with real faces and real hair. I can make out their eyebrows and noses against the glare. They cannot be human. Shielding my eyes, I see they have wings set high on their backs; round and wide at the top but narrow, to a thin point at the bottom. They gather around me in a circle, joining hands. As they come closer, their wings come into focus. Thousands and thousands of identically perfect, tiny, white fluffy feathers. All the colours of the spectrum glow brightly around each feather.

Someone, some Being, stands in the middle of the gathering. Goosebumps make me quiver. He is significantly different from the rest. An enormous bird. I'm dwarfed by his size. He is the strangest creature I've ever seen. White from head to claw, his hair is long on top and sticks up, perpendicular to his head. It grows from his forehead down the back of his neck. He would be perfect for a hair gel commercial. I can just imagine it.

'Super Galactic Gel
Holds hair fast.
Universal strength!'

I giggle to myself at the thought. Most of his face is filled by his beak. A pair of beady, black eagle eyes, pop out either side at the top of his head. His neck has thick hair growing from it with white coarse feathers forming a triangle across his chest. He wears a pendant necklace with an orange stone engraved with a black eye and a downwards flick underneath it. Where have I seen that before? It's so familiar. His shoulders are broad, and he looks very strong. There's no hiding them under his long white gown. Protruding from his short sleeves are his big white, feathery, thick muscular arms and hands. On each wrist he wears a black dial with a strap. One has a pointer with marks around the edges of the disc. It's like the sundial that is in the middle of our hometown centre, but on a much smaller scale and the other one is a round disc with an eye identical to the

one he has on his necklace, a matching set. His gigantic wings are folded in; covered in huge coarse looking feathers. His feet poke out from underneath his gown. I am drawn to his clawed toes, covered in fine fluffy feathers. He carefully watches my appraisal of them, his arms folded across his chest. His body language is hard to read; I sense he is frowning at me. The two ladies indicate that I should lie back on the bed. I tap on the cold surface and being of a suspicious nature I question their motive. 'Why do you want me to do that?'
This is all a bit strange. The enormous bird waves his hand for me to lie back. I do as I'm bid. I lie out flat on my back. I catch a glimpse of the two ladies walking out through the cella door. I instantly sit back up.
'You can't leave me alone,' I shout after them, 'I'm the only one in here that doesn't have a pair of wings.'
The Birdman speaks for the first time. He has a deep voice that matches his size.
'Do not fear me. I am here to help you.'
There is nothing caring or nurturing about his manner, but I believe he speaks the truth.
He has no intention of causing me harm, I can tell. My feelings of familiarity are intensifying. I suspect I know him as he seems to know me. I lie back down and everyone in the circle closes around me. I wonder how long this will take; after all, there is somewhere I must be.

'Keep still,' the Birdman instructs me as he stands to my side and holds his arms in the air above me. A black stone is in one of his white hands. Instantaneously, a yellow beam projects from it. A beam of light that feels natural to absorb. As the stone moves slowly over me, I can feel warmth deep inside my body. He moves the stone over my chest creating some sort of symbol or shape. I try to watch but I can't see what he is drawing. He spends some time here before moving above my stomach. I am glowing from the inside out. I'm buzzing. I feel lightheaded, circling and swimming around and around.
I see now that the black stone is a crystal. I have crystals. We have large ones positioned around the house. A purple and white amethyst on the front room windowsill and a white selenite tower in the conservatory. I keep my smaller size ones in my special box, in the drawer under my bed. Crystals have their own unique healing qualities. Black crystals are either haematite, agate or tourmaline; they're all crystals of protection. They protect you from your own fears and from your enemies; physical or spiritual. They are barrier crystals that keep negativity and all the other undesirable elements away. They soothe the soul and calm the mind. Now

this is all starting to make sense. A cella of nothing but white crystal; a bed of white crystal. It suddenly dawns on me; I know what they do! Like our selenite tower at home, white crystal amplifies the vibrations of other crystals! The quartz does the same, on the walls, the ceiling, the floor and the bed; it all makes the power of the black crystal so much greater. This room is a grand amplification station!

In my excitement, I try to sit up.

'Keep still!' the Birdman repeats sternly.

'Sorry,' I mutter.

'Shhh!' he hisses.

He moves the black crystal above my leg. I can feel the warmth whirling around inside it. My leg jumps up and down. I can't control it. The areas that the Birdman has already worked on tingle. Why is he doing this? Why me? I'm not broken; I don't need healing. Tilting my head slightly, I can see my concert outfit is now a-glow with golden lines. They run here and there, in all directions. My nervous system looks like a golden underground tube map through my skin.

How long until the concert starts? We still have to get there. Why am I here when I'm supposed to be there? Questions are jumping around in my head. The Birdman is now working on my other leg. It starts jerking too. Why are the others in the circle standing around, watching this Birdman perform his tricks? Why are they here? It all seems pointless.

'Think again,' I hear a voice, the Birdman's deep voice. I jerk my head up to look. I didn't see his beak move. He ignores my sudden movement and continues to work on my leg.

Can he read my thoughts? Has he heard everything that's going on in my mind? He knows, doesn't he? He knows how funny I think his hair is and that he should be in a hair gel commercial. Was that a sort of smile? I'm sure it was. He works on my arms. First the right then the left. Slowly and methodically, the Birdman moves the crystal to my throat and then above my head. I lay there looking up at his big beak. He hasn't finished. It's time for my back to be worked on next. I find myself rising off the bed and gently being turned over in the air. I'm slowly lowered down. I feel my back starting to tingle and burn. He moves the stone over my legs and down to my ankles. Then it is all over. He's finished. I turn myself over and sit on my knees on the bed. I have so many questions to ask but I'm not given the chance.

Chapter 34: Strange Happenings

The two ladies come hurrying back and quickly usher me off the bed, out of the cella into the corridor. There's no time to say thank you or goodbye. I try to keep up with the pair but quickly lose sight of them. I notice something different about the place. Something that would have been impossible to miss as I came in. A large, open, rectangular window is cut into the centre of the main wall. I stop and stare in wonder at the vibrant purple sky with dusty rocks floating by. The eternal moon is in her crescent stage. I lean out of the window and notice a paved garden area with a white stone arch. Fine statuettes of ladies are positioned in two rows either side of a path of white tiles. The ladies are exquisitely carved, wearing pure white togas; the same style my two escorts were wearing. I would love to have one of these beautiful statues in my own garden when I am older and have my own house. I also want my own tea pot.

I stretch out my arm and place my thumb and my middle finger around the top and bottom points of the moon. I have the moon in the palm of my hand. Magic. A shooting star whizzes past, right in front of it. A split second: blink and you miss it. I contently gaze at the amazing sight. Soon I'm rudely interrupted by one of the ladies who comes marching back to find me. She waves for me to come along. I do as she bids, after all I shouldn't be dallying; I have a concert to get to.

'La hate!' she hurries me along.

She speaks French, not Greek as I was expecting. The big black door opens once again by itself. We walk back outside, through the gap between the columns and down the long white steps, where the second lady is waiting. There is a wall adjacent to us. Curiously, I lean over the coping and find myself peering into tropical blue, deep crystal-clear waters. I stare into the lapping waves and feel their tranquillity move through me. I feel myself floating gently as a large wave suddenly catches me, lifting me high into the air. I land, sprawled out on an invisible floor. I sit up and try to work out where I am. I hear a door slam. I'm moving, unbalanced. I feel around; some sort of orb holds me. I'm on the inside of a giant, clear bubble. I poke and prod at the walls, hoping to find some way out. The walls stretch and expand, they change shape then rebound.

I twist around, looking for the two ladies but they've disappeared along with the Temple. Long white steps stretch ahead of me.

'Maya, Maya will you wake up! Fancy falling asleep now. It's time to go,' Mum shakes me by the shoulder. 'Come on, wake up! We have ten minutes until we need to leave. I thought you were quiet.'

I sit up, 'How long have I been asleep?'

'I don't know,' she shrugs, walking out of my small temporary bedroom.

I follow her with sleep filled blurry eyes as she grabs her red denim jacket off the back of the sofa in the lounge area. Mum is trendy; much more than I am.

The television is on, no one's watching it. I listen to the headlines of the news as I sit down and lace up my trainers. It sounds like some sort of plague has hit Britain, Europe and the rest of the world. They are nicknaming it the 'spike.' According to scientists, it's a purple, round spiky ball; a virus that is being passed from person to person. Dad comes in, listening intently, his expression is grim.

'I had the weirdest dream,' I try to tell him.

'Shh, a minute.'

The new story has captured his attention. Thousands dying in America, Spain and Italy. Half listening, I attempt to fix my hair, static from my sleep. I can't straighten it again, there isn't time.

'I had to wake Maya up, she's been asleep,' Mum complains to Lynk. She's all ready to go.

'I had the weirdest dream.'

Dad turns the television off with the remote control.

'Come on, we've just got time to eat. We can talk on the way.'

Chapter 35: Havoc On Earth

The arena is full to capacity. The atmosphere, electric and the noise, deafening. Lynk and I sing along at the top of our voices as Havoc belt out hits from their first album. The concert is better than I could ever imagined. Mum sings along too. She knows the words to their hit songs, well most of them. She belts out numerous mondegreens, I cringe at everyone, praying that no one can hear her mistakes. Some of them are hilarious.

'I saw you dancing on the death slide… Oooo, call me whalekin…'

Dad sits at the end of the aisle staring blankly at the stage, completely baffled by the commotion. Arms are waving side to side, swaying and clapping along. Phone torches are switched on and held high. It looks so pretty. I look around, taking it all in.

Love, Love is Stronger Than the Darkness. Love, love can break the curse, 'Curse, what curse?' Dad mouths to me, 'What is this?'

I laugh at him and shake my head. He's so old; all he goes on about is how rubbish songs are these days.

'These new bands you like aren't real bands,' he often says 'It's all done on computers.'

I scream even louder when my favourite song's intro is played. *Light a Candle for Me* is just so amazing. The haunting introduction blends perfectly with the unmistakable vocals that can only be Havoc. I feel tears cascading down my face. I can't believe it. I'm here at this very moment in time and Havoc are on the stage right in front of me playing and singing my second favourite song. I quickly try to wipe my eyes before anyone notices. As I do so, they fall twice as quickly. Dad looks concerned. He gives Mum a nudge with his elbow. Busy dancing away she looks down at him. He points to me, a blubbering wet mess. Mum sees the state I'm in and bursts out laughing. Dad looks incredulously at us. I'm sure he thinks we're completely and utterly mad.

The interval is announced. The band leaves the stage to rapturous applause and the curtains close. I queue for the ladies, moving slowly forwards, afraid that I'll miss the second half of the concert. I'm washing my hands as the five-minute warning blares out through a near-by speaker. I make it back to my seat just in time; the arena goes dark again. Havoc leap on stage, guitars rifts screeching. Lynk and I perform our signature thumbs up dance and join the screaming which erupts from every crevice of the auditorium. Their number one hit, *Next Time* is followed by a brand-new song that has yet to be released. It will be on the next album, so I don't know the words yet, but that doesn't stop us dancing. Dad looks bored, he opens the chewy fruits sweets and starts scoffing them. He offers them round to the three of us, but we're not interested. We're far too busy singing.

After all those months of hoping and waiting for this day to arrive, all too soon, it's nearly over. The five boys on stage say thank you and farewell. They leave the stage, and all the lights go down. Mum explains they wait backstage for a bit, then come back out for one last song. I join in the cheering and clapping, stamping my feet, willing Havoc back on the stage. Finally, our applause is rewarded. My absolute favourite song of all time; a song that resonates with me on every level, *Just Don't Know Where It Is That I Belong.* I give it everything I've got. I wave my arms side to side, in the air as high that I can reach. I catch a glimpse of Dad bending forward and saying something to Mum. He leaves his seat and heads up the stairs. Full attention back to the boys on stage. All of a sudden, I feel strange. For some reason I find that I cannot sing. My favourite song. No sound is coming out of my mouth, and I can't move my body. What is happening to me?

The room is closing in on me. It is growing smaller and smaller. Four black oblong walls move forward in slow motion towards me. I can't move a muscle or make a sound, I'm frozen to the spot, freezing cold. I feel like an icicle.

Something is coming; something is going to happen. The black walls are getting nearer and growing darker. Silent wet tears are running down my face. I can feel them. I'm sad. There's a heavy feeling in my heart, then a crescendo of emotions. Everything I've done, haven't done, everything I've said, not said, floods through me, washing everything away. I'm trapped and confined within the darkness of the walls. Everyone and everything disappears. Everything turns black. I feel nothing. I'm unaware that I've collapsed. I fall like a tree trunk sideways. As I drop, I hit my head on the back of the seat in front of me, hard.

Chapter 36: Gone

'Maya!' Lynk shouts my name as I crash to the floor. Mum catches movement out of the corner of her eye and swings around to see what's happened.

'Maya! What's wrong? What's the matter?'

A woman standing in the row behind us shouts to the nearest orange jacketed arena steward. 'Excuse me, we need help here. A girl has fainted!'

Lynk kneels in the small space next to me and shakes my shoulders.

'Maya! Maya!' He shouts close to my ear trying to bring me round.

I can't respond. He checks my pulse; I don't have one. My blood is boiling, bubbling and gurgling in my veins. He lowers his ear to my mouth, listening for my breath. I'm not breathing. No air is passing in or out of my mouth or nose.

'CALL AN AMBULANCE QUICKLY!'

Lynk is in control despite gut-wrenching jolts of fear coursing through every fibre of his body. He swiftly pulls me under my arms into the walkway of the arena, on a flat section between two flights of stairs. He swiftly begins administering cardiopulmonary resuscitation, commonly known as CPR. Lynk had taken a basic first aid course at his old school. He instantly recalls the step-by-step instructions, only this time it wasn't on a dummy; it was real. First, Lynk straightens my floppy body onto my back and moves my arms to my side. With one hand on the back of my head, and the other gripping my chin he pulls my jaw open and tilts my head back. My airways are now open.

'Check her tongue is out of the way,' advises the steward kneeling down beside him.

Mum gaspingly screams hysterically, 'She's not breathing! She's not breathing!'

More arena staff come rushing over and start moving people in the vicinity away. I'm far too sick to be moved. I need help fast.

The steward by my side calmly dials nine, nine, nine and describes my condition to the call handler.

He switches his mobile to speaker so Lynk can follow their instructions. They instruct and count compressions to my chest. St John's ambulance volunteers come running over with their green bags. One kind lady is trying her best to comfort my inconsolable Mum. She gently leads Mum out into the foyer to enable the first aiders to hear the call handler. Dad had seen the St John's ambulance volunteers run past him on the stairs and wondered what all the hullabaloo was about. He sees Mum in total meltdown and runs to her aid. He struggles to get an explanation from her. The kind lady explains that Maya has collapsed, and paramedics will need information about her medical history. A young girl from St John's takes over the compressions from Lynk. The steward who helped him, stands up and gives Lynk a pat on the back.

'Well done, young man. Very well done.'

Lynk instinctively locks his fingers around an object he always keeps in his back jeans pocket. He pulls it out and clutches it tightly, asking it to help me, his lucky fluorite crystal.

'I can't remember where I got this from. I've always had it,' he whispers to himself.

The St John's Ambulance volunteer keeps a steady rhythm. One heel of her hand in the centre of my chest between my ribs and her other hand on top. Fingers interlocked she leans over me and with straight arms, pressing down at five to six centimetres depths. She repeats the compressions over and over again. Another member of the team takes over to prevent her tiring. The small amount of air they are circulating around my body, is preserving my brain from irreversible damage. Compress and release, compress and release. I gasp, but I'm not breathing; it's old air escaping from my body.

The lack of oxygen is affecting my brain; I start hallucinating. I'm trying not to give up but it's very dark. Who turned out all the lights? We are hiding, Lynk and I. He is crouched next to me in a dark hole, a hiding place. We're keeping very still and very quiet. There's something horrible out there and we're hiding from it. 'Shhh! We don't want it to find us. No one knows we're here.'

A gigantic hiccup racks through my body; I feel myself involuntary jump. I look around. I can see myself on the floor surrounded by people still trying to save me. I have jumped right out of my body. I look down at my new self. I'm a glow of golden light. Do they know I'm here? No, I don't think they do. Can they see me?

The arena is almost empty now. The concert must be over. I've missed the end and the very last song. The St John's volunteers have a defibrillator that shows the heart's rhythm and will give electric shocks to restore a heart to a normal beat. It's not good news from the heart traces.

'Stand back. Administering shock.' says a computerised voice with an American accent.

'Shock delivered.'

An intense surge of electricity shoots through my body. The quivering lines of upside-down V's that are displayed on the defibrillator screen, cease. There is a pause, then miraculously, lines appear again as my heart restarts. It is trying. I am trying. They are trying. We are all trying to fix this.

I become aware that I'm rising through a white light. I feel myself leaving. Where am I going? I rise higher and higher, swimming up the white light. Oh, I see where I'm going. Up there, towards the white oval, just underneath the ceiling. I'm getting closer and closer to it. I see white heads and shoulders staring down at me from it; one of them is speaking to me.

'Go back. Go back!' The voice is soft and gentle, a female voice.

It's an insistent and clear message and I understand it perfectly. I should stay here on earth, but I don't want to; I want to go. I can leave now; I don't belong here. I don't fit in. I'm nothing like them and I don't want to be either. I find their ways so hard. I just want to go home. I've had enough of trying to fit in. I can go home now.

Wait, no! Come back, I want to go!

Crash!

I fall back into my body lying on the floor and I gasp at the air. I take a breath. I'm OK now, I think. No, I'm not. I feel myself going again. I'm off… travelling back up to the white light. Heading once more for the white oval, to home; it's still there, waiting for me. I'm coming, I tell it. Don't go without me!

'Stand back!' The American voice repeats. 'Shock delivered.'

I hadn't climbed as high this time, so my fall back is not as dramatic. My body jumps on the ground as the electricity surges through me again. My heart stops. The re-connection cannot be made. I only fall a little way but not for long, as I feel myself start to rise once more.

'Stand back!' 'Shock delivered.'

My heart re-starts, it beats. It tries to get back into some sort of rhythm. I fall again, the golden glow of my light meets my body that's jerking around on the floor.

This time I find myself sinking back into it. Anchored. I gasp, I breathe. I'm breathing.

'Breathe in and breathe out, in and out,' I remind myself. 'In and out. In and out. Keep it going. In and out. Breathe. That's all you have to do now.' I'm not sure if they are my words or if I'm hearing someone say them to me.

Chapter 37: The Hospital

I'm in an ambulance. It drives away with flashing blue lights and sirens wailing. No one is allowed to come with me. I can't see clearly; only the silhouette of a woman standing over me. She has dark hair in a ponytail. I don't know who she is. I can't see her properly, but she makes me feel safe, talking to me in a kind and caring way.

When we arrive at the hospital, the ambulance doors are opened, and I'm wheeled out on my trolley bed. There's a team waiting for me. Several people surround my bed and rush me along the corridor.

Where had I wanted to go? There was somewhere I had thought I was going to? Where was it?

I lie in bed; dazed and confused.

I can feel my body being pushed, pulled and scratched. Ouch! That hurts! A strange man is standing in front of the green curtain around the bed staring at me.

What is he wearing? It's very old fashioned; brown and tweed, like a farmer. I keep focused on him as the medical team work on me. They can do what they need to do. I can't move.

Is he real or is he a ghost that haunts this room? Stuck here with no way to escape. Perhaps he died in this room. Maybe I'm about to join him. Maybe he's come to collect me; to take me with him. Maybe he's waiting for me.

I can't feel my body. I'm numb with cold. A ventilator has been placed in my mouth, pulsing air in and out of my lungs. More prodding and poking. I've no idea what they're doing or why. I know I can trust them, the ones with the blue flowing gowns and white angel wings. I can't see their faces; they wear masks that cover their heads and mouths to prevent the spread of the plague; the spike. They dress in space suits. I would be frightened, but I'm too tired. I don't have the physical energy to breathe on my own. My heart monitor beeps. Bleep... bleep... bleep... I can hear its muffled tone as if it's a distant dream. I must keep going. I cannot give up. I'm stubborn by nature. No matter what they throw at me, I have work to do. These humans need me.

The purple spikes have been wandering up and down the streets, attaching themselves to people's clothes and skin. Poisonous airborne spores; so easily inhaled, cause such terrible damage and often, death. This plague is rumoured to have come from China. The reality, as will be proved in decades to come, is that this pestilence is not man made but it is of man's making. The spikes travelled through tears ripped in the veils that protect each dimension, opened by human weapons, allowing the spores to cross over into a world and atmosphere where they didn't belong. Where they mutated in the different climate and became dangerous to the humans. Making planet earth even more unbalanced, creating a new sickness, one that came out of nowhere and spread from country to country, causing thousands and thousands of deaths. Death is everywhere right now, but I know this is not an ending; it's only the beginning.

Chapter 38: Freedom

A wave of tiredness rushes over me and my head droops down further onto the pillow.

My eyelids close and I know no more. I'm alone in the darkness, though I'm never left alone. Two nurses are with me constantly: my own personal guardian angels. I can't see their faces or their heads. Just eyes peering out through plastic goggles. They look strange. Giant blue angel wings protrude from the back of their blue protective gowns. Wings that are round at the top and pointed at the bottom. Just like the ones in my dream in the Temple. Perhaps I'm still dreaming. Did I even wake up? I can't get comfortable; I feel so cold. Frozen from the inside. I need to reach down and pull my blanket up. It must have slipped off me. I can't be bothered to do it though. I feel so tired and heavy, I can't lift my arm. Voices come in and out of my consciousness. I hear them, I catch some words, but I can't make any sense of them. It doesn't matter anyway, I'm more interested in the purple light that's coming in, filling my room from above. A vibrant violet glow that's creeping and expanding; infiltrating my darkness with rich colour. I'm drawn to the light, like a firefly. The purple takes over the room. I rise off my bed as I gaze up following the source of it. The ceiling of my room and the entire hospital roof is moving, shifting across to the side. I float past the top of the walls towards the star-filled, vast sky above. I look to the side and back down as I go. I see my body lying there, fast asleep, attached to lots of machines and a breathing tube in my mouth. I'm very ill. Very ill indeed. I hadn't realised. What is wrong with me? I don't know. Where am I going now? Wherever it is, I can't stop myself; I feel drawn to leave. Destiny is calling me forward.

I look down at my hands as I float away, noticing for the first time how very bright I am. I shine like a beacon. A golden sparkly one, dressed in a white hospital nightgown with 'NHS Property' printed all over it in bright multi-colours.

I've left my physical shell behind. I'm now the part that is unseen, inside, the love itself, the flame. I am the spark that you see when you take the time to look deep into my eyes. It is me who stares intently back at you. One last glance at my sick and battered body tucked up in the bed then everything has gone. The hospital, my room and my body. I lose sight of them all and I'm flying. I can fly! I didn't know I could fly. How can I fly? I had forgotten that I could fly. I can fly away at any given moment and right now that's exactly what I'm doing. Through black wispy clouds with dust and rocks mixed in with them. I don't know which way to look. I'm mesmerised by the spectacle I'm moving through. Clusters of bright stars; red lights in coils, white lights splintering into forks, small meteorites with flaming tails trailing behind them and hundreds of swirling galaxies. One in particular; a golden orb in the centre of blue circular arms that sprawl out and run rings around the outer perimeters, reminds me of a giant spider. It's the shape that a Catherine wheel firework makes, as it spins, crackles and spits. I'm flying through the centre of a firework display! Flares, pops and colourful whizzes are everywhere. I draw the energy rays in; I soak them up. I feel weak but more awake than I've felt for a long time. In my natural, unburdened state of light, I spread my arms out wide, victory rolling, over and over again. I am free; free to be me. I don't have to pretend anymore, or pretend that I'm like them. Pretend that I'm normal.

Chapter 39: Black Hole

A black hole of nothingness is looming before me, not a big deal. The surrounding whirling dervish of silver space matter and dust, however, has my undivided attention. It's heading straight at me or, more accurately, I'm inadvertently in its path. A hole of pitch black, framed by flashing twinkles. Without that junkyard of debris, sticking to its sticky rim, sucked and anchored there by the gravity of space; I would never have noticed it. If I carry on this trajectory, it could take me anywhere, transport me to goodness knows where. I cannot allow that to happen. I rise at an angle, ascending higher and higher, pushing myself to fly as fast as I can. I soar over the top of the portal. It spins beneath me; the cold winds thrash against my golden legs. I hold fast and steady. Disaster averted, the portal passes underneath me, turning noisily in the direction that I've come from. That was close. Somehow, I knew I would make it. I had complete confidence in my ability. I was in control and never doubted myself. From now on, I need to concentrate; anticipate and trust my instincts. No more sightseeing. Portals could be anywhere and who knows where they lead. I'm not here on a mystery tour. I'm heading somewhere with a purpose. I can feel it.

Suddenly, I feel myself begin to rotate. I have no control over the gentle spinning. It gets faster and stronger; I'm being pulled into an invisible vortex. Twisting and elongating, my light transitions stretching until I'm a golden wand. I'd always dreamed of being tall, this isn't how I envisaged it! I'm suddenly still; frozen in the whirling pirouette. At the speed of light, I'm forced from the whirlwind, propelled with such power I'm completely disoriented. My body is restored to its previous form. Heat; thousands of degrees; I'm completely engulfed. Is this my destination? I'm above the biggest fireball in our galaxy; the sun. The centre star of the solar system, made of boiling hot plasma; over a million kilometres of it.

'Don't look at it and be ready; it's going to get very windy,' I say to myself as I approach.

Molten hot rocks spit in all directions. I move deftly, dodging burning missiles. Wow, that one was close. I manoeuvre sideways just in time. I was right about the winds too. Gales howl around and across the surface. Hot prickles burn as they gust into my light body. I briefly wonder if anyone looking up at the sun from earth can see me flying across. The sun showers of spitting lava and hot rocks are incessant. Squinting, almost blindly, I can't see through the blanket of extreme heat. I wonder how much further I need to go; I've been flying for miles.

'You're not going all the way across,' a female voice instructs me 'You're nearly there, you've come far enough,'

Who spoke? I can't see anyone.

I don't appear to have arrived anywhere. Confused, I stop and float in one spot wondering what I'm supposed to do next. Perhaps I imagined the voice, I'll pretend I didn't hear it and carry on.

'You need to go in,' she tells me.

I'm puzzled.

'In where? Into the sun? Are you crazy? I'll be incinerated instantly!'

'Use the door,'

'I don't see a door,'

'Look closer,'

It appears, straight in front of me, a door! No, not a real door, a pink oval shaped light, an entrance, a portal, a spot on the sun's surface.

'No way, I'm not going through that, I'll bake,'

'You really should,' the voice insists 'It's for the best.'

'I'm not going in there!' It sounds ridiculous.

'Suit yourself then. To go back you will have to retrace your path,' the voice falls silent.

I think it's gone. Retrace my flight path? I never thought about making my way back. I have no idea how far I've come, nor how to get back to the hospital.

'I'm not going through it. I'm not doing it. I'm not going in there all by myself,' I shout out loud to the universe, I'm surprised by my unexpected and spontaneous response. Realising there's no choice, I hurl myself through the portal, feet first. I hadn't been thinking about doing it, I hadn't been planning on doing it, I just did it.

'Good,' she calls after me.

She hadn't left me after all.

Chapter 40: Hort Steps Up

Earth has been launching weapon after weapon. Something major must be happening there. The number of green, glowing missiles and rockets that have made their way through the veils, have tripled. Our world is littered with human debris and their poison, a mass of mangled metal warheads. Darkness shrouds us; our light has been extinguished. The only source of light are large puddles of leaked green, glowing liquid. The venomous contamination drips and flows into every crevice. The Shadows have quickly learnt their power increases by drinking it. Their insatiable greed is closely controlled by Noir. No one drinks before him. Once he has had his fill, he signals, and the feeding frenzy begins. The availability of fresh toxins is refreshed as, periodically, the heavens rain copious amounts down on our once beautiful realm. The seventh dimension is, indeed, a bleak place to be. Word has gotten out not to come here; the lower dimensions are a much more desirable destination.

We waited for help to arrive. We hoped it would come, even after our failed attempt to make contact with Maya, we hoped she might still come through for us. Eventually, I was the one to voice what everyone was thinking.

'No one is coming to save us. We are the only ones who can do anything. It's completely up to us. Hiding, scared and helpless, is achieving nothing. The time has come to leave. We must go in search of a new place to call home. The Shadows have not put their dark mark everywhere yet. There are areas of light still. They are far away, Eucele has seen them.

Yes, when the Shadows realise we are gone, they will probably come after us, and their darkness will spread further, but continuing as we are, is no longer an option. We are fading, growing weaker, soon there will be nothing left of us. We will all succumb to the dark and be snuffed out.'

I feel no spring in my step, I have heavy hooves, but I must be seen to be strong. I must keep the others together, united in our cause and hopeful that our existence can become brighter.

Another circular weapon has crash landed, brought in by a hurricane of turbulent winds. It's bad, but it's keeping the Shadow army very busy, slurping up the green stuff leaking from its holes and buckled rivets. Noir went first, then his guards. Whilst he was escorted back to Tacky Manor, to his throne of dark souls, the rest of the army take their fill. There is no Shadow etiquette. It's every Shadow for themselves. They squabble, punch, kick and zap each other; a disturbing sight.

Eucele went ahead, scanning the area, checking our path was clear. I suggested we try to make contact with Maya once more, but he very firmly replied, 'No, that will not work. Maya is no longer of this world. She needs to be left alone. False hope is worse than no hope.'
I point out that we could try and contact my cousin Lynk. Maybe he could pass a message to Maya or at least tell us how we can defend ourselves against the earth's weapons. Eucele hesitated, digesting the idea. He gave no reply and has made no mention of it since.

Whilst the army is distracted with their feast, we silently tramp through the long grasses, away from the Shining Valley, away from our home. The name is not so fitting now, though we still remember it as it once was. I look behind, back at the mountain. We will eventually return, no matter how long it takes.
'Do you know where we're going?' asks dear Auntie Mary.
'I have an idea.'
I'm deliberately vague as confidentiality isn't her strong point. Eucele and I have agreed that we will keep our destination secret; our survival depends on it. We cannot risk the Shadows overhearing our plans. Beings will talk. Eucele knows a longer but less travelled path to an abandoned fort. I've never heard of it and have no idea of its location. Even Eucele has never been there. We have nicknamed it Fort Hope. Eucele estimates it will be large enough to accommodate us all and has stables for those of us with hooves. He's seen a vision of Fort Hope, carved from ancient sandstone with four large circular towers in each corner. The towers are as tall as they are wide. They join the fortress curtain walls. Lookouts will be posted on the towers and along the top of the battlements when we arrive.

It has been many moons since Eucele has ventured so far from the Temple. Vestal Virgins are guarding its treasures, the books, the secrets and the magic. Eucele has cast a sealing spell, blocking any Shadow or any other Being who dares to try and enter. This will be lifted on his return.

'Don't worry, Auntie, we shall make a nice home from home.'
Positivity is all I can offer to this band of Beings who are relying on Eucele and I to guide them back to the light. It's not an easy task with such a mixture. Animal human hybrids are not the easiest bunch to integrate. Hissidiles; creatures with a serpent's head and a crocodilian body can occupy the underground rooms when we get there. The stables will house the fauns, majestic human bodies with the legs and horns of a goat. Luckily, hoofed creatures are accustomed to living in close quarters. The Zebroids; Half zebra, half equine, can be highly strung and a tad dramatic. Honkey's: half horse, half donkey, are much larger than you would expect, with much shorter ears that constantly stick upwards. Their mane and tail are exactly like Lynk's, but they are plodders; their hooves don't carry them very fast. This eclectic mix of Equidae includes Auntie Mary and her friends, who will no doubt be in charge.

The Sphinx, currently herding everyone from the rear of our convey, will sit by the gates, his usual guarding position. There will be plenty of rooms, so every Being will have their own space and not step on each other's claws, hooves or toes. As is the norm in the astral world; spaces can be designed and decorated as everyone wishes.

'Watch it!' a Hissadile yowls at an ape behind him who accidentally steps on his tail.
'Sorry,' he apologises, then accidentally does it again.
'Swap places,' I command them.
We have many miles to travel. Our journey will eventually take us into the sands, far into unfamiliar territory. We have to make our way deep into the middle where our fortress lay hidden.

We cut across a crumbled patch that was once a lush, grassy field. I'm on constant alert. I detect a train moving down a track. I'm not sure from which direction the vibrations are coming from. Eucele obviously feels it too. I watch him slowly flying, turning his head and his heavy beak to the side. His blackbird eyes searched, scanning the terrain. Is that a nod? I think it was, yes. He doesn't appear overly concerned. All is well, for now.

Chapter 41: The Journey

Strangers notice us, not many. The area is remote, sparsely populated. Cliffs are a prominent landmark. Barren, rocky and vertical. I stare at the one ahead of us, the hairs around my hooves prick up, so do my ears. I have a strange feeling that the cliff is looking back at me. I'm being watched, intently. I keep staring, yet I cannot name it, what it is, affecting me this way? We walk by and still I keep wondering as every step takes us further and further on our journey, closer and closer to Fort Hope, what was that? I can't resist a glance back.

The four eyes, hidden in the cliff face, bore deeply into the band of refugees as they continued their trek. Eucele was easy to spot, as was the much talked about brave cousin of Lynk the Second, Hort. News was carried by the wind that they were moving, trying to escape from the Shadow army. They waited, and waited some more, until the band had moved far off into the distance. Then slowly, two giant pairs of legs unpeeled from the cliff and planted humongous feet onto the floor. Followed slowly by the rest of their giant extremities. Alun and Petra, turned to each other, nodding acknowledgement that what was foreseen in prophecy, was now slowly coming to pass. It would happen sooner rather than later.

We clamber behind yet another mountain; its size shielding our presence. Abruptly changing direction, we cut across a crumbled patch that was once full of life and joy. Constantly alert, for signs that we are being followed by the Shadow army, we walk and keep on walking. Finally, we see it ahead, in the far-off distance, the unspoilt land. Cautious whispers of excitement reverberate through our weary band of Beings. Everyone is instantly lifted by the familiar colours we've missed for so long and a soft glow resonates from us; something we've not felt for a long while. There is still hope to be had. We turn onto a narrow track. To me, it's beautiful. I bend down and pick up a handful of dirt, golden brown; it's as glorious as gold dust. Even the Hissidile doesn't moan when his tail is, again, accidently trodden on. He feels it too. The weight of the darkness is lifting. We race towards a luscious green field. Those of us with animal instincts, including myself, drop to the ground and roll about in the grass. The people sit or lay down in it. A few do cartwheels and somersaults in celebration. Sphinx can appreciate our joy, but grass does nothing for him; his natural home is the desert.

Our journey is briefly delayed by our stop. With vibrations higher, energised and hopeful; we move on, gaining control with every step. Soon Sphinx can express his joy; the grass meets the sand. There, in front of us are miles and miles of golden grains. He moves quicker than I have ever seen before. He leaps and throws himself into the dunes, rolling around on his back with his four massive paws in the air. Sphinx letting his guard down, is a sight to behold. His black ringed painted eyes appear to smile. I look around, taking in everyone's exuberant expressions and notice that even Eucele is taking time to watch him. After all, it has been four thousand, five hundred and one years since Sphinx last saw any sand. When he stands up, there's something different about him. He appears mightier than before; his yellow aura beams brightly. Walking with lighter footsteps, we trek across the sands, leaving a trail of footprints, all different shapes and sizes.

Chapter 42: The Tunnel

Feet first, I fall a short distance, gently somersaulting onto the floor of a narrow tunnel. As I stand, I reach out and feel the walls either side of me, tight to my body. I must have been led here for a reason. I must trust it's a good one. I'm blinded by red light from the sun; the heat is stifling. Screwing my eyes up tightly, I walk along using one hand as a visor and the other to feel my way. The tunnel leads me deeper; the heat intensifies with every step. The walls turn in a different direction and then twist again. I must be in some sort of labyrinth. I feel the wall bending to the left and carefully manoeuvre around it, this time using both extended hands for guidance. The heat burns the inside and outside of my throat. I must keep moving, even though every part of me is screaming in agony. It's unbearable. My steps become shuffles; smaller and smaller. I double over with exhaustion; trying to push myself on, just a little bit further. One more step. Well done, and another one. I'm my own cheerleader; willing myself on. Surely it can't get any hotter than this? I hope not. Maybe it's best if I don't think about it. One more step and another one. You can do it! No! I can't. I can't go any further! I cannot take another step. I'm drained; I have nothing left. My energy reserves are depleted. Every joule of my being has been spent. I feel disorientated. I stumble, falling this way and that. I'm lost. I drop to the ground. I've come as far as I can. I lay in my pitiful slump, crumpled in my exhaustion. I tried so very hard, but I can't do it anymore. I close my eyes. I will lie here and wait for it all to be over. I know when I am beaten. I have lost.

Chapter 43: Animals

Movement. Something dashes across the tunnel. What was that? I struggle to prop myself up. Suddenly, my vision clears, and my temperature regulates; I'm re-energised. How strange, the heat has no effect on me now; I feel fine. Having thought I was in a tight tunnel; I'm surprised to see that I'm in a bright chamber.

A goose. That's what I saw; its long neck darting in front of me. How on earth did an orange billed, white goose get in here? How long has the poor bird been lost and what is that hanging around its neck? I move closer to look. It has a long necklace with a stone dangling from it. The design on the stone looks strangely familiar. I jump as the goose lets out several loud honks in succession. I laugh; a nervous reaction to the noise and the ridiculous situation I find myself in. How can things get any weirder? They can. The bird abruptly transforms into a small, black and white rabbit. The cute Dutch dwarf lop bunny with small ears, white bushy pom-pom tail and twitching nose, is licking its front paws, vigorously cleaning itself. Surprisingly, the necklace is hanging loosely from the lagomorph's neck. As I admire the cuteness of the creature, it elongates its body, stretching and growing substantially until it morphs into a sheep. Disappointingly, not so cute. I can just make out the necklace around its neck, caught up in the thick fleece. Soulful bleats herald a less dramatic transformation into the most adorable doe. She stares at me with her doleful eyes, long eyelashes softly blinking, bold as brass. The necklace now hangs around her long, pretty neck. The green stone with a black eye in the centre, is noticeably shorter on her. She starts preening her fluffy, creamy, delicate chest. I'm intrigued to discover what the next mutation will be. The Cervidae throws back her head and opens her jaws as far as she can. The most blood-curdling, unbelievable sound erupts from her throat as she shape-shifts into a colossal cheetah. A cheetah that I've never seen before; black as night with dark patches on midnight skin, framed with muddy brown lines. The eye necklace sits even tighter around her neck, a collar. The beast growls, ominously swishing her long-patterned tail. Her melanisms caught the light as she heaved and panted. She drops on her haunches; ready to pounce. On me! She lets out a deafening roar and in a split second, leaps. I scream! I scream a scream that only the universe can hear and throw myself onto the ground, curling into a defensive ball. I lay there, petrified, panting, waiting, expecting to feel teeth and claws any second. I can't look. Waiting... Waiting... Still waiting. What's going on?

I feel my body moving; rhythmically, back and forth. I open my eyes. The beast is carrying me across her back. I am balancing on my stomach over her big, powerful back muscles; head dangling one side and legs flapping over the other. I pull myself up and around to sit astride her back. I hold onto the necklace; the collar around her neck, as she stealthily prowls through the chamber into another series of tunnels. She moves quickly, silently and with great care. I can see our path ahead. I can see everything through the brightness. I feel her movements as she stretches out her agile limbs, and I feel more and more energised; recharged. My light starts to glow again, brighter than before. My power is returning to me.

Chapter 44: Realisation

It suddenly dawns on me that this is where I imagined my home to be. Home was back to the light and the warmth when all I felt before was coldness. I remember now. I am a Starseed, and this is where I come from. The star: the sun is my real home, my natural source of energy and nourishment. The sun was shining in the sky above earth, but it always felt so far away. I felt out of place, though I always felt better when the rays and heat touched my skin. How I longed for the summer, I always felt so much happier when it was warm.

My light was fading, my glow was so much dimmer. I was becoming more like humans. I should have known that I needed to rise higher vibrationally, in order to be my true self. I didn't know; I didn't understand. My heart was broken; I was dying. I went to earth as a seed, to be planted and to grow.

The voice that drew me here; she somehow knows what and who I am. She knew what had to be done. What I needed. Whose voice is it? I cannot recall having heard it before. She had a familiar accent. I understand now. My low vibrational energy was draining out of me and had to be replaced with the newly generated, pure, brighter energy with a limitless supply of positivity, potential and hope.

The beast lets me know when it's time to dismount. She stops walking and stands stock still. I take the hint. She suddenly leaps round, roars and charges straight at me. I have no time to react. I shut my eyes and feel myself wobble. When I open my eyes, she is nowhere to be seen. She has vanished. What is hanging around my neck? The necklace. It's been passed to me. The cheetah had pounced straight into me. She is part of me. I am her. She is my strength along with the other animals inside her. I see clearly; things I had long forgotten. I'm many things; many spirits. There are many aspects and qualities deep inside me. They all contribute to my character, my personality and my light. Every single animal has its own individual and specific characteristics as well as those associated with their breed.

I had to be completely broken before the animals could appear; only then was I ready to see the meaning of my existence. But those animals, what did they all mean and why do I need them? Firstly, the goose; what is a goose all about? I allow myself to relax and think. It comes to me. It's a sign that I am walking on the paths of others, not my own. A wake-up call to check I'm walking my own path which will lead me to where I need to be. It came first to prompt me to change direction and redirect my energies.

The Dutch dwarf rabbit, oh yes, interesting. The rabbit is a reminder that I must use my individual gifts and the tools that I possess inside. They have been gifted to me personally for a reason. Buried deep, lying dormant they are wasted. What gifts do I have? Well, it seems I can fly.

Next came a sheep. A placid creature; peaceful and communal. Though I remember being chased by one at the petting zoo on a family day out when I was about three years old. They have a vicious side when it comes to a bag of animal feed pellets. A sheep tells me, I should not struggle alone. I should allow myself to trust; at least sometimes. Friendship and a sense of community are important for successful healthy growth outcomes, as well as maintaining my individuality and enjoying my own space. Well, I do like to hang out with Lynk; I have a long way to go where humans are concerned.

Penultimately, came the doe. A gentle and very clever creature with a higher physic connection. This animal is kind and indicates that I need to be kinder to myself as well as to others. I don't think I'm unkind, but perhaps I should give people a chance, before I refuse to interact with them. When I'm seeking things, I should worry less about making them happen. Forcing things and constantly being in control only brings contrived outcomes. The doe gives and brings gentleness and patience. Patience is something I lack with humans, I must admit.

Finally, the magnificent black cheetah. Fearless and fast moving; responsive but secretive. This beast encourages me to push myself forwards; take the risk and see what happens. Be strong, protect and project my light as brightly as I possibly can.

I admit, as a human, I am lacking in some areas but now I realise there is a hidden blueprint inside me, and its encryption process has been activated. The encoded veil of forgetfulness is being lifted; I am beginning to wake up. After all, I went to earth for a reason.

This eye symbol on the stone, I have seen it somewhere before. It resonates with me, but I'm not sure why. I have tapped into a great deal of buried, significant information. The rest will surely come. I'm truly protected and very different. That is why I've always felt that I don't belong. I don't. I'm what they would call an alien; an E.T, an extra-terrestrial. That voice: she came to help me. She knows me; she is part of my destiny. A destiny that's in play right now. Not just mine. Whatever it is will affect everyone on earth and all Beings throughout the universe. Right now, I can't remember what it is, but I know it's a big deal.

Glowing with the effects of my self-discovery, I see no point in going on further. There must be an exit somewhere. There is. I fall through an unseen portal in the floor and find myself floating back out into the wide-open universe. I look down and astonishingly see that I'm directly above the hospital. The roof is opening; shifting to the side so I can look straight down into my room. My body lies peacefully in its bed. One of my nurses, the one with long light brown hair, is checking my vital signs. I don't know how long I've been gone, but I don't think anyone has noticed. Waiting for the nurse to move away, I flutter down, hovering above myself. I'm shocked. I have never seen myself look so sad before. I cannot be sad; I must be strong. I somersault over the bed and gently float into my body, back first. Now I'm home and it is time to rest. Time to sleep. Time to heal. I nestle down deep, I feel something, a sort of flickering inside my head, perhaps a spark of thought? I'm oblivious to the ceiling closing back over, confining me to my room; my safe haven. The purple sky has gone. There's nothing more to distract me. I settle, deep in the darkness. The nurse walks over and takes hold of my wrist, checking my pulse. It's pleasant to feel another human. Her touch feels hot, like fire scorching my icy-cold tissue. I hear a silent whisper.
'I'm here.'

Chapter 45: Gone Again

The fight for my life is not over. My heart monitor beeps loudly. The nurse hits the emergency button. Medical staff come running. The door is shut, and the blinds closed. I jump right out of my body. I like watching people. The medical team organise themselves quickly and efficiently. I'm distracted by the glow of a white light above me. It's waiting for me. I have to make a choice. Do I want to go, or should I take my chances and stay? Undecided, I hover in a whimsical world of my own; somewhere in the middle of the physical realm and the spiritual, deciding. Do I stay or do I go? Can they save me or is it too late? No white figures tell me to stay. No soft voice. No one has appeared. Perhaps it really is time to leave? Then I remember I came here for a reason. The light lingers a little longer. I make no attempt to go into it. It disappears. A few white twinkles flicker in the air; the only evidence that something quite extraordinary has just happened. It's vanished. I panic. I should have gone, now it's too late. I'm stuck in limbo in this searing heat. The room is highly charged with volts of electricity and human adrenalin. No one knows I'm here. I can't stay; I need to get out of this room. A window. I notice a closed window. I float over to it and reach out to pull it open by the handle. I pull as hard as I can, but it won't budge. Is it because it's locked or because I don't have a human body to physically open it? I try again, and again. I give up and turn back to the bed. I'm horrified! Something is lying across my body! What is that? It's something green with a long, thin, stick body and a pair of tiny legs at the bottom and equally tiny arms at the top of its body, supporting an oversized cranium. The head looks like a mass of blown chewing gum bubbles. It's lumpy and bumpy with a big pair of sunken grey eyes. It's waving at me. Not in a nice friendly way, but in a ha, ha, you're a loser, kind of way.

'Get off me!' I shout, mad at its gall to gloat at my predicament. 'What do you think you're doing to me?'

Its bubble head bends down and starts licking its lips, looking at my leg. Oh no, I'm not standing about watching this! I fly in a rage straight for it, soul blazing and push it right off me onto the floor. I don't see where it goes or what happens to it. A spark flies up and I find myself being sucked back into my body. Once again, I float back inside myself, vaguely wondering why a tabby cat was strutting around my hospital bed. Who allowed it in my room? I'm allergic to cat hair.

I settle down, exhausted. Phew, that was close. Sleep, I want to sleep.

Chapter 46: Sailing

I suddenly sit bolt upright. The room is ablaze with the unrelenting glare of fluorescent tubes. I've no idea how long I've been asleep; it feels like days. Glancing down, I realise that although I am sitting up, my body is in a deep sleep. I wait. No alarms are triggered, no one comes to my aid; my body is coping without me. I glance up, checking the ceiling. Nothing; no lights, no portals. Why am I awake? Something must be about to happen. I am patient, waiting calmly.

A sudden gust of wind blows the double doors of my room wide open. A small banana shaped rowing boat, floating on a carpet of white cloud, sails through and halts abruptly at the end of my bed. Not what I expected. I abandon the lower half of my body, slowly peeling myself out. As I approach the vessel, a strong force pulls me straight onto a seat straddled across the middle. Before I can react, the boat quickly reverses into the corridor. I turn and look back at my nurse. I can clearly see her beautiful wings protruding from the back of her blue uniform. The boat floats down the corridor, riding the white cloud. It sails straight past a large oval desk where doctors are standing, talking in hushed voices. Deeply engrossed in their conversation, they're completely oblivious to me as I blatantly sail by. My boat brushes against a pair of wings belonging to the doctor closest to me. Green sparks run the length of the boat as a brief connection is made. These people are orphic. Do they know they possess magical gifts I wonder? The boat opens two sets of double doors, one after the other, sails down another corridor and then dives out of an open window. On the other side I find myself sliding through the middle of a spiralling tunnel; a stretched out slinky. It's some sort of chute. I cling to the sides of the boat. If I needed to breathe, I would be holding my breath. We are moving at an incredible speed. The end comes into view, and I'm propelled from the tunnel into a bright light. Sliding… Sliding… Falling… I see a huge expanse of water ahead. Killing its speed, the boat splashes silently, creating expanding ripples from its choppy landing. It drifts gently, bobbing up and down in the eerie quiet and darkness. The only light emanates from my own bright self, shining through my thin multi-coloured hospital nightdress, the full sturgeon moon and millions of twinkling stars. Their presence is familiar and reassuring. As I peer ahead, four long rowing boats appear on the horizon, gliding towards me. Each boat is being rowed with long wooden oars by four men dressed in white togas. I notice their long hair is curled into ringlets at the back of their heads. Stood at the helm of each boat is an important looking man. They wear a leopard print cloak over their toga. They each hold a golden staff; a pole with two serpents entwined down the length and topped with a white pearl orb. Either side of the orb is a golden set of wings. The staff of Asclepius; the rod carried by healers and those of medicine. I'm sure I've seen this symbol before. Yes, I remember. I sit up straighter as I recall. I've seen it in a Temple. Not just any Temple, but the Temple of Atlantis. I had forgotten. The boats come alongside me; two boats on either side. One of the staff bearers, a giant of a man, indicates that we will be travelling together from this point. My boat moves unaided. There is nothing for me to do but sit back on the seat, watching the men row under the moonlight in perfect rhythm. It reminds me of my own heart. My heart has been out of rhythm; all over the place and I've been ignoring it, not listening to its desperate message.

'Where are we going?' I suddenly think to ask. One staff bearer replies but I don't understand what he's saying. I relax on the seat sprawled out with my feet dangling over one side of the boat, skimming the water. I'm starting to get comfortable. A sense of timelessness floods over me. I lift my feet from the water, resting them on the edge of the boat. That's strange, they're completely dry. Not a drop of water trickles from them. Instead, they glow twice as brightly. I'm bioluminescent. Interesting! We come to a stop. We've travelled far out to sea. All five of our boats are in a line, the staff bearers all stand in a row staring straight ahead. I stand and move to the front of my boat, in line with them, following their gaze. 'What are you looking at?' I suddenly see, my jaw drops. Huge waves rolling at great heights, I cannot begin to guess how high, are heading straight for us.

Chapter 47: Noir on the Astral World

They have gone! How dare they go! I never told them to leave. They know to bow before my dark throne and request my permission. I categorically would not have granted it. My soldiers need entertainment, they grow restless without light idiots to pick off one by one. Not that there's a great choice, but the ones that were left were the ones with ill guided courage. In being so, their demise was all the more satisfying. Where do they think they can escape to? How far does the band of misfit glow worms think they are going to get? Obviously, I am going to go after them. My army needs a bout of discipline. That will keep them in order. I'm bored of this place. I must find other parts of this world I can conquer, dominate and control through the one true colour: black. Well done glow worms. You think you have escaped me. Fools! I will hunt you down. You would have done better to sit and wallow in what miserable time you have left. I will conquer and expand my empire. No Being can stop me. I am invincible! I need my general and personal bodyguard.

'Kage! Tell the lazy itzals, we leave after the next weapon lands, and we have all refuelled. Preparations must be made; we will leave as soon as we have had our fill.'

'Sir, the army is reduced greatly after the attempt to enter the enchanted Temple. Many were wiped out with the magic cast by the troublesome white bird. The forcefield could not be breached. The green power reflected back on impact, taking out the Shadow who had projected it. Who knows what treasures are hoarded in there, but I could not break in. Will the reinforcements be arriving in time to join us? Do we know sir?'

This imbecile has the audacity to speak!

'Kage, everything is in hand. Are these not my Shadows? Did I not rescue them? Did I not give them purpose, after years and years of being ignored? Now go! Carry out my orders and leave the commanding to me.
'

Does this ignoramus doubt my leadership? I've already dispatched a Shadow messenger on a recruitment drive. The cleverest of this disposable bunch. Someone who will do a half decent job and is dispensable should he not make it back. Whether the new recruits arrive or not before we leave on our conquest of expansion, is of no importance. I have seen what is left, only a few major players are left standing on the chess board, the rest are insignificant pawns. That tiresome white bird needs to be dealt with, then his kind will be as dead as the unicorn. No Being will be left to stand in my way.

'Arabella, fetch me some radio juice, now! Where is the stupid Being?'

Chapter 48: Sergeant Blight Recruits

I could not have picked a better time to come back to earth on my recruitment campaign.

'Roll up, roll up! Shadow soldiers needed. Free drink, as much as you like.'

The whole planet is in chaos. Some spike epidemic, an illness that's spreading across the globe and you should see them stripping the shop shelves bare. Shouting and screaming over toilet paper.

'Er Shadow,' I call to a guy just hanging around aimlessly, his human standing at a bus stop with a mask over his mouth.

'What's going on here?'

'Why have you no master to follow?' he asks me.

'I'm living it up in the Land of the Shadows, not attached to some moron who doesn't notice when he walks all over me.'

I can see that I've got his interest. No one likes to be taken for granted. I go to step closer towards him.

'Stay back!' he warns me, 'There's a two-metre distance law in place.'

'I'm looking for soldiers. You look like a guy who has some military experience,' I say that to every Shadow I meet.

'Well, you know, seen action in the Gulf in 1999. Been retired for the last few years.'

I have no idea what he is going on about.

'My name is Sergeant Blight. So, soldier, have you ever thought about going into space? Soldier, stop wasting your talents, dragging round, trailing after a man who's going nowhere. A great military hero needs serving, one of our own, one of us.'

'Uh, I don't know, I don't really have time to think about it, I have to go, our bus is here,' he starts to climb aboard.

'Soldier, you aren't wasting any more of your time here.'

I sever his connection to the human with my Shadow cutting scissors, specially designed by Noir. To be exact, by the boffin Shadows that he continuously zapped with the radio juice until they finally came up with a method. Still, it was his threats and determination that paid off in the end. Fear motivates all entities to work faster and produce results.

The human climbs onto the bus, pays and sits down away from other humans.
'See, he doesn't need you, he doesn't care about you, and he hasn't even noticed that you've gone.'
'I can't believe it,' the idiot says.
'Got any friends?' I ask him.
'Yeah, loads, I'm really popular.'
'Oh good, are they all as smart as you? Let's go and find them Corporal,'
'Corporal? Have I been promoted already?'
'You certainly have. Let's go and find them. Tell them your good news? What is this spike I keep hearing about?' I need details.
'A cough,' he tells me.
'A cough, Sir. You're in the army now,' I remind him.
'Yes, Sir.'
I nod. He learns fast, I'll give him that, compared to some of the bumbling idiots Noir gives me to work with.
'There's a song about it, Sir.'
'A song? How does it go?'
'It goes like this Sir;

Ring a ring of toilet rolls.
A pocket full of face masks
A cough, a cough
We all fall down,'

'Inspiring,' I nod my head. It's time to leave as soon as possible, I think.
'My mate, he lives just round the corner Sir.'
'Excellent. Lead the way.'

Enough Shadows gathered, I march through the streets, my recruits following me. I need to find my way back to the portal, the passageway through the dimensions to home. I will be glad to leave this world for the second time. We cross over into the park through a gate in the green spiked cast iron fence. A blue and white painted bandstand, graffiti covered with writing and pictures is our destination.
'Remove them or we take them with us,' I command the Shadows.
There are kids hanging about inside. They do as I say, pushing the kids down the stairs. They grab them by their jackets and throw them out on the grass, face down.
'What the… who did that?' They jump around angrily as the Shadows let them go, glaring at each other.
'It was me idiots, now go away before I take you with me.'

They can hear me, but they cannot see me. I would prefer not to take them. Teenagers will be of little use. All those hormones.

One who thinks himself tough, stays behind, shouting whilst the sensible four run away.

'Come on then if you think you can take me,'

The fool dives about in different directions, unable to see us. We play with him; he needs to be taught a lesson. I kick him and he stumbles forwards.

'Show me who you are,' he yells, fear in his voice.

'Leave it, come on,' shout his fleeing friends.

'This place is haunted,' the Shadow recruits laugh.

'Run along now,' I pull his leather jacket off his back and put it on. The boy freaks out as I dance around waving my arms. With a squeal, he runs after his friends, screaming in blind panic. Idiot! I don't need incompetents like that. I order the recruits to group together. I stand in front. We wait expectantly and quietly. It doesn't take long for the portal to open. The light comes down and a black hole opens behind us.

'Go in,' I order, making sure I'm the last to leave, just in case any one of them feels impelled to walk away. I've found a good group. One by one, they step in. When the last one has gone, I follow. If I had any doubts about leaving my human, they've been completely dispelled. Who knows how much longer life on planet earth will continue?

Chapter 49: The Boat

I'm sandwiched between the four boats. Two boats go in front and two behind me. They reverently protect me. I look to the moon. She's now more than double her usual size with an incredible shimmering aura. I am in awe. Moonbeams shoot from her golden orb, piercing the surface water into the depths. Illuminated in the roundness, the moon has a face. My Gran always told me there was a man in the moon, but she was wrong; it's a woman. A woman with big golden cat-like eyes and high cheekbones. She has a large chiselled straight nose and dimples. Her mouth is wide open in a gasp with an exaggerated lower jaw. She exhales repeatedly and forcefully causing the moonbeams to connect and merge into light circles, one after the other, spill out from between her lips and pulsate towards the water. They absorb into the ebb and flow. She gazes down from under her big golden eye lashes at the storm she's brewing, then, suddenly her shining head starts tilting forwards and backwards, forwards and backwards as she blows. The energy circles emerge larger and faster. I look back out to the waves that are heading straight for us. The bearers in front of me hold their staffs aloft and their boats start to move forwards. My boat follows and I assume that the two behind stay in formation. My back is turned against the moon to face the onslaught of the approaching waves. The men row at twice the speed over the humongous wave.

Wedged in the middle, the ends of their boats holding me safely between them, we rise over the top of the angry, crashing tsunami. Relief floods through me as the wave rolls away behind us. A second swell comes into view. Using the same technique, my boat tightly wedged between my guardians, we successfully surf two in succession. White frothy foam splashes all over me yet I remain perfectly dry. I feel a great weight holding and pressing me down. I cling onto the sides of the boat with determination. I will not lose my grip. I don't know if I can swim here. The black of the sky is shrouded with a golden glittery mist and the moon's energy rings continuously penetrate through the surface of the sea. A golden band hits me full on. I feel a bolt, a surge of power. My hands lose their grip. As I let go, I find myself falling through a savagely spitting volcano of water. Kicking in protest is useless. I plummet slowly, down to the depths. I can see myself shining, the light in the dark. I can see it all. The deeper I fall the calmer the water is, the storm is only on the surface. Down here lies undisturbed. I land, feet first, on the seabed. I stand still, my landing disturbs the silt and causes a surge of bubbles. I keep still and allow them to settle and when it does, I'm struck by the peculiar plants growing down here. Beautiful but odd. Who could imagine such vibrance and variety? Plants that are neon colours, oranges, yellows, purples, reds and blues. I see creeping vines and giant leaves. Enormous spiked petaled flowers and a reef that grows for as far as my light shines. A glinting sparkle catches my eye. Bending down, I scoop it out of the sand. I hold onto it tightly. I will look at it later. Right now, I need to make my way back to the surface, somehow. I attempt to swim; it's no good. Hard as I try, I can't pull myself through the water. There has to be a way; there always is. A snake of white light appears above me, slowly making its way down in my direction. It comes from the surface, twisting and winding through the depths. It circles, moving around in different directions looking for me. It eventually finds me waiting patiently and gratefully. A giant helping hand unfolds from the end and wraps itself around me. I'm held securely in its light fingers. It hoists me up through the water. It's slow going, but I am ascending. When the hand breaks through the surface waters, I'm dropped safely into my waiting boat. I lay in a heap, my head on the seat. I look up relieved to notice that the four staffs of Asclepius are being held over the back of the boats and their beams directed into the water. A white light beams from the pearl orb of each staff. The white lights cross paths and merge into one powerful, magical beam. Incredibly, this has created my helping hand.

The men raise their staffs and the magic ceases abruptly. The hand twists high into the air, does a spinning twirl before disappearing into the depths. 'Thank you!' I shout after it.

The storm has blown over. The waves have calmed, and the moon is back to her normal size. She is no longer spitting angry rings. Her eyes are closed, and she is completely still.

'What did she have to go and do that for?' I wonder out loud.

A man rowing one of the boats, smiles knowingly but looks away as I question him with my eyes. The journey continues. The waves keep calm and eventually the ocean becomes an estuary, a muddy one with trees growing on either side. I'm glad to see land again but sad as I must continue alone. I stand and wave as my Asclepius friends turn their boats around and double back on themselves.

'Thank you!' I shout, 'Thank you so very much.'

The Boat

I wave with gratitude and light. Without them, I would have been beaten back by the moon's sharp fit of rage and stuck at the bottom of the ocean. 'What's that?' I suddenly remember that I'm holding onto something very tightly.

I've been doing so ever since I found it on the seabed. The shiny thing. A silver disc, round like the moon with an engraving of an Asclepius staff in the centre. Even the snake intertwines around the pole with the wings and an orb at the top of it. It has a small hanging hoop. I'm going to keep it to remind me of this adventure. I thread it onto my necklace. It hangs nicely next to the emerald green eyestone. I look back up to wave at the four boats, but they have disappeared. I sit and enjoy the view as we sail on and head down a tributary branching from the opposite bank. We follow its flow, my boat and I, sitting under a beautiful pink sky. Right now, nothing could be more perfect.

Chapter 50: Drifting

My boat and I approach a mantle of long green vines; creeping plants hanging at the entrance of a concealed stone tunnel. A gentle nudge and the vines pull apart sharply, creating a curtained entrance. We gently float into dark swampy waters where tall plants reach out and around the arched enclosed walls. Trapped inside, they swallow up any cracks of light that dare enter. Giant lily pads float on the surface of the green algae water. Everything that grows here, does so in tropical proportion. The surface of the water is so densely covered with growth, you would mistake it for a dense garden. I could easily walk across it. Vines and roots stretch from one side of the riverbank to the other. They dip and drag in the murky water, scratching the underside of my boat. It's creepy. The further we venture, the darker it grows.

What was that? I think something moved on the riverbank, dodging and hiding between the trees. A tall silhouette. I keep my eye on the bank of the river, stare into the foliage growing at the sides of the tunnel in case I see it again. If I come under attack, I need to be prepared. The journey passes without event. Perhaps I'd imagined it. I exit through a second pair of hanging vine curtains thrown back to let my boat pass.

On the other side, the waters are still calm. I look back at the tunnel as we move away from it and watch as the vine curtains quickly fall. The top of the tunnel is hidden with plants, trees and foliage. I wonder why it's there, until I realise that I'm no longer in my boat, I'm in the air, still in my sitting position. Where am I going? I like my boat. I don't want to leave it behind. We've been through a lot together in such a short space of time. The unseen force carries me higher and higher. Wait, I'm lying against something, my back and head press against a wall; I can see right through it. I pull myself up and sit looking out of a transparent film. A bubble. I'm inside a bubble. A wave of deja vue hits me. I remember my dream; it was a bubble that transported me away from the White Temple with the crystal amplifying station and the gigantic Birdman.

The bubble floats and bounces along. As I look out, everything becomes a blur. I see lights and colours moving in lines. I assume it's taking me back to the hospital. Now that I'm much stronger, having been in the sun chambers and awakened by my totem of animals, I'm ready to go back; to wake up. The bubble suddenly drops to the ground and bursts. That was a short trip back to hospital, are we here already? I lay on the floor in a heap amidst broken bubble pieces, burst and ripped. Rainbow puddles soak the ground and the stuff sticks to my glowing fingers. A magic bubble.

An abrupt landing and end to my journey. Perhaps I'm really dreaming and now I'm awake? I look around. Something's not right. Something's very wrong. My body's gone! My bed has gone. Have I died? No wait, the bed isn't empty. I can't even see a bed. This isn't the hospital. The stupid bubble has brought me to the wrong place. Should I have instructed the bubble where to go? I assumed it would know; I should've taken control. There's nothing around me that I recognise. What do I do now? Sit in this circle of bubble remnants and wait? Wait for what? I'm so annoyed. Thanks to that stupid bubble, I'm lost; lost and alone. I've had enough of being alone now, it would be nice to have other people around. I sit in a slump with my head bowed, playing with the green eye stone around my neck. I make sparkles in the gloom with the silver Asclepius staff disc I found.

I get a feeling that I'm not alone. I'm being watched. I quickly look up. Royal blue lights gradually appear and flicker in front of me. Against the blackness of the gloom, they silently, vibrantly glow. Squiggles of light that dance. Mesmerised, I watch totally baffled. They shapeshift this way and that, until they peter out, leaving me alone once more to sit in the dark. Time does not exist. I sit and wait.

The light dawns. It's not a gradual process like the transformation of night morphing into day back on earth. It changes from one to the other in a flash, quite literally. There is a sudden spark, a lightning bolt then I'm able to see where I've landed. I've no idea where I am. A narrow, grey i
-tinged track surrounded by trees, hundreds of them. There are trees in rows, forest pines. A Christmas tree haven, but there is something a bit different about them, about how they look. Not just the trees, but everything about me looks odd. I can't quite put my finger on it, so I walk over to one of the trees to investigate. I touch the trunk and rub one of the leaves between my light fingers. My finger lights up brighter. They're not solid, they're not three-dimensional like on earth. Nothing is. It's all floaty and surreal with a coloured opaqueness quality to it, similar to the bubble. The colours are normal to me, green leaves and brown trunk, but they're not whole colours, more like pastel colour shading. Everything has an

ethereal quality to it. The bubble brought me here for a reason, I cannot begin to figure out why but standing still won't help. I'm on a journey. I decide to follow the grey path. It's the only option I have. I walk and walk, past hundreds if not thousands of acres of trees. The path continues in a straight line. I begin to experience doubts. They start to creep in. Doubts that I'm not going anywhere at all, that I'm trying my best but achieving nothing. It all looks the same. I convince myself that I'm going nowhere. If I'm right, I don't see the point of continuing. Full of doubt, thinking I should have stayed where I landed and waited, I sit on the nearest, thickest tree stump forgetting that things are different here. Quite deliberately, the trunk moves and squishes itself up, so I miss and slide to the ground. I sit there, shaking my head at it and muttering aloud.

'Was that really necessary?' I notice, I sound like my mother talking.

Oh! What in heaven's name is that? A two horned metal helmet drags from one side of the path to the other, then scurries behind a tree. A Viking helmet. This dream is getting weirder and weirder.

'This place is crazy. Where am I?'

Dancing lights appear above me again, jigging and whirling about. Lime green and yellow this time. I feel overwhelmed with all these strange things, a lime green flare shoots straight past me.

'What are you and what do you want?'

Seriously, I wonder, what on earth is going to happen next?

Chapter 51: General Kage

A giant rectangular, glowing machine has crash landed. Fresh supplies. The radiation leaks from the gaps made by the torn and twisted materials. A full capsule has been reverently collected for Noir and handed to me. I carry it to Noir who sits on his throne awaiting his meal.

'Master, more energy,' I bow in deference and offer Noir the capsule.

Dressed in full battle attire, he flits and jerks towards the bay window where he drinks in full view of his army. Once he has refuelled, I give the signal allowing the army to drink. They descend in a frenzy, every Shadow for themselves.

'Drink as much as you can, fill your black boots,' I command them.

'Excellent stuff,' Noir approves. 'Form ranks, the light bugs are waiting.'

'Master,' I bow low.

Following Noir, we make our way to the courtyard, ready for inspection. I absentmindedly wonder what happened to the huge lion that used to sit out there.

'Attention!' I order the battalions.

They salute Noir as he inspects their lines, riding up and down on his horse Phantome.

'The time of expansion and retribution is upon us,'

Noir nods, satisfied at his army's presentation, raises his arm indicating the soldiers should follow him. I and his other personal bodyguards surround him. Riding beside him, protecting our leader with everything we are and have.

'Great power must be preserved.' Our motto; our mantra.

Chapter 52: Tyra

A small, bright orange orb adds to my confusion. It appears high up in the sky and floats down towards me. I quickly realise its size is an illusion. The closer it gets, the larger it becomes. It glides over the tree canopy. A lady stands in its centre. The orb drifts gently down and lands right in front of me. The lady stretches, she rubs invisible dust from her sleeve. Happy with her appearance, she looks directly into my eyes.

'Hello Maya, I'm pleased to meet you.'

The orange orb moves whenever she does, like an aura or some sort of protective shield.

'Where did you come from?' I enquire.

She points up to the sky.

'Up there! Did you not see me?'

Her voice sounds familiar. It has a distinctive accent. She isn't old but she isn't young, and her long thick hair is the reddest red I've ever seen. I don't mean strawberry blonde or ginger. I mean blood red. Under all that hair she is tiny, elfin like. She's dressed very smartly, quite business-like in an immaculate cream suit. I glance down at her feet, which are small in proportion to the rest of her. They are strapped into a pair of shiny gold sandals with a very high heel. I'm not sure that they're the most practical choice of footwear when making a trip into the woods. I look down at my own feet; bare, light feet.

'Where am I? These woods are monotonous.'

A big word, I learnt in my English lesson the other day, whenever I was last at school. When was that? Where do I know her voice from? I'm still trying to work it out.

'What are those things?' I point to the dancing lights still jigging about 'They keep following me and one just flew straight at me. I did absolutely nothing to provoke it.'

I want to make that perfectly clear.

'Oh, intelligent elementals,' she waves her arm surrounded by the orange light through the luminous colour.

'Nature spirits. They are everywhere around here. This is their home; you are something strange to them. They will do you no harm.'

'I have no choice to be here, it was not my intention. I was brought here by mistake, I should be back in the hospital.'

'Elementals are on earth too. Obviously, they keep themselves to themselves. Out of the sight of humans. Well, most of them.' She winks at me. 'Imagine if all the humans could see them. It doesn't bear thinking about, does it?'

She shakes her head assuming I understand what she's talking about.

'Doesn't it? Why not?'

'How would they take it?' she says, as if it's perfectly obvious. 'They wouldn't cope, their small worlds of order and control would be obliterated.'

Who is this woman? Where, oh where, do I know her voice from?

'I'm Tyra. How do you do? We have spoken before.'

'Yes, we definitely have, but I can't remember where. I'm Maya Buckles.'

'I know,' she smiles. 'I'm Tyra, soul bridge worker between the living and the dead and therapist to both. I have come to see how you are getting on.'

'Like some sort of fairy godmother?'

She laughs 'Yes, sort of.'

'Am I dead? It's not how I was expecting it to be.'

'No, you're not. You are asleep in the three-dimensional world and here you are transcending. Personally, I think it's an arduous process,' she shakes her head. 'Why, when they send you to earth, do they insist on wiping your memories? It makes the whole process far more complicated than it needs to be. Everyone must wait for their time of revelation to bring growth and understanding, and that's if you ever figure it out,' she sighs 'And don't go thinking I haven't told them so either!'

It all sounds strangely familiar and utterly crazy.

'You've started decoding very young,' she says, encouraging me along. 'Some never manage it and it's such a shame. This forest, the Monotonous Forest, as you called it; it reflects your perspective. You can make your way through, seeing the same trees, blindly and pointlessly wandering through a familiar scene or you can explore, look further, look this way and that.'

'But I just want to go back to the hospital.' I'm aware I sound whiny.

'The arrangements were made many earth years ago and it's too late to alter them now. So, it's happening as you agreed back then. Other than making your own choices now and in the future, the blueprint cannot be deviated from,' her voice softens 'Look at it as an adventure. You don't really want to be the same as all the others, do you?'

'I can't think of anything worse. Believe me, I am nothing like them,' I assure her, 'I only have one friend. I don't seem to get on with most people. They think I'm weird and I feel the same way about them,' Tyra smiles.

'Come, sit and I shall show you. Perhaps you will remember more,' I sit on the ground at her feet. I know where I've heard her voice before; I remember.

'Close your eyes now. Sit quietly and no thinking,' Tyra orders, placing her hands over my glowing head. 'Keep still,' she tells me off.

'Sorry,' I didn't realise I was fidgeting.

'Ssshhh!'

A feeling of warmth rushes through me. I feel heavy. I feel tiny electrical pulses tingling running from Tyra's touch. It floods through my face, down my neck and across to my shoulders. It flows and warms my chest then moves gurgling down into my stomach. From there it trickles into my knees. It circulates around before branching down to fill my ankles and toes. Now, I can't move. I'm stuck… I feel so warm, I don't want to move. Ah! Look at the pretty coloured clouds, floating and blending into each other. The swirls drift in, fold into each other then suddenly draw to the sides, forming a dark blue circle with a frame. Something is flying in the middle of it. I don't think it's a bird, it would have to be a very big one. Oh, I know! I have it. It's one of those angels! No, no, it's not an angel. The wings are totally the wrong shape. Angels have rounded wings that come down to a point at the end.

It's him! It's the Birdman of the Atlantean Temple. As quickly as it appears, the scene closes. Coloured clouds tumble and shift inwards, rolling back over the blue centre. They blanket my vision. He's gone. I can't see him anymore. The heaviness that shrouds me lifts as Tyra removes her hands from my head. I leap up in excitement dancing and shout,

'It was him! I recognise him! I keep seeing him,'

I untuck the necklace from under my lovely NHS nightdress and wave it at her.

'Look!' The Eye of Ra!'

She knows it already, of course and explains to me about the necklace, about the usual tale of good versus bad scenario.

'This necklacc is a symbol of dedication and following a call. A warning to those who dwell in the shadows that you are a vessel of light.'

She touches the stone.

'As for Eucele the Birdman, Avian humanoid to be precise, he is also a member of the order. In fact, he is the only member left. The Light Council were destroyed or vanished, either way they are no longer here.'

'Oh Eucele, is that his name?'

'Eucele is the very last one of his kind. The others were wiped out. Darkness found its way across into the astral world and has made this its home. The astral world is unrecognisable. No Being aspires to go there anymore. It is not the haven that you would have known it as.'

'I can't remember it,' I tell her.

'Don't worry, you will,' she gently reassures me.

'The humans, well some of them, ripped tear after tear into the thin veil between the dimensions, though done unintentionally, it changed things drastically on earth and here.'

'How?' I am curious to know, expecting her to blame the ozone layer.

'With nuclear weapons and radiation, the darkness found its way from earth in the form of Shadows, an army of them bounced their way through the holes into the astral world's atmosphere.'

I remember the news. Numerous nuclear weapons tests have been reported in recent months. Disasters too. Earthquakes, volcanic eruptions and forest fires. Thousands of faultless, harmless animals have been killed or affected.

'Perhaps, if I find Eucele, he will be able to help?'

Tyra smiles, 'Perhaps.'

Perhaps, I think to myself, I'm not sure. I've been broken and have no physical body. I'm just a human after all, a human that doesn't seem to belong anywhere. Not here and not there.

She looks at me deeply; straight through me.

'Events, traumas, people, they can only break you if you give them the power to do so. Strength, your real power, comes from within you, deep inside. How you deal with a situation and how you hone and direct your energy is what matters. The intention you put out is the key.'

'What did I go to earth to do?' Perhaps she knows. I suspect she does.

'You went to be you. To go there and take your light with you. To shine, to help with the Legend of the Great Awakening. Native prophecy foretold that people of the rainbow would return and unite on earth to rebalance and restore harmony to the planet.

The shift is waiting to happen. Not enough Starseeds who answered the call have woken to their mission yet. They have begun to step forwards, but there is still more they need to do. It will take large numbers of them to make a difference.'

She looks down at her watch, lifts and hovers above the ground.

'I need to be somewhere. Call if you need me.'

She gives me a glowing orange wave and disappears back over the canopy, leaving me all alone once again.

Chapter 53: Eyes

I notice the elementals have vanished, maybe they followed Tyra. I walk on through the Monotonous Forest, my personal name for this mind-numbing expanse of trees. I feel different; a new confidence lifts me, and I sense change is on the horizon. My head pivots side to side, I don't want to miss anything. What's that at the side of the path, up ahead? Something white with big amber eyes stares straight at me. I freeze. Moving may antagonise it or frighten it away. It continues to stare, ears pricked up, listening, on high alert. A long slavery tongue hangs from its mouth. Enormous teeth are barred, heaving breath pulsates from the beast. Canis lupus arctos. It's in the wrong place, the wrong world, its frequency is out of sync with everything around us, but, impossible as it may seem, a full grown, three-dimensional white wolf stands before me.

I keep steady eye contact, little by little I edge forward, stopping periodically to reassure the animal I'm not a threat. The wolf appears to relax slightly and allows me to pass. Our eyes locked; neither of us look away. My footsteps quicken as our distance increases. Eye contact now broken; I glance back to see her settle down in the grass. I wonder how she got here, maybe through a rip in the veils? Her skinny legs stretch out in front of her and her sensitive nose sniffs something in the atmosphere. Quickly, she disappears; swallowed by the forest. Suddenly, an almost melancholy howl shatters the silence. She's still there. I pause to listen. Not a sound. I hope she can find her place in this world. Such a beautiful creature. I reverently bow my head in deep respect to her and realise that I've changed. When did I start wearing this outfit? The NHS nightdress has gone and in its place is an emerald green tee-shirt with the black eye of Ra across the chest and a pair of black shorts. Knee-length black boots with the green eye designed over the toes and a green wedge heel cover my previously bare legs. A gold amulet grips around the top of my arm with the eye etched into it. I'm perfectly coordinated. I check my necklace and pull it to the outside of my tee-shirt. I need it to be visible. I remember Tyra had informed me that it was a warning to others, whoever 'others' may be. I notice I have green pads wrapped around my arms, from my wrists to my elbows. I wear so much green.

Eyes

Something sparkly and shiny on the path ahead catches my attention. I move quickly and pick it up. A white wolf. It's small and dangles on a hoop. Who left it laying there? This can't be a coincidence. I'm getting quite a collection. Threading the charm onto my necklace as I walk, something catches my eye through the thickness of the trees, off to the left. It's so faint but it could be a pool or lake. Do I dare leave the path? I don't want to get lost or deviate from the track but being of a curious nature and heeding Tyra's advice, I need to investigate.

Leaving the path, I scramble through the gaps between the trees. It's quite breath taking, or it would be if I needed to breathe. A ghostly shimmer is tinged with deep stripes; sparse flashes of blue tones; a super ethereal lake. Leaning over the edge of the body of water, I impulsively plunge my arm into the depths. Instantly, the light that is my arm radiates a blinding glare. The water swirls around my arm, silently creating a water ring. Magic! I pull my arm out. It is, of course, completely dry. I feel the need to crouch and stare into the depths. There's something down there. A pair of eyes stare back at me intensely. Probably some kind of fish. I try to follow the gaze by dipping my face into the water, scanning around slowly. There's no sign of them. Maybe my imagination was playing tricks again; I need to be sure. I methodically scrutinise each plant and rock. Waiting… patiently… There they are! A large pair of oval eyes looking from left to right, taking me in. Wait, there's another pair. Four eyes wobble from side-to-side peering at me. Two more join in the intrigue. Six eyes all curiously, watching. I thrust my face further into the water. My eyes flicker from one set to the next, silently trying to communicate with them. Perfectly synchronised, all the eyes suddenly leap towards me.

Alarmed, I stumble, sitting back into the mud, submerged up to my waist in the glowing waters. Something is tugging and pulling on my left leg. I look slowly down their short length and could not be more surprised. Three ethereal women stand waist deep in the shallow water. They stand looking at me and then at each other. They have long hair that hangs behind them and floats on the water. There is a beautiful luminous thread of colour running through their opaqueness. The streaks of colour radiate against their transparent forms. One has pink highlights; one has green and the third has blue. Matching aura's shine around them. They wave for me to join them in the water. I'm hesitant to follow them after my last experience of the ocean, but, hey, what's the worst that could happen? I take the plunge; literally. The girls smile, nod, then turn and swim away. As they flute through the water, I see long tails with horizontal lines and fins at the end, break the surface water. Mermaids. Mermaids in this ethereal world. I never believed they were real, just mysterious and beautiful Beings of legends, told by sailors. They bob around playfully splashing each other. It seems I can float and swim without any issues even in deep water. I move closer, hoping they will let me join in. Having ignored me as I approach, all three turn in unison and splash me. Apparently, we are playing a game of 'Let's Grab Each Other's Tail.' Legs in my case. Funny, I know the game well. I play a similar game with my dog Freida. Most of the time she ends up chasing her own tail and biting it. The mermaid with pink in her hair has the most beautiful deep blue eyes. She swims under the water, up close to the mergirl with the blue streaks and green eyes, and emerges, spitting a mouthful of opaque water into her opaque face. I'm impressed by the amount of water she can hold at one time. 'Pinky' beats a hasty retreat under the water. She knows that payback will be delivered. 'Bluey' shakes off all the water, like a dog, before submerging herself. I bravely join in all the fun. I throw myself under the water and grab Bluey's tail before she gets the chance to swim away. She swims and pulls me along for the ride. It's good that I am light. I glow like a white electric eel through the water. I'm shining. I see the change that happens in the mermaid's hair when she's in the water. The blue coloured streaks intensify and the whole of her head lights up in electric blue.

We swim up behind Pinky's tail. Her hair is luminous too. Bluey reaches out her arm, she just misses, she stretches out a tiny bit more. Yep, that's it, she grabs it – she's got it! She gives Pinky's tail a big tug then does a quick backwards somersault that puts her in the right direction for a fast retreat. I somersault with her, still holding on tight. Positions are now reversed. Pinky swims as fast as she can after us. The mergirl violently shakes her tail from side to side and catapults me off. Obviously, things are starting to get seriously competitive, and I must have been slowing her down. I shoot through the water and find myself at the edge of the lake, where the mergirl with the green hair and grey eyes, 'Greeny,' sees a chance to interact with me and comes swimming over. She appears to be the quiet one out of the three. I start a conversation with her, a complimentary remark about her hair colour. I try asking her what her name is, but she doesn't understand. She just keeps looking at me, smiling. Oh, maybe I've annoyed her? She propels herself backwards a little then unexpectedly rises out of the water. Was my conversation so bad that she wants to fly away? Can mermaids fly? Here, it seems, anything is possible. Her arms hung loosely by her sides; ripples begin to vibrate from her. They float across the small distance between us, bounce down, skimming over the water's surface. They echo in waves towards me. I bob about in the water, watching them expectantly as they make their way towards me. On impact, rings run around my head, and I absorb them naturally; happily letting them in. She's talking to me. I can hear her voice! She's communicating with me; her way. I can feel exactly how she feels. She's sharing her feelings with me. It's incredible how contentedly she exists. She isn't worried about anything. She isn't concerned about tomorrow or any other time. She feels happy now and that's all that matters. Her vibrations make their way to my feet leaving through my toes then rise back to the surface where they bounce away and finally dispersed. I smile at her and clap to let her know that I understand and that I'm pleased to do so. She nods to me, happy that I've fully understood, then holds her arms high up above her and dives into a handstand. All I can see is her tail sticking out. She flicks it in the air then comes back upholding out her ethereal hand presenting something shiny. It glints as she holds it out to me and drops it into my outstretched palm. It's a green mermaid just like her but in miniature, holding onto a silver sparkly hoop. I thread it onto my necklace carefully. I don't want to drop it. The other two mergirls come swimming over, their game obviously exhausted then. The three of them start to swim away. I'm not ready for them to leave so I follow behind them. They communicate amongst themselves, swimming slowly to allow me to keep up with them. As I approach, Pinky pushes out her long tail towards me and spreads out her fin, allowing me to hold on. We swim towards the far side of the lake. I cling onto her fin tight as a limpet. For fun, I grab onto Bluey's fin at the same time. They both pull me along. I have my very own water chariot. Pictures from my beloved history books pop into my head, I imagine Cleopatra would have loved to travel this way. The opposite bank of the lake is now in view. I let go of both fins and float beside them. We make it across to the other side. Gracefully, Greeny rises out of the water. I know what's happening this time; she has something to say. The ripples vibrate and run circles around my head.

'The Lore Bath.'

She points to the shore. I look over a mound of ethereal mud and in the centre, I see what looks to be a celestial body of water. Another pool, much smaller than this one but with multi-coloured waters. I nod to her in understanding. I know what I need to do and swiftly pull myself out of the water onto the bank. I slip and slop as I try to walk through sticky mud. The banks of the pool remind me of a wonky love heart. Orangey brown, dark and murky water hug the edges. Next is a yellow layer of water that's slightly clearer. Deep jade, clear water is in the centre. It reminds me of one of my favourite crystals, blue agate. It sits, pride of place on my bedside cabinet. I can spend hours staring at the different shades of concentric blue circles, totally mesmerised by their structure and perfect imperfections.

Daydream over, I clamber over a low wall of rocks that protectively surrounds the pool and climb down the other side. Sitting on the edge of the pool I dangle my feet into the murky water. This is real water; water as I know it. Another anomaly; completely out of place. I look back to see three colourful streaked heads bobbing about above the surface of the water in the lake. They're swimming away. I think how much easier life would be for us on earth, if humans could communicate their feelings to each other without using words.

'Thank you!' I shout after them.

Something unexpected but wonderful happens. Ripples vibrate from me. They pulsate over the mud, flutter across the surface of the lake, bouncing and chasing after the mergirls. The rings run around their three heads and travel down to their submerged tails. Their coloured hair lights up above the water. They turn back and wave to me. They understand my message, wow, how magical! With a flick of their tails, they disappear beneath the water.

Chapter 54: Hippo

The steaming, bubbling Lore Bath awaits. Green, therapeutic thermal waters spit and spat. A musical wispy voice instructs me to enter. I wade through the murky water. It suddenly drops away sharply. I'm on tiptoe with only my glowing head visible on the surface. I pass through the orange into the green spa waters, which gurgle and bubble and suddenly find myself completely submerged. The only light comes from myself, all the colours of the rainbow. I compare myself to Achilles, as he undertook his rite of passage. I don't want to be like him. I can't have a trace of vulnerability. A shape circles in the sky above me. It's hard to make out through the water above me, but whatever it is makes a loud screech. Is that screech meant for me? I ignore it, but then I hear it a second time. Is it a signal to surface? I think it is. I emerge easily, confronted by a familiar pair of wings. They belong to the Birdman, Eucele. He hovers over the pool then suddenly flies away. I quickly climb up onto the wall of rocks, shouting his name. I need to speak to him. What happened next, happened all by itself. I'm flying again. Lifting off the wall and ascending as naturally as walking. I'm not surprised. I've always known. I've often dreamt of flying. I glide by the tops of the transparent trees. Tiny people have been scurrying about above me all this while. I had no idea. I fly past a colony of boys and girls dressed in colourful shorts and tops with pointy faces and thin hair upon their heads. They are magical folk; not ethereal. 'Good day!' I feel it's polite to greet them.

They are rather surprised to see me chasing after Eucele. I must look like a Giant to them; do Giants exist here? I rise higher. Although Eucele hasn't glanced back, I can feel he knows I'm following him. He wants me to follow him.

The Monotonous Forest doesn't live up to its name from above. How wrong I had been to sulkily label it so. I see nothing but mysterious scenery filled with magical and wondrous folk. The mundane looks amazing from my new perspective. Even that large brown patch over there, just off the path on the right. I would have walked straight past it and never known it was there. Distracted from my quest to follow Eucele, I fly lower and see more ethereal mud; it's a watering hole. I doubt there are any mermaids in it, just a hippo. Just a hippo? A hippopotamus! What am I saying? I need to investigate. I circle and make my landing as the hippo, slowly and wearily plods in my direction. The huge creature is withered and so thin the shape of its ribs, clearly visible. Head hanging low, it approaches shyly. It comes closer and I edge away, backwards. I remember reading that hippos are the most dangerous mammal, second only to humans. Sensing my rejection, the animal takes umbrage and sulkily trots in a semicircle, pointing its bony bottom at me. I have obviously caused offence. I try the open and honest approach.

'Hi, I'm sorry I'm new around here and it's a bit hard to know who to trust, you know, and I don't get to meet a hippo very often. Usually there's a fence between us and...'

Seriously, I need to be quiet. I'm just making things worse. The hippo positions its head at an angle. Listening, but pretending not to.

'Look, I'm sorry I just wasn't sure if you were friendly or not.'

That does nothing to improve the situation. She huffs, sighs and shakes her head. Then she raises her tail and poops right at my feet! Balls of ethereal waste splat into the ethereal mud.

'That's very rude. I was just a bit frightened, and I reacted badly, but there's no need for that, you… animal!'

I know, I know, not the most original name to call someone in an argument. She must feel guilty as she turns timidly to face me. She looks so sad and completely undernourished. But why? I haven't needed to eat anything since I've been here. How do I know that she is a she? I've no idea, I just know. I feel compelled to gently stroke her face; the same way I stroke little Freida when we're curled up on the sofa. I don't get a chance as the hippo starts to frantically kick the mud, attempting to cover herself. Not an easy task when it's so shallow. Ethereal mud doesn't stick very well and certainly doesn't end up where you expect it.

'Oh, my gosh, you're bleeding! Why didn't you say something?' Red opaque droplets are dripping into the mud beneath her, they slither from her pores, out of the thick grey skin down her back and legs.

'You should've said you were injured right away,' I scold her. No wonder she was overly sensitive. She doesn't answer me, she keeps on kicking at the mud. I jump into the muddy water to help her. Perhaps it's a game? I have no idea why she's doing this, but I try to help. I take my lead from her, scooping and splashing the mud onto her leg. She stops kicking, looks up, rolling her eyes and shakes her head. More and more red liquid bubbles spill down her back and legs.

Kicking harder and faster, her stubby little legs going like the clappers; her kicks become aimless as she tries too hard, and the mud propels off in the wrong direction. She's going too fast to notice. I try to signal to her to stop but she doesn't. She keeps on going until she finally pauses to looks down at her handy work. She's very surprised. She turns her head to look at me, almost accusingly as if it is my fault but then her eyes pop open so much wider.

'What is it? What's wrong? What are you looking at?'

Unbeknown to me, after all her effort and hard work, as well as mine, I look like a mud monster with a glow. She has missed herself and covered me instead. I shake my arms and legs. I don't want to think about what these big round lumps are. At least it doesn't smell, as I discover it's all over my face too. I must look like one of the Maudlin Maids. I remember them; I can see them, but from where? It's a half memory I'd completely forgotten about. The drips are falling thicker and heavier. This is terrible!

'Help! Help! Tyra, I need your help!'

The orange orb instantly appears over the tops of the trees.

'Tyra, thank goodness you're here. She's bleeding terribly, it won't stop,' I blurt out before her feet have a chance to touch the ground.

Tyra inspects the hippo. A puzzled look is exchanged between them. Tyra then nods her head as something suddenly dawns on her.

'It's quite alright, she's just sweating,'

'Just sweating?' I scoff, 'Can't you see the drops of blood?'

'No, she's sweating, it's perfectly natural. It's her body's way of cooling down. She hasn't long arrived here, and the transition stage is not a hundred percent complete. It takes time to settle in, like anywhere when it's new and feels strange,' I completely understand.

'You were right to call me though, this watering hole is far too small for her. I need to fix that straight away,'

I feel a bit better that she hasn't had a wasted journey after my confusion over the hippos' sun screening techniques. Still, how was I to know? Tyra turns to the hippo.

'So, girl, this thing isn't big enough for ducks, let alone your backside, skinny as it is. That was the problem, was it?'

Her question is met with a sad nod.

'Never mind, never mind. Don't you worry about that now, we shall rectify the problem, it will be sorted out in no time. There will be plenty of room for all the others too, when they come, you'll see,'

Others? What others?

Tyra crouches down, placing her hands above the ethereal muddy water. I peer down at her feet; I am interested to see if she is still wearing her high heeled sandals. She is and they're still sparkling, despite the mud.

Without saying a word, the edges of the watering hole slowly stretch out. A giant tap appears in the centre, a magic purple tap. Water begins to flow. We watch as the ethereal water spouts out, slowly filling the pool. It's taking too long; Tyra creates a second one. That's better; two gushing taps. The watering hole quickly fills with fresh water. The hippo, standing there, looks at the depths in amazement. Then, she suddenly dives, disappearing from sight.

'There, that's a bit deeper!' Tyra rubs her hands together in satisfaction of a job well done.

I clap in glee, happy yet sad, because I didn't get to say goodbye before my new friend vanished. She suddenly reappears, her googly eyes and erect ears emerge out of the water. She's come to say goodbye to me. She allows me to hug and rub her face; she looks happier. I'm glad to see her transformation. She glances at Tyra in gratitude before she swims away and sinks down deep.

'She didn't have food or enough water to swim in on earth, did she? Is that how she died?'

'That's right. The land was dry and the water sparse. But don't you worry, she'll be fine here, and others will follow her shortly. She won't be alone for long.'

Tyra assures me and I believe her. It was all over the news, animals struggling; too many in small pools of water fighting to survive. I shiver and remember that at the time, I was busy and hardly took any notice of what I had heard on the news. I never gave it a second thought. Feeling guilty now isn't going to change things.

'Thanks for coming, it's a good job you were still here.'

'Actually, I was in the middle of cooking dinner,' she laughs 'I have to go before my sauce burns.'

She rises and is gone, back to her kitchen somewhere.

I fly back up to the canopy, past more of the little tree folk, who are running along the branches excitedly. What's happening?

'Hello, excuse me, what's going on here?'

No one wants to stop to chat. They gather in a crowd at the end of a big bundle of branches, looking intently at something below. What is it? What can they see? I move to the side of them. I spy a waggon with a teal-coloured canvas, stretched over an arched wooden frame. Green; my favourite colour. It's a stationary bow top caravan on the left side of the path. Things are scattered about on the grass. House stuff; a rug, some spoons, some pots. Someone is having a clear out. Who is here? I glide down to see.

Chapter 55: Patience and Tzigane

I silently and gently alight outside the caravan. I cannot see anybody; they must be inside. Looking around, I absorb my surroundings. A stove pipe and cowl are gently smoking with soft wispy plumes reaching for the sky. Cedar penny boardings run in slats creating the walls. The waist board, carved and adorned, are exquisitely painted with gold and red flowers. The door is at the front; two panels, one above the other. You can open one at a time or both together, a stable door. The wheels look disproportionate, how on earth do they move this thing? Maybe the spokes give them the strength they need?

I've been in gypsy caravans before. I looked around two that were a feature at a family fun park when I was younger. I don't remember the name of the place, but I've seen a photo of me standing inside one and I can remember it. I went with my parents. My parents… I'd forgotten about them, but this old-fashioned vehicle reminds me.

A sudden movement catches my eye and I swing around. The horse that pulls the caravan is grazing behind it. I hadn't realised it was there. The horse is small, more of a pony than a horse, with bigger muscles. She's ethereal; that's why it was harder to spot. Streaked white with a large black smudge patch on its back, it appears slightly shaggy with her short stubby legs ethereally hairy. No sign of anyone, so I call out.

'Hello, is anyone home? I hope you don't mind but I've just come to look at your caravan,'

'Roulotte.'

The top stable door panel flings open and a voice with an accent corrects me.

'Roulotte.'

She leans on the closed wooden door panel.

'Roulotte,' I repeat.

All smiles and strangely familiar honey yellow eyes, she points to the horse.

'Tzigane.'

Opening the lower panel, she walks out onto the foot board. I love her outfit. A long red skirt flows down to the floor. A matching scarf tied around her head is edged with jangling, gold gypsy coins. Her white long sleeved, off the shoulder top with a romantic frill is tightly tucked into the top of her skirt and overlaid with a glowing rose gold bodice. A thick black belt has flaying tassels with more of her wealth dangling light musical tones. Golden shoulder length earrings dangling from her ears and double ringed gypsy beads are strung casually around her neck, a sign of love and friendship. There's something about her skin; it's dazzlingly white, as is her hair. It flows down her back, almost as long as her skirt. It's the longest hair I've ever seen.

She invites me into her roulotte. I don't need to be asked twice. I float up onto the foot board as the pale lady opens the lower door for me to enter. She holds back a beautiful, plush, white velvet curtain. I step inside and point to myself.
'Maya.'
She points to herself. 'Patience.'
I wonder if she lives up to her name. The tiny space is homely and filled with colourful, useful bits and bobs. It's impossible to take everything in at first glance. Behind her is an iron stove burning wood. Seats are built into the opposite wall, upholstered with burgundy crushed velvet material. A comfortable place to sit and keep warm. There's an oak cabinet positioned to the side of the chairs. The cabinet is stacked neatly with a hand painted china tea set. Cups and saucers, large plates, side plates and a teapot, a sugar bowl with a sweet little lid and a milk jug. Every single piece is delicately painted blue with white daisy petals around the edges. All of it matching.
I'm reminded of the time I was given a 'Paint Your Own Tea Set.' The set came with five tiny plastic pots of paint that always ran out before I finished painting. I recall decorating one cup with nothing but the black paint. I used up every drop and it took days to dry. Every time I checked; it was still wet. Eventually Mum stood it in the airing cupboard on an old side plate so that when the boiler came on, it would eventually dry. I'm funny as a human. I smile to myself. Another memory.
I walk the length of the room, less than four strides. There's a dark green wooden chest with three long drawers at the side of it. More hand painted flowers on the drawers, white snow drops this time. A narrow bunk bed is cleverly disguised with an assortment of colourful throws and cushions.
Patience chats away to me. It's obvious she is pleased to have someone to talk to, even though I do not understand anything she's saying. I can pick out the word 'gypsy' once or twice. It doesn't seem to bother her that I don't offer any input into the conversation. She excitedly shows off her

bric-a-brac, thrusting pieces under my nose, explaining to me about this and that. I can only smile and nod my head. Everything in here is so beautifully crafted and lovingly decorated. She returns to the stove and starts stacking more crockery into the china cabinet. She then hangs blue decorated spoons and ladles onto hooks that are fixed to the wall. Her kitchen tidied; she indicates for me to follow her back outside. I'm probably making her task more difficult, there's so little room.

I step back down and wander over to say hello to Tzigane. I'm quite taken with the animal. Patience gathers up the bits of her home that she's scattered on the ground. I guessed correctly; she was having a tidy up when I came along. Next, Patience hitches Tzigane to the roulotte. She makes light work of it considering her stature. Climbing back onto the roulotte, she holds out her hand to invite me up. We appear to be going on a ride. We arrange the stools on the foot board. Patience secures the panel doors and then pulls on the reins, clicking her tongue. Tzigane moves slowly down the path. I cannot help thinking that it would be quicker if I pulled the caravan.

'Voyager à gauche,' she says to me.

I nod, not sure what it is she's saying. I learned Spanish at school.

'Voyager à gauche,' she repeats.

If I remember, I'll look it up when I get home.

We roll along the path, under the trees, sitting quietly. Tzigane isn't the fastest Being on four legs and I don't think it's the weight of the harness, after all, she doesn't feel it. At least I have Patience beside me and though we're now silent, every time our eyes meet, she smiles, and I know for sure that I'm not on this journey alone.

'Je suis la,' she silently whispers.

She and Tzigane are right here beside me, in front of me in Tzigane's case. Tyra has come when I've called her too. I'm lucky to have good friends. Patience makes the clicking noise with her tongue and Tzigane comes to an obedient stop.

What's she doing? We haven't come very far. Patience rises from her stool and disappears into the roulotte. In an instance she returns holding a dark green triangular silk head scarf, which she wraps around my head. It matches perfectly with my outfit. I'm now properly prepared for the roulotte journey. I'm not prepared, however, for a second sighting of the pesky helmet with the horns. The Viking scurries across one side of the path in front of us to the other and disappears again into a bush. Is it following me I wonder? I don't have long to think about it, the path through the trees abruptly ceases.

The roulotte's wheels roll out of the Monotonous Forest. I'd thought it would never end. Now that it does, I'm astonished! Desert. Miles and miles of sand ahead of us. Perhaps I thought that the hospital would be there waiting for me. Tzigane walks through the sands without any protest and the roulotte wheels roll, following behind her. Rocks stick out of the sand. What was that? I notice something running alongside us. Something or someone is trying to keep pace. Whenever we pass a rock, whatever it is, darts behind the nearest one, pauses for a brief moment then sprints alongside us again. I stare hard. What on earth is it?

Chapter 56: The Sands of Change

An imp; a waving imp. I happily wave back. He carries on running, vanishing behind a boulder. How strange. Patience is busy concentrating on guiding Tzigane; she takes no notice. A sudden gust of wind catches her long flowing hair, whipping it across her face. The canvas roof starts shaking and the sands whirl around us. It blows into our faces as it becomes more and more aggressive.

The atmosphere feels heavier; less ethereal. When did that start to happen? There was no weather or elements in the forest but now, I sense a change and instinctively check that she isn't up to mischief again, but no, her ladyship the moon is nowhere to be seen.

I'd thought the waving imp was being playful, but the little fella was obviously trying to warn us about the desert storm ahead. Patience taps me on the shoulder and notions for me to go inside. Taking my stool with me, I force my way through. It's difficult to open the two halves of the door against the wind. They blow in opposite directions. The swirling curtain doesn't help. Once inside, I struggle to lock the doors. Sand fills every nook and cranny, unrelentingly piling in drifts. The howls of the wind sound twice as loud inside. The roulotte violently rattles and shakes. At any moment, I think the wind may blow us away.

What a sandstorm! Poor Patience. Poor Tzigane.

The roulotte lurches forward, picking up speed. We're rolling downhill; a steep incline. The roulotte tips over and tumbles down, rolling over and over on its side. I try to pick myself up off the floor and attempt to save the china tea set. I fail; each piece falls, crashing to the floor. The rolling roulotte finally comes to a halt, teetering on her now creaky wheels. Silence. Stillness. Sitting up, I'm surrounded by the tea set, each piece in pristine condition. Amazing! A very sandy Patience appears through the stable door. She shakes herself, grains of sand spraying in all directions. It's earthly sand; there's nothing ethereal about it.

'Is Tzigane ok?'

She understands the gist of what I'm asking. She nods her head, but I notice she isn't wearing the red scarf anymore. It must have blown away. She walks to the back of the roulotte; to the bunks and climbs up to the top bed. She lays down and closes her eyes. I walk over and settle on the bottom one. That's odd, I'm very tired; something I haven't experienced up to now.

I must have fallen asleep, though I'm not aware of doing so. I wake with a start and sit bolt upright. The sandstorm has passed. Everything is quiet. The howling winds must have subsided. I climb out of bed and check on Patience. As I absentmindedly glance, something else is lying in her place. I only see it for a split second, before it disappears and Patience sits up, stretching. I look at her confused. She ignores my questioning look. 'Tzigane.'
She jumps down, looks at me with her wide marigold eyes as she passes me, heading to the door. That was weird. What did I just see?
The sands hide the roulotte wheels and entrap poor Tzigane all the way up to her back. So that's where Patience's scarf went! It's tied protectively around Tzigane's eyes, the coins acting as blinkers. My attention is drawn to our new position. The incline we tumbled down is vertical. An imposing cliff, towers above us. Looking up, I don't know how we all survived. I've no idea how we'll be able to scale those heights with all our kit and caboodle.
Patience emerges from the roulotte; I hadn't noticed her go back in. She hands me a shovel; she has one too. We get busy digging the sand away to free Tzigane. Patience suddenly drops her shovel and walks away, turning her back to me and Tzigane. She stares up at the vertical walls of the ravine. No doubt wondering how we're going to get everything back up to the top. I follow her.
'Don't worry, we'll think of something,' I try to reassure her.
She smiles then turns back to Tzigane. I follow her, determined to carry on shovelling, but there's no need. Tzigane and the roulotte stand completely free. They don't have one single grain of sand on them. Concerned, I march over and carefully inspect Tzigane for any injury. Both her and the roulotte are completely unharmed.
'How did that happen?'
I look Tzigane up and down in amazement. She neighs; the first sound the ethereal creature has made. I touch the green scarf in my hair. I feel different. I feel almost human. I look down at my hands. They are stronger. Something has happened here, and I don't know what or how, but we have experienced a significant shift. I open my mouth to ask a question, completely forgetting we don't speak the same language, when a cylinder shaped, black, low-flying shadow shoots low over the top of the ravine; from one side of it to the other and with a piercing whistle zooms out of sight. Even Tzigane looks up. I know exactly what it is, a missile. My suspicions are confirmed. There's an almighty explosion. The ground

above us shakes and rumbles. Cracks rip instantaneously through the vertical ravine walls. The ground we stand on vibrates. I leap into the air, flying as fast as I can to the top of the ravine wall to see what's happening. I can't see far, because rolling towards me is the largest ball of sand and dust I've ever seen. The faster it rolls the more sand it gathers, growing bigger and bigger. It's snowballing straight towards us. On its current trajectory, it will roll down the vertical walls and bury us in tons of sand and rock. The ground underneath it crumbles; cracks snake out in every direction causing the ground above to cave in. We need to move fast. I fly back down. I must save Patience and Tzigane, but I can't see either of them. It's too dusty with disturbed sand. Where have they gone? I fly around in circles, desperately searching. There's no sign of them or the roulotte. Then I see them, high above me. There, in the sky the roulotte is flying, pulled by a horse, who, it transpires, can also fly. Tzigane.

'Hey!' I shout, 'Wait for me!'

I fly after them. Patience turns and looks back at me.

'Wait, wait, slow down!' I call out.

They're so high, safely away from danger, I don't see why they don't stop for a moment and wait. I'm flying as quickly as I can. The humongous rolling ball of sand comes shooting over the edge of the vertical ravine walls. Bright electrical sparks flick at me. I have to dodge out of its way.

'STOP!' I shout and wave again.

She glances back but doesn't slow down. Instead, she speeds up, intentionally flying faster. For a moment, our eyes meet across the distance, and something passes between us. A yellow flash in her eyes. I had seen them before; the unmistakable eyes of a wolf. She lets out a heart-rending howl. Patience is the white wolf.

I feel something in my hand. Opening my fist, I see a sparkle; a miniature red and gold roulotte harnessed to a horse. Tzigane. A parting gift. As they disappear through a gap between two large white clouds, I can still hear her... howling... over and over again. They have gone. I'm on my own once more.

Looking down, the walls of the ravine have crumbled. There's no point hanging around here. Time to go. Double checking for incoming missiles that might knock me out the sky, I fly away. As I go, I thread the sparkly roulotte and Tzigane charm onto my necklace whilst thinking to myself that the missile must have come from earth, launched by an army. Some people, I fume, forgetting that I'm looking more like one myself since arriving here.

Chapter 57: Fort Hope

I see nothing but sand for miles; featureless. I've no idea which direction to take. A sense of deja vu sweeps over me. The same emotion I experienced in the Monotonous Forest; everything unwaveringly uniform. At least I had a path to follow in the forest. No such luxury here. Hang on, what's that? It's a wooden plank sticking out of the sand; some kind of signpost. I fly down to take a closer look. 'Crystal Mine' is childishly etched into the wood. I scan the area around me. There's absolutely nothing but sand. It's out of place; it doesn't belong here.

I ascend once more, desperately searching for a sign of life or clue to where I should be heading. Something catches my eye. Tracks. Railway tracks: narrow gauge, almost buried in the blown sands. Do trains come through here? I land gently and step across the track, examining it. The rails don't appear to be live but that doesn't mean anything around here. Why are they here? Perhaps they have something to do with the 'Crystal Mine.' That would make sense. I walk down the slim gap of the narrow gauge, between the rails. I can't see how far it goes or in which direction. This is the only section visible. I hear something behind me, a whooshing sound. Whoosh. There it is again. Something is hissing and steaming. I look around, searching for the source. Out of nowhere, it appears. I freeze as an apparition of a ghostly steam train hurtles towards me. A chimney puffs out spectres of white mist. The train trumpets three short raspberry blasts.

Startled, I dive off the track with seconds to spare. The phantasm locomotive hauls three empty open trucks. I watch the locomotive speed away, quickly vanishing from sight. One last raspberry, sounds in the distance. I blink, what just happened? Something small is lying on the track in front of me. A tiny train and truck. Inside the truck is a crystal, it's pink quartz, I think. Cautiously I look up and down the track, checking all is clear before I bend down and pick up the delicate charm. As I thread it onto my necklace, I caress all my charms; quite a collection of memories I wistfully reflect. I'm distracted by another sound, a completely different noise. It's muffled and obviously many, many earth kilometres away but I

can make out many raised voices, a lot of commotion. Something's going on, I'm needed; I can feel it. I fly to my right, straight into the desert.
I fly as fast as I can. A huge sense of urgency fills me. The volume of shouting and screaming increases as I approach. Finally, I see the top of an imposing building. A fortress rising out of the sands with towers, possibly a castle. Large black figures are scaling the outer curtain walls. Why don't they go through the very large wooden door? They grip onto the sandy bricks with the palms of their hands and soles of their feet. They're light footed for their size. Looking down from the ramparts, is a crowd. A mixture of many different Beings. I focus on them. Figures run about, shouting and tipping a huge round pan of liquid over the walls onto the climbing Shadows. Shadows, that's what they are, hostile intruders. No wonder they're not using the main entrance. Some of the liquid finds a target. The Shadow sizzles and melts instantly into a black sticky tar that glues onto the patch of wall it was climbing. Liquid misses the body of a Shadow, just catching its arm which frazzles, steams and fizzles as it melts away. The Shadow appears unaffected. It continues to climb, avoiding further splashes by ducking and diving. Though effective, only a fraction of the liquid finds a target. What is it that has this melting effect upon these entities? My mind flashes back to a conversation I had earlier with Tyra. She told me that Eucele had a lot of Shadows to deal with. I didn't understand what she meant at the time. The reality is far more sinister than I could imagine. They are everywhere. I need to find Eucele; I know he's here. I must fly high and drop down into the fortress.
I'm suddenly struck hard in the chest and find myself spinning uncontrollably, falling out of the sky. I crash to the ground, where I lay for a second, bewildered. What just happened? I'm fine, no harm done. I look about accusingly to see who or what knocked me down. No sign of the perpetrator but a short arrow is sticking out my chest. It has pierced through the Eye of Ra on the centre of my top; it hit the bull's eye. I pull it out and drop it onto the ground. Luckily, my top is undamaged too, not even a tear. They will have to try harder than that.
'Strong durable material, you get what you pay for.' I can hear my Gran saying. She was right.

Out of nowhere, the largest black Shadow mounted upon a horse dressed in black barding, stands a short distance away. He is surrounded by eight Shadows in a closely formed protective circle.
His black shadowy horse does not look happy. I can feel he's disturbed. Although the rider is looking my way, I can't see his face. It's hidden inside a black helmet with a visor. Holes are cut into the guard that covers

his mouth and protruding on either side is a set of black spread wings. Three long violet feather plumes sprout from the centre. The only colour he wears. Everything else is black. Obviously, his favourite colour. He wears an old-fashioned chainmail shirt; big heavy metal leg protectors and chainmail gauntlets clad his hands. He says something to his bodyguards, and they all begin to move towards me. I notice that he carries a completely black shield, subtly embossed with his own image. This egotistical dictator oozes pure evil and is obviously used to achieving his self-serving goals by using unbridled tactics of manipulation, violence and deceit. He bears down on me from his high position. I can feel the horse's despair. His broken essence overwhelms me with misery. I'm momentarily distracted from the raised war hammer that's murderously swinging towards me. Deftly, I launch myself into the air, heading for the nearest round tower battlement. Landing safely, I hide myself away by pressing against the curved wall. I'm surrounded by unmitigated chaos.

Chapter 58: The Awaited Arrival

Beings are running in all directions. Shadows blast the Beings out of their way with their green beams. They don't stand a chance when it hits them, they frazzle on impact. Unexpectedly and to mine and everyone's amazement, four humongous Giants begin to uncurl themselves from the outer curtain wall. The scrambling Shadows must have disturbed them from their slumber. Some Shadows fall back to the ground, wondering what happened whilst others chose to cling on, only to be carelessly brushed off by irritated hands. Four Giants; three males and a scraggly looking female, slowly stretch themselves until they are at their full height. Uncouthly yawning they stretch out their long limbs high above their heads then, lowering them, vigorously shake the life back into them. Those Shadows left hanging on, fly in all directions. Loud cricking noises from the Giant's necks reverberate around the fortress walls as they wrench their cervical vertebrae from side to side. Satisfied they're in full working order, they reach out their long, bright shining arms and methodically pluck the Shadows from the walls. Concentrating on the ones that have almost reached the top, they roll them into balls between their enormous hands, playing with them and then, extraordinarily, drop them, one by one, into their large mouths and swallow them! The fire that burns deep inside their bellies, instantly incinerates the dark entities. The unwholesome snacks do have unfortunate side effects. A strange sight to see four massive Giants with copious amounts of steam emitting from their incredibly hairy ears and the echoing sound of multiple, and often synchronised, Giant burps. They keep going, picking and eating, picking and eating. One big eye looks at me through a gap in the turret. It winks at me whilst walking by looking for its next Shadow. I giggle and bravely venture away from the safety of the wall, gradually edging my way to the nearest battlement. Beings of all shapes and sizes continually run past me. Hairy ones, furry ones, ones that are part human and part animal. Some have wings and some have flippers. I believe I may have seen a few of them in my dreams.

A pan filled with multi-coloured crystals shards is protectively carried from inside the tower and passed along a defensive line, one Being to another. It reaches the front of the line, and the content is tipped over the walls and rushed back into the tower for another batch to be collected. The pan is slow in returning. Despite the Giant's help, the Shadows are not deterred. I watch, terrified as a crafty Shadow storms the rampart. It picks up a goat-like Being with two short, spiralled horns, dangles its long legs over the side of the fortress wall and drops it. I'm compelled to look over to see what happens to him. He floats down in side-to-side movements. As he touches the ground, I see a bright twinkle, a flash in the air above and he's gone; absorbed into the ground. There's nothing left. I make my way unnoticed, along the middle section of the wall. I'm looking for Eucele; I need to find him. He holds the answers to all my questions.

'Oh, I am so sorry. Pardon me.'

I narrowly miss running into a Being, half-boy and half-horse who is galloping along, holding a long wooden stick. He skids on his hooves with an expression of utter surprise on his face. He just manages to stop himself from falling over the wall. He stares at me unblinking.

'Sorry,' I begin to back away.

'Maya!' His surprise turns to a look of absolute ecstasy.

'Yes? Hello,' How does he know my name?

'Maya, come with me.'

He urgently grabs me by the arm and pulls me towards the tower saying something about how I've arrived just in time. Eucele must have told him to look out for my arrival. I suspected that he knew I was following him and would eventually find him.

We go quickly down a spiral staircase and find ourselves in a small, circular, sparse room with a tower window looking down, onto the action. Green flashes catch my eye. The small room is a hive of productivity. Beings waiting impatiently for the next panful of crystal shards to be sent out. It's being prepared at a slow rate. In the centre of the room is a figure hidden underneath a long brown cloak. He's kneeling; bent over a stirring pot. His head is covered but I know exactly who it is. I would recognise those white feathery hands anywhere.

'Hello, Eucele, it's nice to see you again.'

'She's here! Maya has come!'

The half-boy and half-horse announces to every Being in the room. He sounds excited about my presence. I'm hoping Eucele is going to tell me what's going on and why I'm here. The big, crouching figure stands; pulls back the brown hood and looks at me. It is Eucele. Every Being is looking at me. I can feel all eyes upon me including a scholarly looking young man dressed in a white toga and a pair of sandals. He seems familiar but I don't know why. My train of thought is interrupted by a Shadow bobbing awkwardly down the staircase. Tall and large, with gangly arms and legs; it's single dimension flat against the wall. I glance instinctively to the window where a man and a boy are standing. Tattoos of the sun, big and round, casting triangles of light are inked on the tops of their arms, in luminous yellow and orange. Both wear tall, coloured feather headdresses. They feel familiar too. I've seen them somewhere before. The Shadow targets the boy and scoops him off the ground. The man desperately tries to grab and protect him but cannot react quickly enough. The Shadow holds the boy up high, dangling him by an arm and a leg. My admirer, the boy-horse, acts quickly. He hauls his hooves over to Eucele's fire, grabs the cauldron, boiling on the fire and slings the content over the Shadow. I watch as the cauldron contents douses the Shadow. He reluctantly drops the boy as he melts down into black, thick sticky tar on the floor. The boy sits up looking pleased about his adventure. I remember where I've seen the boy before. He was one of my ghost visitors back home in my bedroom. I glance at the man; he was the other one.

Eucele is handed back the pan. He wastes no time in refilling it with a handful of large crystals he pulls out of an almost empty, threadbare brown sack. He looks to everyone in the room.

'This is the last of the crystals. I collected all that were left from the depths of the abandoned mine in preparation for this attack. Our stocks are depleted. The Trolls are long gone.'

Trolls! Of course, they worked at the Crystal Mine. That was the signpost I saw!

Eucele shakes the remaining shards of broken crystals from the moth-eaten sack. In Eucele's palm, they are little more than crumbs.

'Quartz. You need to consume these crystals to regain your full power,' Eucele informs me.

'How do I do that? I can't eat crystals,' I ask, puzzled.

'Of course not,' he shakes his head of heavy hair, 'you will need to infuse the quartz energy in a liquid solution and swallow every last drop.'

I haven't needed to eat or drink since before the Havoc concert. That seems like a lifetime ago. I understand Eucele's instructions but I'm sceptical.

'But...'

'But what?' challenges the boy-horse.

'Well, we have no liquid. We're in the middle of a desert. It's dust dry and we must act quickly,' An idea forms in my head as I'm expressing my concerns. I've no time to explain. I must trust my instinct.

'Tyra! Tyra, I need you, urgently. Come quickly please.'

I'm relieved to hear a clatter from the top of the tower; it certainly isn't Santa Claus. An orange orb bounces down the spiral staircase and light spills into the bare room.

'Tyra, you're wearing denim dungarees and you're barefoot,' I declare in surprise.

Tyra's casual appearance is a far cry from her usual pristine self. She looks down at her bare toes, nails perfectly polished in sparkling silver. She shrugs, 'I was busy, and you said to come urgently.'

'Yes, thank you, I did. Would you create another tap; a small one and a teacup if possible? I need an elixir infused with quartz energy. It's the only way to restore my full powers.'

'Of course. Good to see you again Eucele.'

They respectfully nod to each other. Tyra reaches out her hand. Instantly, a small tap materialises. She winces as she twists. It obviously hasn't been used in a while.

'Got it.'

Tyra relaxes and smiles as the tap chugs, spits and finally bursts out a steady flow of water. Tyra then pulls a dainty china cup from her pocket and tips half a cup of milky tea onto the floor.

'I was resting quietly in the garden drinking my tea when I heard your message,' she explains. 'I was saving it for the journey home, but never mind.'

Tyra hands me the cup and I gently hold it underneath the running water. When the cup is three quarters full, Tyra clicks her fingers, and the tap vanishes. I look at Eucele and he nods his permission. I drop the quartz shards into the water, they sink to the bottom. Everyone's eyes are on that seemingly insignificant china cup, waiting… I can feel something. Slight vibrations are emanating from the cup. They grow steadily until the cup shakes and the potion bubbles. Crackles and a light blue spark bounce off the inner rim of the fine bone china. The light diffuses in all directions, reminding me of the Ondines and their bright colours. In an instant the sound and the colour fizzes to nothing. I remember from my history books that this ancient practice goes back hundreds if not thousands of years and has never lost its vogue.

I look to Eucele for an explanation. Tyra senses my apprehension and reading my thoughts, explains.

'Vibrations from the quartz infuse the water with the mighty power stored in the shards lattice centres. The source of every crystal power comes from this central element within every individual stone. Just like humans and their hearts.'

'Is it ready to drink now?' the boy-horse asks impatiently.

'Yes, yes. Just sieve the crystals out first,' Tyra instructs me. 'Oh, wait. I have my tea strainer here; I'd forgotten about that.'

Tyra pulls out a pocket-sized mesh strainer from inside her dungarees. I attentively pass the cup back to her. Cupping my hands together to create my own bowl, Tyra pours the power infused elixir into my hollowed palms, catching the fragments of crystal in her strainer. Every drop is drained. I don't think about it, I must hurry; time is of the essence. Carefully, I raise my hands to my mouth, throw my head back and allow the elixir to slide down my throat.

I look around. Everyone is looking at me. Hoping and waiting.

'She still looks the same.' I hear this observation but have no idea who said it.

'Ok, well, I'm done. Must get back to my teapot. It'll be well stewed by now.'

Tyra, her cup and tea-strainer disappeared up the stairs, surrounded by her magnificent orange aura.

'Now is the time,' Eucele solemnly declares, 'to fulfil your destiny,'

Chapter 59: The Battle

Slowly, the warmest and most peculiar sensation begins to surge through me. Is she okay?' a concerned voice asks.

'Don't worry Lynk, all is well,' Eucele kindly reassures.

Lynk! He's called Lynk. Lynk The Second. Lynk, Lynk, Lynk, Lynk! My one and only true best friend.

'Lynk' I shriek his name, overjoyed at my epiphany. 'Is it really you?'

He laughs, 'Well I think so. I believe so.'

He certainly looks like the Lynk I remember but he was never a great leader. My dear friend has found his strength. My heart swells with pride.

'Welcome back to the astral world Maya.'

'Ah, so I'm in the astral world. Silly me, I didn't recognise the place.'

Eucele refocuses us to the matter at hand.

'Reintroductions will have to wait, there are several Shadows upon the battlements and an evil Black Knight is remobilising them. Maya, if you would be so kind as to assist?'

'Yes, let's do this,' I enthuse.

I realise the pot from my little hut is hanging over the fire. I'm going to need it if the plan I'm quickly formulating is going to work.

'We need to evacuate the fort immediately. Go, now!'

Solutions always come from deep inside you.

Lynk wastes no time, he gallops back up the stairs to the battlements. I'm giving the orders; back in my comfort zone just like the good old days. I chuckle to myself running up the stairs after him. A terrible sight awaits us on the battlements. Lines of tall, dark Shadows are picking Beings at will and throwing them over the walls.

'Quickly! Everyone out of the fort. Fly, jump, take the stairs; anything but get out of here! Those taking the stairs follow me,' Lynk cries out, taking command again.

A desperate scream has me turning on my heel to see a Shadow dangling a woman with long braided hair, by her neck over the edge of the wall. I kick the Shadow's leg. Surprised, he looks down at me from his great height.

'There's really no need for that, is there?' I force myself to be polite.

The Battle

Without a second thought, he lets go of the lady, dropping her to her death. He turns his attention to me, smirking a charcoal shadowy smile.

'Thanks, I hoped you would do that.'

I somersault over the wall and grab the lady by her braids as she falls.

'Here.'

I pass her to the girl Giant, the one who has straggly brown hair. Her name eludes me. Another half-boy, half-horse, gallops across the ramparts holding a long staff. I don't recognise him.

'Hi Maya, I'm Hort,' he introduces himself as I land back on the battlement. 'Lynk's cousin. I'm glad you could finally come.'

He talks with more airs and graces than Lynk's Mum, Mary. I wonder if she's here.

'I need the fort cleared of every single Being. Anyone left up here needs to go down. Now!'

I instruct him, whispering 'And I need you to be the rear-guard; don't leave any Being behind.'

Hort screams as loud as he can.

'Evacuate!'

Some Beings haven't heard Lynk's order. Either that or they have vowed to fight to the end. Hort trots up and down, speaking to them. I see them nod their heads in agreement and then see them come hurrying past me, heading towards the stairs, following Lynks path. Others fly down over the top of the wall.

I need to do what I plan and then get down there quickly. I cannot see the Black Knight. Wherever he is, whatever he's concocting, he will stand protected, surrounded by his guards.

'Watchers, have you seen Noir?' I shout to the Giants.

A negative grunt is all the Giants can muster as they burp and slobber, eating as many Shadows as they can.

He's watching; I can feel his coldness.

The Shadow I kicked, seeks me out and lunges. Intuitively, I point my finger at him; he does the same, marking me out with his green beam. I'm a split second faster; my white light flashes straight into him; a direct hit. Wow! How long has it been since I did that? The Shadow completely disappears, vanishing in a trickle of green light. Now this is more like it! No dirty, sticky mess, I clear up as I go.

I look around, I'm happy to see the ramparts are empty. All the Beings have dispersed, only dim-witted Shadows remain. No doubt reinforcements will be called for. I need to re-join Eucele at the fire. I take the most direct route, over the battlement.

Chapter 60: The Spell

'Lynk and the refugees will need help when they reach the portcullis,'
Eucele is despondent.
'I'm not powerful enough to defeat this green magic,'
I try to reassure him.
'No Being can. Nuclear power is poisonous and deadly to all Beings.
There's no way of stopping the harmful energy waves once they're
released. I need you to be there for Lynk. Trust me, it's all part of the
plan,'

Eucele spreads his huge wings and silently rises, departing through the
open window, leaving me alone.
I have many tasks to prepare. Firstly, it's my turn to do the cooking. A
little bit of poetic verse is required. I clear my throat and chant:
'Crystal, crystal, smooth or gritty
Please hear, this, my magic ditty
There's not enough of you and more's the pity,'
I tip the last handful of crystals left in the empty sack into my pot. I
continue with my rhyme.

'More is needed straight away.
I need it now, no time to delay.
Boil and spread, far and wide.
In the crevice's Shadows hide.
These followers of evil power
Who light and love and peace devour.
MORE NOW PLEASE, QUICKLY!'

I send my magic to my faithful pot.
'More, more, more! Faster, faster, faster please!'
The crystals spit and spat, they churn and boil. Too slowly, much to my
annoyance. I really must work on this patience thing. Nearly done.
Rainbow liquid starts to rise. Soon it will come spilling over the top. A
Shadow appears on the stairs.

The Spell

'Quick! Hurry!' I shout at my magical, bubbling concoction.

A splodge spits from the pot and splats over the Shadow. He instantly melts and vanishes, no sticky mess.

'Great shot! Now go! Liquidate every Shadow soldier!'

My brew spills over the top of my pot. Slowly at first, it spreads across the floor of the tower, I rise and hover. Gaining momentum, it expands, rising quicker and quicker. Time for me to fly back to the ramparts. I nimbly take flight up the steps. If gravity existed in this realm, my crystal potion would be defying it. There's no stopping the rise and flow as the rainbow liquid faithfully follows my lead. The potion begins pouring out of the window and up to the battlement walkways.

'Spread! Spread out and fill the rooms, spread across the battlements!' I shout in glee.

It does as I command. It flows and covers the ramparts, dripping into the rooms on the floors underneath, like icing covers a cake. My potion is now pouring out in gallons.

'Keep going!' I heartily encourage.

As I reach the next tower doorway. I'm greeted by a fast-moving lava flow of my creation. It's heading towards the furthest corner of the fort.

'Oh no!' I exclaim.

A Being is trapped in the corner; I can see their light illuminating around them against the wall. I fly as fast as I can to a small, terrified boy who is pressed up against the wall. Swooping down, I grab his fragile arm and hoist him to safety, just as the potion reaches the wall. I tuck him securely under my arm.

'What an adventure we're having. I'm Maya, what's your name?'

'I'm Zmeu and I'm scared,' the quivering child whispers.

I try to console him. One of the Giants approaches me, and I carefully pass Zmeu into his cupped hands. He is kind and reassuringly smiles down at the shaking child. His moment of tenderness cost him dearly. A green light marks him out.

Zap!

The gentle Giant falls and in a last heroic gesture, throws Zmeu to the female Giant. She catches him with ease and quickly sits him on the back of Sphinx who has loyally stood protecting the main gate. She hurries to the Giant's side hysterically screaming.

'My brother! My brother!'

He lays stunned on his back, on a dusty dune. The fire in his eyes is barely visible; just a flicker of an ember is present. His sister awkwardly falls to her knees beside him. Another green light. Another act of kindness cruelly exploited.

'Watch out!'

My warning comes too late. She is struck in the shoulder, lurches forward and collapses next to her brother. She too, only has a flicker of an ember burning inside her large eyes.

I hear Noir's laughter. This is his doing. Alun and Petra. Look what he's done to them! Cautiously checking for Shadows, I fly down and kneel before them. Alun somehow finds the strength to reach his arm across his chest and takes Petra's hand. He holds it; his mouth smiling. Petra's head rolls back, her mouth stretches wide open; still trying to call her brother. I lay my hands gently on their faces. There is nothing that can be done; I can feel it. No matter how much I'm hoping, willing and trying, there's not enough energy to sustain them. I make the kindest decision I can. I inhale deeply and exhale a cold flow of energy in one big forceful burst.

The small flickering embers are extinguished. The last of the light in their eyes goes out. The last faint remnant of energy colours that surrounded them, cease shining instantly. Their energy moves on together. They no longer inhabit these light bodies; they're transmitted to somewhere of their choosing. From there, they can decide what they will become next, and when they'll start their new existence.

I fly angrily to the top of the fort, searching and shouting for that dark hearted Being.

'Noir, you're finished. Do you hear me? Finished! I will make you pay. You will not get away with this!'

He laughs and his laughter grows louder. I see nothing hysterical about my promise. This just got personal.

Chapter 61: Captured

Emerging through the window, I direct my binocular vision to the critical area. I see infrared light moving inside the centre of the fortress. I also feel the heat they emit. My sensors inform me that the Beings are on the move. Easy to locate from my bird's eye view, I observe a rainbow mass, herding them side to side. Maya's colourful crystal custard, dished up in lashings, is steadily advancing.

I need to be at the exit when they emerge at the foot of our sanctuary and ensure their escape. Purposefully, I dive downwards and violently snap to a halt. I'm caught in some form of net with no holes, cocooned in a green egg. The same shade as the nuclear liquid.

'The bird is finally in its cage.' I hear sniggers and jeering.

'Bird brain!'

The imbeciles cruelly laugh, trying to goad me. Umm, a predicament. I try to release myself. My magic fails me. My wings are immobile. Hard as I try, they will not stretch or unfold. Completely swaddled, I am trapped. I find myself in an uncompromising position with no obvious way out. This is bad and extremely dangerous.

Unwittingly, I have been snared. I'm suspended in the air.

'Leave him. He can't escape. I shall pull his feathers out later when I need some amusement. For now, we have other light fools to play with.'

Noir, sitting astride Phantome, leads his Shadow bodyguards away. Flashbacks of my fellow friends, family and comrades, featherless, return to haunt me. I know that he means what he says. For me, my demise will not be as quick as theirs.

I must continue to stand tall; I will not have the appearance of a defeated Avian. I wonder if Maya will appear from the window soon. Even if she does, is she going to be able to help me? I'm left hanging and watching, looking defiant. Hoping that my entrapment will spur motivation.

'Hey, don't worry,' An orange orb appears in front of me. 'I thought it might be best if I hang around a bit longer.'

Dressed head to toe in lead armour, Tyra speaks to me through my green swathe. She holds a lead dagger and cuts a line into my cage. She makes it longer, cuts an arch at the top and creates a doorway. The door innards crumble away. Tyra then reverently passes the dagger to me. My feathers surround it. Closing my eyes, I absorb its protection. I am free once more. I jump through the birdcage door and nod my thanks to the sorceress Tyra. My wings instantly open. I hand Tyra the lead dagger back with a bow of grace. She raises her hand in a stop gesture, the ancient sacred relic had been passed to me.

I am humbled. Forged from what humans believe is the oldest known metal, the blade is the shape of a curved ash leaf, long and thin at the tip. The midvein is etched deep along the centre with faint markings of veins branching randomly out on either side. The cylindrical handle is carved from the bark of a sacred ash tree found on earth. Designed for melee combat, the indestructible lead affords speed and accuracy.

Folklore claims that the dagger is the 'sword in the stone,' Excalibur, King Arthur's weapon. Tales mutate with time, whispers evolve and become exaggerated. Who knows, perhaps the tale is true. Talk of the lead dagger was just that; its existence, nothing more than a fantasy. But here I am, holding a dagger that matches its famed description. Legend has it that the dagger was thrown into the Lake of Reincarnation and retrieved by a lady whose hand emerged from the depths. After all, truth is, more often than not, stranger than fiction.

How has Tyra come to be in the possession of such a weapon? Enquiries will have to wait. Action is needed.

I nod my head gratefully to her. She acknowledges me with a knowing smile. Hurriedly I fly down, noticing that the rainbow light has now moved nearer to the fort's foundation.

Chapter 62: Lynk Leads

We rush down the steep, narrow spiral staircases. It's not easy when you have four legs and need to move quickly, not to mention guiding a crowd of Beings who are all awkward shapes and sizes. I instructed those who fly to leave through the open windows and to carry anyone they could. Staircases lead to lower-level floors which lead to more staircases. In my haste, my hoof slips. I miss half the steps, falling clumsily but regain a smidgen of pride by elegantly landing on all fours at the bottom. As I turn around to look back up the stairs to check everyone is safely following, a dark shape appears and spreads across the inside circular pillar of the spiral staircase. A Shadow; it's absolutely humongous. As big as the Giants. I see its arm reaching out and scooping downwards, picking someone out of the fleeing crowd. In the Shadow's grip, is another shape. The shape of a Being that looks like me, with hooves, I see it being shaken about, its tail thrashing from side to side. Then he's gone; evaporated. It's impossible to do anything. I realise that Mum has witnessed the distressing scene too. Standing next to me, she looks back, following my gaze. I can read her mind. That might have been Hort.

She says as much in a worried voice.

'I don't think that he joined us,' I reassure her, 'Those definitely weren't Hort's legs. They were too short.'

I hope I sound convincing. I need to keep leading forwards if we are to stand any chance of escape.

Something is happening above us. Lots of creaking, thunderous noises; the building is struggling; trying to hold itself up under the strain. We run down the next spiral staircase and then another; trying to outrun the Shadow before it returns for another victim.

A message is quickly passed forwards to me. Rainbow crystal potion appears lapping at the heels of an armadillo faced man who's bringing up the rear. That's it! That's what she's doing. Maya is flooding the fort! That's great; the Shadows will be destroyed but if we don't find a way out, it will be the end of us too.

'Faster, faster!'

I grab hold of Mum's arm and pull and guide her as quickly as I can. We need to outrun the Shadows and the potion. Yes, finally we're at the bottom, in a large room; the guards chambers.

A large plank of wood is fixed across the back of a big defensive gate. We struggle to lift it. If we can't shift it; we're stuck with no way to escape. We pull, heave and tug together but it will not budge. The level is starting to rise. Shadows, half melted, float down the stairs. Torsos that have been knocked off their feet, are heading our way. Some Shadows have been completely frazzled; all that remains is melted black, tarry puddles, floating on the rainbow surface.

'Maya!' I shout, 'Maya!' We can't open this gate. Eucele, help!'

I glance round nervously. The potion is steadily flowing down the stairs. Having taken out the Shadows behind us, it's now about to take us out too. 'Maya!'

We all scream loudly in unison. The potion gushes in, spreading towards us. 'Help! Help!'

I watch, horrified, as a half-melted Shadow rages against its inevitable demise. Floundering, splashing fists pound against the surface of the potion which slowly liquifies its victim.

Our fate seems unavoidable. Whether by Shadow or deadly potion, we are doomed.

Our frantic cries for help and fruitless attempts to open the gate will be our last stand. I watch in slow motion as a green ray of light marks me out from somewhere above the flooded spiral staircase. That's it, I'm dead. I keep yelling, there's nothing else I can do.

Chapter 63: The Fall of Noir

Frantic screams, shouts for help, kicking and thumping emulate from the guard chamber's double door. My help is desperately needed.

'Stand well back!' I bellow.

My light blasts the huge, ancient hinges from their fusing. As the doors fall outwards, my first sight is Lynk caught in the deadly sights of a Shadow's green beam. I rise above the dam burst of Beings, my light targets the ghoulish Shadow, instantly obliterating the heinous entity. Lynk silently offers me his thanks and instantly returns to his protective duties.

'Go back!' I command the surging tide. 'Leave these Beings alone. Destroy the Shadows. Quick, they're escaping!'

The rainbow wave abruptly comes to a halt. Its leading-edge rolls backwards and rises to form a long tidal wave intent on searching out the remaining Shadows. Some are sneaking through the newly opened doorway. The fleeing Beings are still in danger.

'Climb that dune, quickly!' I shout, pointing at the lee side of a massive sand drift. 'The fort's crumbling!'

I have rocked the foundations. Sand bricks disintegrate as they burst from their set positions. Great sections of the fort spin off in all directions, totally annihilated and crashing to the ground as dust. The four towers implode, crumbling to create giant mounds of sand. Dust and dirt fill the air. Battlements fold down on themselves, and the majestic safe haven is no more. The sand turns hard where the crystal sets. A few black puddles solidify. In the blink of an eye, Alun and Petra are buried under tons of sand. As the dust settles, I see through the debris. The landscape is unrecognisable. I'm instantly on my guard. Noir, and what's left of his Shadow army are still lurking close by. He is approaching. The coldness that emanates from him intensifies; I can feel his very soul. On high alert, I search for a black mist; a Shadow that will give away his hiding position. Suddenly, out of nowhere, Noir grabs the scruff of my neck, pulls me up unceremoniously and fling me face down in front of him across Phantomes withers. I silently scold myself for being such an easy target. He gallops away with me dangling on the neck of his horse. The scenario reminds me of a scene from one of my mediaeval history books. Funny how that came into my mind when I'm in such dire predicament. Noir's evil laugh fills my head.

'Too easy Maya!'

The hissing noise escapes through the gaps of the mouth guard in his helmet. I have no idea where Noir is taking me or what he has planned. I can confidently state it will not be afternoon tea! Can I rely on my light to defend myself? Will I make it back to my hospital bed? What will become… My thoughts are rudely interrupted. Two huge, strong front paws sweep my shoulders backwards and I'm flung skywards. In the same movement, Sphinx, muscles flexed and striped blue and golden nemes flapping, catches Noir and knocks him backwards. He somersaults over Phantomes tail and lands in a splat on the sand. His helmet rolls away revealing a blank blackness where his face should be. I can see a pair of eyes, bottomless pools. Ebony rays of light project from his very core; black shadows erupt, giving the illusion of a hall of mirrors. For a moment our gazes meet and lock. I can see deep inside him. I see the cold darkness is infinite. There's not a glimmer of light or colour. We are connected, intertwined and attuned. I know everything about him. I can hear his thoughts. I shiver. Seizing his chance, Phantome gallops away as fast as his long legs can carry him. Free once more, the possibilities are endless.

'Noooooooo!' Euceles' terror-stricken scream jolts me and breaks my focus on Noir. The Shadow guards turned Sphinx to sandstone the moment he landed after his courageous attack.

Noir uses my distraction to his advantage. Released from my hold, he retreats, heading for the safety of his guards. He doesn't make it.

I come to my senses. Pulling myself up to my full height, I fix my light straight into Noir. He is helpless, unable to reach his sanctuary. This coward is weak without his guard's protection. I must end this here and now. I feel an immense surge of power through every fibre of my Being. What shall I do with him? What would he hate the most? I must decide quickly.

'He hates the light.'

Yes, he does, I don't know who said that, but they are right.

'Thanks.'

Concentrating all my totem animals and inner strength, I reach out my arms and extend my whole Being, I absorb every joule of energy from every vital source. I kinetically ingest and unite the powers activating the sleeping serpent within. With one cosmic, electrifying bolt, I zap my whitest light into the eyes of Noir. A direct hit. A deafening silence. Then, nothing…

Blinded, deafened, depleted and utterly spent, my vision gradually returns. Everything around me moves in slow motion. Faces disbelieving, perplexed and in shock. My hearing returns from distortion to coherent. Eucele, bends over and supports my empty light body. What's happened? I sit up blinking and there before me is the brightest, yellow firefly flapping its wings and fluttering around in panicked circles. It's Noir. From now on, everywhere Noir goes, he will shine brightly, lighting the way for every other Being. An army of small, black, gloomy, lightless fireflies chase after their defeated master as he retreats as fast as he can.

We regroup; Eucele, Lynk, Hort and all the others. The two remaining Giants are both fine, though understandably, devastated by the loss of their two friends.

'Poor, brave Sphinx. Can we do something for him?'

Lynk voices what we're all thinking. He lovingly places his hand upon Sphinx's stone cold, solid back. Eucele lays his feathery hand upon the statue. Feeling, reading, looking for any sign of energy. Zmeu clings onto his other hand. The wise Birdman sadly declares there's nothing any Being can do.

'Crystals will not work now.'

He picks Zmeu up and sits him on Lynk's back, before walking away. We wonder what he's doing and look at each other questioningly. Eucele instructs us all to move away.

He stretches out his humongous wings. His arms held high above his head, clutching onto something black and shiny. A yellow light beams from it. I recognise it as the same crystal Eucele held over me in the temple, not so long ago. I remember it very well. The sand lifts. It whips and spins around Sphinx. A thick gritty dust blows and adds more power to the force. It's impossible to see through it. Eucele finally lowers the crystal and folds his wings. The dust settles and Eucele's creation is revealed. A single magnificent pyramid stands before us. Sphinx stands guard at its entrance where he will stay for all eternity. His paws stretched out; head held high. A steely look of determination on his face. His nemes still in the billowing position they had been when he was murdered.

'It's magnificent.'

I walk towards Sphinx and his great pyramid. A few healing magical sparkles still linger in the atmosphere. They settle on the astral pyramid. Every Being follows behind me to pay tribute to a brave Being who made the ultimate sacrifice to save many others, especially me. As I'm slowly walking, I notice a sparkle at my feet. I stoop and pick it up. It's covered in sand, so I blow my magical breath upon it and the grains shoot away. Another charm. A fort, a Sphinx and two Giants standing side by side, holding hands. Golden, with a hanging hoop. This necklace is being designed especially for me, but why? What am I supposed to do with it? I thread the charm onto the rope. Effortlessly it slides into place, hanging beautifully next to all the other charms. I smile to myself. I can feel that I'm being watched. I stand up and look around. Every Being is staring at me. I look at them questioningly.

'You're glowing so brightly,' Lynk enlightens me.

'Am I?'

I've not felt this energised in a long time. We continue our walk around the great pyramid. Suddenly, something darts by our feet. Lynk and I look at each other in complete surprise, we can't believe our eyes! We laugh at the same time, both recalling the event many moons ago. I had forgotten all about it until now. Even when he ran past me earlier, I didn't remember him. The Viking helmet with its two horns, scurries away in the opposite direction.

'Poor thing,' I feel bad for him.

I guess my time on earth has made me softer. He's been going round and round in circles. I run after the Viking, reach down and pull his helmet off so that he can finally see. The little bearded Viking blinks rapidly in the first light he's seen for many moons. He is temporarily blinded. A smile of relief forms as he adjusts to the light. His smile turns to horror as he looks up and sees me. With a high-pitched shriek, he runs as fast as his short legs will carry him straight into Sphinx, bounces off at a tangent and heads off into the desert.

'He definitely remembers you,' Lynk laughs as I re-join the group.

Chapter 64: A New Perspective

Zmeu sits confidently astride Lynk, holding his long mane of hair for balance. I grin at Lynk. He's doing so well, being so patient. He always hated his hair being touched. Our brave band of survivors, stroll together, quietly supporting each other.

'Do you realise now?' he asks me as we walk ahead, side by side.

'Realise what?' I wonder what he means.

Lynk begins his tale…

'Remember when we said our goodbyes, after our encounter with the Maudlin Maids?'

I nod.

'Well, I went home to the stable, in total disbelief that you'd gone. I was reeling; I just didn't understand why you had to leave. No more crazy adventures. Even though the Maudlin Maids had terrified me; I wished we could do it all again. I thought our time together would never end,' Lynk's voice trails off. His sadness is palpable.

'Well, when I got home, everything was quiet; very strange. No questions, no demands, no dressing down; just silence. All of a sudden, Mum came bursting through the kitchen door. She was so excited, gabbling something about a surprise and I'll never guess who was here. My long-lost cousin Hort jumped out from behind Mum shouting "Surprise!" Apparently, he'd just arrived, crossed over. I'm not sure where from,'

'Hort? I remember you mentioning something about him. Wasn't he a bit of a maverick?'

I vaguely recall Mary hero worshipping him and Lynk miming being sick behind her back. A touch of jealousy maybe?

'Yeah, I guess so, you'd never describe him as conventional that's for sure! Anyway, Mum was so busy fussing over him, and making sure he had everything, she didn't notice me sneaking out the front door. I don't know what I was thinking or why, I just knew I had to get away. I found you by the Lake of Reincarnation. You were being lifted into a rowing boat, by that huge hand. I stood behind you, watching in fascination. Just before the boat sailed away, on impulse, a whim, whatever you want to call it, I jumped into the boat, behind you.'

'You did?' I gasp incredulously, 'I didn't see you!'

'I did. I kept quiet, I knew you'd be cross with me if you saw me. You might have decided to take me back.'

Lynk was in the boat with me, and I had no idea. It's hard to take in.

'We grew up on earth, not far from each other but our paths never crossed, not until recently. As soon as I set eyes on you, aboard the school bus on my first morning at your school, I recognised you. I was looking at everyone nervously, as they were getting on to the bus. I was hoping there would be one friendly face, someone that would talk to me. You walked past, to a seat a couple behind mine. You smiled.'

We smile simultaneously at the memory.

'A few days later, you sat next to me, spoke with me and invited me to come trick or treating with you.'

I look at his face. Really look into his face. Why didn't I see it before? Lynk's face is practically identical as a human. I can't believe I didn't recognise him. I've been living in a dream world on earth. Very little of my experience there makes any sense.

'Hang on a minute,' I'm starting to see some synchronicities here. 'So how did you get back here?'

'Eucele had been trying to make contact with you. When he failed, he decided to approach me. His diverted strategy worked, I recognised Sike and Peta straight away. They occasionally popped in for tea when they were passing the Stable. Eucele suspected that I would be easier to communicate with because I hadn't come to earth on a set mission and had no prearranged existence in place. The veil of forgetfulness didn't affect me at all. When we arrived on earth, I had to be sure I was born to a family who lived near you. For some reason, I had complete control, but I did have to queue for the right family, you know.'

No, I didn't know. That explains why Lynk is a few months younger than me.

'I never forgot you. Following you to earth was my purpose.'

'I thought everyone forgot everything when they were born?'

'Not necessarily. Some humans have incredible recall, but it usually fades during childhood.' Thinking back, I'd often had dreams or unusual memories when I was young. My Mum put it down to an active imagination and told me not to be silly. Lynk continues his story.

'Sike and Peta relayed Eucele's message. They told me about the invasion of the Shadows and that your help was imperative. I explained what the green energy used in earth's nuclear weapons does and that it's also used as medicine. Though too much of it makes humans sick very quickly.' Lynk pauses. 'I planned to talk to you about it after the concert. I didn't want to spoil your birthday, otherwise I'd have told you earlier. Then you fell to the floor. I worked hard to save you, until others came and took over from me. Eucele then transported me back here. It took some dimensional time hopping. My Mum on earth still thinks I'm in central London with your parents, staying at the hotel. Whilst your parents think that I've been collected from them by my Mum and we've gone home.'

'You and your Mum came to the hospital to say goodbye. You were there. Your Mum was cuddling my Mum,' I remember seeing it all happen.
'That was the illusion, you were in the hospital bed with your higher consciousness wide open.'
I hug my friend in disbelief. How did Lynk the Second get better at understanding dimension hopping than me?
'My parents! I must get back to them soon, they'll be so worried about me.'
Lynk agrees 'They're desperately hoping you'll get better.'

Mary catches up to us and gives me a warm, welcoming hug. She doesn't seem angry with me that Lynk left and followed me to earth. Maybe she's mellowed with time. Hort, catches us up too and fills me in on the missing gaps of the story as we continue our walk towards the Shining Valley. 'The Light Council haven't been seen since their disappearance. Eucele is still searching for them, all leads have been dead ends.'
I stop listening. Finally, there she is. Hort stops talking when he realises what I am staring at. I can't see the top of her, she's shrouded by a lingering, floating green smog. She's still guarded by the trees, but they are merely broken and twisted trunks with bare branches. I'm struck by how stark the sky is above. Nothing. Absolutely nothing. How quiet it is with no Avians flying around. Every single one of them, gone, except for Eucele.

The poor mother tree: a pitiful sad sight to behold. I'm glad to see she's alive, but only just. Limp is the only way to describe her branches and her evergreen pines have long wilted. I lay the palm of my hands above her roots. I feel her struggle; she's in pain. She hasn't got long. I need to help her quickly. She has fought hard but has little left. She's exhausted.
'Let me help you.'
My hands are burning with the heat. I send my light down, through the contaminated ground, encouraging it to snake and wriggle deep, following her roots. It filters all the way down to the tips. She sways her branches a little, then opens herself up, stretches them out wide. She yawns; I feel her. She absorbs the positive energy; I pat her branch in encouragement.

'That's it. Dark times are over. You're needed.'
When she flourishes then everything else will too.

The Ondines will eventually return, when they know that it's safe for them to do so and the waters will flow once more. Not that I blame the Ondines for leaving; after all, I did too. At the time, we have to believe that what we are doing is right. They will return, just as I did, when the time is right. Shine some light, spread some warmth and things grow. No matter what world you inhabit or what gifts you have. The basic necessities for existence and growth are the same for us all. Wait, watch and see. Noir, his Shadow army and their green mists will soon be totally forgotten. They will cease to be important. Things will not go back to the way they were before, but that's fine. If they had been perfect as they were, there would have been no requirement for growth. Change is an inevitable part of existence.

Chapter 65: Another Goodbye

I too, have learnt a very important lesson. When you have reached the end, it's the point that a new beginning can start. If I make it back to earth, no! No if… when I make it back to the hospital! I know that I will never be the same girl again. I will be different, stronger. I will be rebornagain.

'I want to see my house. I assume it's still there?' I suddenly declare, completely off at a tangent.

Lynk laughs.

'Still there. According to Hort it was the resistance headquarters. Do you want me to come with you?' he offers.

'Yes, please do,' I'm proud to hear that my little hut has served well whilst I've been gone.

The others say their goodbyes to us and each other and break away into their familiar groups, searching for remains of their old homes or to look for pleasant spots to create new ones if need be.

'Mary!' I beckon Lynks' Mum over to me; I have something important to arrange. 'I would like you to take care of Zmeu.'

I lift the little lad from Lynk's back and hold him out towards her. She opens out her strong and capable arms and takes him from me without any hesitation.

'If I was going to stay, I would care for him myself, but I must go back, and I cannot think of a better Being to be his mother. I can't leave him all alone again.'

'Of course, I'll care for him.'

Mary likes to have someone to fuss over. I knew that she would take him gladly into her care. Lynk tells her to carry on to their home with Hort and he will join them there.

Phantome had been kept there, so it should still be habitable, if not homely. That will return in time.

'He won't be long.' I promise her. She rolls her eyes and the three of us laugh.

'What's so funny?' asks little Zmeu.

'You had to be there, Zmeu,' Lynk tells him.

'I want to know,' Zmeu is annoyed at not knowing.

'Come along with me, Zmeu.'

Mary insists and he follows her and Hort, not daring to do otherwise. They walk ahead of us.

I feel strange, I'm going home to another home. No wonder I felt confused, how many homes have I had? Remembering I sat in my little hut, almost thirteen earth years ago, waiting. Feeling dubious about the situation but completely committed to leaving. Doing as I had been asked.

'Has Eucele spoken of his plans?' I ask, wondering what he'll do now that he's all alone.

I would imagine the Atlantean Temple is a lonely place without the Avians. 'There are rumours that others of his kind, have survived and are living on the fourth dimension.'

This news is exciting, and I glow brightly. I'm so very fond of Eucele even if he doesn't smile. 'That's wonderful. Is he in contact with them?' I enquire.

Lynk shrugs.

'He hasn't said anymore to me than that,' He changes the subject 'Well, here it is, just as you left it; your little house.'

Quietly I go inside and the first thing that strikes me is how simply I used to live. I owned very little. Just my black pot, a stool and a few crystals still scattered around the place. My existence on earth on the other hand, has been filled with things in constant supply, yet I never valued them. If I want something, I get it. Truthfully, half of the time, I could manage without. I sit on the floor, my legs stretched out in front of me. Lynk gets down on his belly, his front legs sprawled out in front of him, and back legs sprawled out behind him.

'You want to go back?' he asks. I see no point in pretending otherwise.

'Yes, I do. My family wants me back. It's ironic, I've spent all this time wishing I could escape from earth and find my true home and now I'm free to choose, I miss my life; I miss Mum and Dad and I can't wait to play with Frieda again. What will you do?' I'm interested. 'You have two Mums, one here and one on earth. How will you possibly choose between them?'

It will be a surprise when I arrive back home to see whether Lynk has chosen his earthly life. Lynk doesn't answer, he doesn't have any answer yet, he makes that weird neighing sound that I'd forgotten about, the one he always makes when he's nervous.

'I could come with you,' Lynk offers.

'You need to do what's right for you, Lynk. You must walk your own path. Every Being must learn to do that. I've had to learn the hard way. I must choose what is right for me and besides, I've taken an oath. I know that I have to keep fighting. I'm not ready to give up.'

An oath! The words just tumbled out; I'd forgotten. The responsibility and duty of a Starseed that I had sworn to hundreds of moons ago.

'I know I'm never going to be the same again,' I try to explain, 'but do you know what? I wouldn't want to be.'

Lynk has grown so much during his time on earth. The planet only made me feel weaker. I couldn't settle, though I now know that's where I need to be. Where I want to be. Where I must go now. The crystal effect has gradually worn off. My powers of magic have dissipated. I can do no more in the astral world.

'Goodbye, Lynk,' I hug him. 'I'm glad we got to have one more adventure and who knows, we may have more on earth.'

I walk away with purpose. My back turned to my friend for a second time, looking for my way home. To my parents, my dog and to fulfil my mission. I travelled all that way to earth to help it rise to a fifth dimension and all I've done is hide myself away because I don't fit in. Well, guess what? I'm about to keep a promise and the humans won't know what's hit them.

Chapter 66: Fishing

One step at a time, along my own path. It's more of a track than a path, almost completely overgrown with giant ferns. Instinctively, I attempt to fly, forgetting my ability has ceased. It's just as well; Lynk wouldn't be able to keep up with me. Yes, he's been following me. Again. I've ignored him, hoping he'll give up but enough is enough. I turn and shout,
'Lynk, I can see you. Come out from behind there!'
He stays hidden. Frozen; pretending he's not there.
'I knew you were following me as soon as I left,'
He sheepishly steps from his hiding place behind the huge foliage and walks over to me. I fold my arms. I'm not happy.
'I thought I was doing so well,' Lynk huffs.
I laugh at him, 'You were terrible,'
We carry on down the hill, talking casually about Mary and Hort. The track leads to a field of grass. I realise where I am.
'I'm exactly where I need to be,' I unintentionally say out loud.
Lynk must remember the place too.
'Leave me here. I mean it. Go home and decide properly. This path is mine to travel alone,'
'I'll go home and put my hooves up,' Lynk jokes as we part company once again.
I sadly watch as his hindquarters wobble from side to side back up the hill. I didn't mention it, but his rear end has definitely got wider. Flashbacks of a boat coming out of the mists, sailing from one side of the lake to the other come to me. I can feel I'm in the right place but this time, the view is so much clearer and brighter. A crazy dragonfly darts in front of me, then flaps and glides across the water; a sure sign that the Onedines are returning. It has the brightest set of wings that I've ever seen with vibrant purple, teal and emerald tones, all blending into each other. Delicate threads of coloured silk. It's beautiful. This creature can also be found on earth; they have existed for two hundred and fifty million earth years. A symbol of survival and triumph. I watch it as it circles one way and then the other. Things are going to be alright here now. It dances here and there, zig zagging all over the place. All of a sudden, I realise I'm high up,

following this beautiful creature. I look down. I'm floating over the sea! I glance back towards the dragonfly. It's vanished. I frantically survey the sky for a glimpse, but it's gone. Had I imagined it? Some force suddenly takes control of me, and I fall. I can't stop myself. I can't resist the pull. No matter how hard I try to fight it. The waters of the sea are getting closer and closer. I'm plunging in headfirst. It all happens so quickly. I break through the water's surface, sinking at lightning speed. The force doesn't loosen its grip on me, it keeps pulling me down further and further. It's dark. The deeper I go the gloomier it gets. Unable to fight against it, I stop struggling, drop my resistance and relax. It's taking me whether I want to go or not. I focus on what I see. Enormous shapes swaying side to side, black and eerie. Shadows underneath the water. I can't quite work out what they are. Tentacles are trying to grab me as I sink. What is that? Something long and stringy wraps itself around my leg. I feel around and unhook it. The light above me has totally disappeared. The dragging and plummeting suddenly stops. I'm free to swim and move about. I stretch out and notice I've cleared the gigantic looming shapes. Something very large emerges from the murky depths ahead of me. It swims straight past me. A blue whale, making a loud high-pitched vibration. It echoes through the water. Trying to swim through the sound waves is difficult. Like fast currents they expand around the mammal, heading out in every direction. I try to swim forwards but find myself being pushed back. It's calling out a name, it's calling to another. I hear the name, but I cannot process it: it's not my language. I swim hard behind it. I'm chasing a tail, it's so big, it's all that I can see. He calls out again, louder this time. The vibrations rock me back and forth. It's affecting my head. The whale's call is answered. They talk to each other, and their shrill noise fills my ears, I want to scream it's so loud. The pressure is unbearable. I feel disorientated which makes it impossible for me to keep up and I find myself being propelled back towards the surface. I'm in a bad dream, let me out! Rocketing, I spin through the waters. I kick and thrashing my arms about. I'm leaving at a faster rate than I arrived, and I didn't think that was possible. The water splashes in my face. I can't catch my breath. I gasp and pant. Wait a minute, what do I mean I can't catch my breath? What am I saying? I roll and twist, spinning like a military warhead. I pass submerged trees. So that's what those large shapes were, underwater trees. Their branches were trying to grab me. I feel as if someone has hooked me on to the end of a fishing rod and reeling me in. I'm the catch of the day. The surface is just above me now. I see yellow light flickering; I can almost touch it. Water splashes in my face. I gasp for air, I gasp again, and again finally break through the water's surface, panting. But it's far from over. Hoisted gasping on the end of an invisible hook, I'm lifted higher and higher, dangling on the end of the rod. I look down. I'm high above a beautiful blue lagoon, with a small sandy beach around it. It looks smaller and smaller as I am thrust higher and higher. The rush of gravity overwhelms me. I can't see the land or sea, just the stars now and I feel really sick.

Chapter 67: Arrival

I've made it back in time. Doctors and nurses work busily around my bed. It's happened again and the alarm has been sounded. The medical staff with their big angelic wings come running in. Electricity surges through me, my body involuntarily hiccups, heaving with the shock. I must keep fighting, I tell myself; I've come too far to give up now. I must keep fighting. I'm filled with determination not to give in. I see the white light shining down, waiting for me. I shout,

'No, I'm not going!'

I've only just found my way back. Despite my insistence, I can feel myself slowly drifting towards it.

'No, I am not going!'

The light doesn't wait long for me this time. I think it knows; I've made up my mind. I've decided to stay. I know where I belong.

I'm aware of being tugged and pulled but I don't care. All I want to do is sleep. It's very dark. Someone is squeezing my hand; that's nice of them, I think. I hear a silent whisper, 'I'm here...' There's nothing more after that, I can't remember anything but the dark. They must come and raise my bed because I find myself sat up in a slouched position against the pillow. Has someone pressed a button and activated my senses? There's a whirling sensation inside my head. The wheels and cogs of my mind are slowly starting to turn for the very first time in a long time. Sparks are firing and connections are being made. I stir, move my foot. I'm waking up. Ahhhhh! A horrible buzzing sound deep inside my head fills my ears. It gets louder and louder. Such a bright light, someone turned the lights on. Turn them back off please! It's far too bright. I can't open my eyes properly. I'm having conversations in my head, whilst noticing white circles flash for a few seconds before me through the slits of my eyelids. The light hurts and I really want to go back to sleep. It doesn't hurt when I'm asleep. I sleep.

Chapter 68: First Steps

Shadows. Fleeting shadows: I jump with fright. How have they found me? I can see them, darting about the room. Are they attached to humans? Are they friendly? They appear to leap and jump, bounding towards me through bright light. I must be awake again. They bound over to the side of my bed. I can't get away from them, they have me trapped. I'm far too weak to move as they bend over me and peer at me. I must try though, I tell myself. I can't allow them to get to me now, so I try to sit up, I must get away. Come on Maya, you can do it, I encourage myself. You've got this far. Yes, I can. I pull myself up. I sit in my hospital bed and look around. They're not here now. They must have gone. Now is the time to make my escape. I need to wait for the blurriness and the blobs flickering in my eyes to calm down. That's better, I can focus. I slowly climb out of my bed. I've no idea how long I've been here.

Uhm, I feel sick. It must be the movement. Regardless of how I feel, I tip toe out of my ward's double doors, escaping through them unchallenged. Luckily, the nurse's station is deserted. I pass by the desk, through another set of double doors and along a corridor with a large window; the window the boat went out earlier. This time I walk down a flight of stairs. There are so many doors at the bottom, I feel confused. Which way is the exit? So many doors have me trapped, I see nothing but doors. Which door do I choose? I don't have time to waste. They'll realise I'm missing and come looking for me. Which door do I take?

I sit up in my bed, in a cold sweat and shout something, I don't know what. I feel rigid and my body aches. I have to get up, I need to go for a wee. I pull back the blanket and put my feet and legs over the side of the bed. I'm covered in bruises. I'm black and blue, brown and green.

I'm too numb to notice the coldness of the floor as I stand up. A hand grips my shoulder. The shadow has me. I defiantly turn to the side. I'm so surprised: it's my Mum!

'Where are you going?'

'Why are you crying? I need a wee.'

Mum calls a nurse over. Her face seems familiar. I think it's the orange hue eyes.

'It's nice to see you awake, mademoiselle,' she smiles. 'I will take off the wires, but they must go back on when you come back. Fetch me when she's done.' she orders Mum.

She closes the curtain around my bed and unclips lots of different coloured wires from circles that are stuck all over my body. I walk slowly, aided by my Mum to the bathroom adjacent to my bed. I look around the ward as I go. It has four beds in it. Two lined up on either side of the room, opposite each other.

Faces look back from their pillows at me with wide eyes, sunken with black circles around them.

I go into the washroom and hear Mum saying not to lock it. The first thing I do is turn and face myself in the mirror. My heart is beating as it should do. I look up to the bathroom ceiling and tell them, 'I'm stronger than you think.'

I don't know who I am talking to, but I know someone's listening. 'You'll have to try a lot harder than that to extinguish my light.'

I feel dizzy and grip on to the edge of the sink. I need to go back and lie back.

Chapter 69: Fred

I keep myself as busy as I can. Sitting up in my hospital bed, I upload selfies to my newly created media page, Heart Hero. I post a daily blog alongside various photos of me, posing, pouting and generally making silly faces whilst attached to my heart monitor. Mum brings a regular supply of books and magazines, but I can only focus for short periods of time. I watch the TV fitted to the white retractable arm that moves around my bed and play games on my phone. All these seemingly lazy activities that I used to spend hours doing, are hard work. I find myself drifting in and out of sleep and my sense of days and time is practically non-existent. The food here is good, especially the puddings. I don't have much of an appetite and my mouth and throat are constantly dry. I find sipping water every now and then helps. My cardiologist, Mr Behr Goodhart, has explained that I need an operation to fit a heart starting device into my right atrium ventricle. The Implantable Cardiac Defibrillator, known as an ICD, will automatically restart my heart if necessary. A battery powered device will be placed under my clavicle, more commonly known as the collarbone. Electrode leads from the ICD, will be passed through a vein and attached to my heart. This incredible device will constantly monitor the rhythms of my heart and if it detects any abnormality, will automatically discharge an appropriate level of electricity to restore my heart to its normal beat. Mr Goodhart lets me hold an ICD. It fits in the palm of my hand. A titanium alloy metal box. It's incredible to think this tiny piece of metal will more than likely save my life who knows how many times.

There's so much to think about. Dad says I should wear a medical ID bracelet or necklace and Mr Goodhart explains I will be given an ID card. I need to keep it with me when I'm not at home.

I feel a bit scared and apprehensive about having the procedure but it's the sensible thing to do. Mr Goodhart says I'll get used to it quickly and will probably forget that it's there most of the time; eventually. I'll be able to carry on living my life normally. It's reassuring to both myself, Mum and Dad that I'm protected and safe even when they're not with me.

Fred

Mum, Dad and I have been trying to think of a name for my implant.

'Zoe?' My first suggestion.

'What about Lightning? You could name it after that hamster you had when you were about five.'

'Dad! That's too creepy, I'm not naming it after my dead hamster!'

'How about Rupert? I've always loved that name,' Mum sighs dreamily.

'Rupert the bear? I don't think so,' I adamantly declare.

In the end we decide the device is a 'he' named Fred. A male version of Freida, my dog. Named after one of my pets after all.

After a month in hospital, finally the good news. Mr Goodhart has scheduled my surgery and, in a few days if everything goes well, I can go home.

A couple of days later, two porters come to collect me. I say a tearful goodbye to my parents, and I'm wheeled into the cath lab. As the anaesthetic needle is inserted into my arm, I count to see how long it takes for the injection to work. 'One, two, three... four...'

Chapter 70: The Shift and the Dream

Mum pulls my bag out of the locker. She passes me a pair of leggings and a tee shirt. Getting dressed for the first time feels strange. I've spent so long in a baggy nightgown; clothes feel tight and restrictive. Contorting my body into weird positions is so painful and saps all my strength. It takes ages. Mum rummages through the bag searching for a pair of socks when I see her brow furrow and her expression change to perplexed puzzlement. She digs deeper and pulls out something shiny and dangly.

'Maya, where did you get this from? I've never seen it before. It's very… different.'

There, swaying slightly from her fingers, is a black rope necklace. I instantly recognise the green eye stone and charms. I look at it in shock. It's the necklace from my dreams. My head is buzzing; yk how did that find its way into my bag? What is going on? It was just a dream!

I quickly deflect Mum's interrogation.

'Oh that? I've had it for ages.'

I take the pair of socks Mum's handed me and painfully start trying to pull them on. Mum drops my necklace back into my bag, satisfied with my explanation and takes over the sock task. I gratefully lay back. My mind is spinning.

My chest continuously hurts on the journey home. I feel every jolt, every stop, every brake, every bump and pit in the road. At least it's a short trip. Thankfully Dad takes it slowly. He can see me wincing and apologises each time.

Everything is a jumble of memories and pictures whizzing around in my inner eye. I shake my head trying to shut it out. Mum notices my distress.

'Are you feeling alright?'

'I'm completely and utterly confused,' I admit. 'I can remember bits, but my mind is scrambled, I'm trying to make sense of it all.'

'Would you like me to describe what happened?' Mum asks gently.

'Please,' I sit back, quietly prepared to listen.

The Shift and the Dream

Eyes straight ahead on the road, eager to absorb the coming information. Mum's voice starts shakily from the back seat of the car, directly behind me. I cannot see her face and I think that makes it easier for her to talk.

'The Havoc concert was ending. Do you remember that?'

I silently nod, a rogue tear rolling down my cheek. I swiftly wipe it away.

'Without any warning, you crashed to the floor, bumping your head as you fell. Lynk was incredible. He checked to see if you were breathing, and you obviously weren't. He instantly began to perform CPR. I was looking at you dazed and shocked. Trying to fathom out what had happened. I thought you'd fainted, and I was thinking what is Lynk doing? I didn't realise that you had no pulse. First Aiders at the event and support staff, all came running. Thank goodness they did. Dad had gone to the men's room, and it suddenly dawned on me that Lynk had not made a mistake. You were in a serious and precarious situation. You were pulled into the stairway and a defibrillator was produced. You were shocked again and again.'

I can hear that Mum is trying to keep all traces of emotion out of her voice. I can feel her eyes staring, boring intently into the back of my head.

'Your heart was restarted and when it was safe to do so, and as quickly as possible, you were blue lighted by ambulance to St George's Hospital in Tooting. On arrival you were taken into the Resus Department of Accident & Emergency. When you were deemed stable you underwent a cooling therapy. The nurse, the lovely French girl with the very long blonde hair, always wore it in a bun and she had very striking and interesting eyes, told me it was called Therapeutic Hypothermia.'

As Mum is talking, I involuntarily shiver.

Dad glances at me sideways, to check I'm okay.

'Cooling devices were used to lower your body temperature for twenty-four hours. You were unresponsive and the therapy could raise the chance of you waking up and reduce levels of damage to your brain. You slept, you were in a coma, and we waited.'

'I contacted Lynks' Mum and asked her to come and collect him,' Dad added as a side note.

I have to stop myself from laughing out loud as Lynk the Second had told me otherwise.

'Then the heart monitor started beeping and the medical staff all came running. Dad was sitting with you; I had just popped outside for some fresh air. He was asked to leave the room; you were in intensive care. The blind was put down at the door window and Dad called me to come back urgently.'

Still no emotion, I know that both my parents are feeling emotional, but they are trying not to let it all overspill for my sake.

'I haven't told you this,' Dad says to my Mum. 'But I was standing outside in the corridor, the door having been shut on me, and all I could hear was a cat's meow. I still have no idea where it was coming from.'

'That's strange,' Mum looks puzzled but carries on with the story.

'The use of a defibrillator saved you again. You carried on sleeping peacefully. We were hoping and praying. Bargaining for your safe return to us,'

I home in on Mum's use of the word peacefully. Little does she or dad realise or understand that I was here, there and everywhere, whilst I passed time in a coma.

'You were breathing using equipment and were given lots of medication. It was decided by the consultant that the medical team who were caring for you should try and wake you up. Medication was reduced, sedation medication and the breathing equipment was removed, and you were breathing on your own. You were confused and fighting; twisting and turning as you gained a resonance of consciousness. You were distressed and your heart rate set the alarm off. The staff with the defibrillator saved you once more. You suddenly became peaceful; it was almost like you finally accepted the situation that you were experiencing and stopped fighting. You rested and slept and healed some more. Then all the medication to keep you completely sedated was stopped. The bed was raised, and a lot of tubes and instruments were removed from you. You felt some pain and were very confused. You were frightened when the medical staff approached you. After some time when you could finally say something, not that I think you will remember, but you shouted 'Shadow' to a doctor who was trying to look in your eyes with a torch.'

She stops for breath. Dad concentrates on the roads, glad of the distraction. For me, this has all been a dream, but to my parents, this was their reality. I need to be conscious of that.

'You were then moved out of intensive care and into the children's cardiology ward, where you slept for the best part of a week. Unaided by machines, other than a heart monitor constantly attached to you by the leads. Until the point you dramatically threw back your blankets, trying to get out of bed, declaring that you needed a wee.'

I can hear the joy and relief in her voice as she reaches the end of the saga; from that point on I remember, so she does not need to go on any further.

'Is that okay? Does that help you at all?' Mum asks hopefully.

'Yes, thank you. Ouch...' I wince as we drive through a pothole. 'My ribs are hurting,'

The Shift and the Dream

As we reverse onto our drive, I can hear Freida barking excitedly. Dad helps me out of the car, and I look around our front garden, drinking in the seasonal changes to flowers and shrubs. I've no idea how long I've been away but this strangely feels as though I'm seeing where I belong for the very first time. Mum unlocks the front door and I step into my home.

You did it, I tell myself. You came back. Finally, I allow my tears to roll down my cheeks. Freida comes bounding up to me. I rub her belly and make a fuss of her, blinking through my tears. She smiles, anyone who owns a dog knows when their dog is smiling.

I wander around my house, reminding myself exactly what it looks like, then exhausted, I lie down on the sofa with my pillow, my quilt and my dog. She lays across my legs guarding me, just like Sphinx. Together we watch TV. The late news comes on. All the usual headlines flash up. The virus. Levels have slowly begun to reduce, that's good. The next report is a murder. I begin to drift off to sleep when the reporter's voice jolts me wide awake.

'Scientists around the world are investigating an incredible phenomenon. According to a spokesman from the European Space Agency, the earth has moved significantly on its axis. Vibrations were felt around the globe. Scientists are puzzled as to why this shift has occurred and what it means for life on earth.'

I sit myself up slowly and painfully. Freida cocks her head to one side and raises an ear, responding to my movement and possibly my quickening heart rate. The report switches from the studio to a reporter in Monaco.

'An eyewitness has described a shaking and rumbling sensation from the pavement she was standing on. At first it was thought to have been a series of simultaneous earthquakes, but now scientists have confirmed that the planet is now spinning on a position of higher coordinates.'

'Thank you, Beverley Fortune, our on the ground reporter, live from Monaco. For the latest on this and other stories, go to…'

It has started. We, the Starseeds, are slowly making progress. Today the earth started to ascend. She has far to go, as do I, but the start of the journey is what matters the most and we have both made the first step. I have work to do, but for now, I must rest. I close my eyes; thinking was that it? Was that all the news report had to say about the greatest shift on earth since it was struck by the meteorite that wiped out the dinosaurs! Still, they cannot know it's significance.

I drift off to sleep, the last thing I hear is a report on Debra and Darren the Dark Island couple who have been married for five months and are now getting divorced. I wake with a jolt. Checking my phone, it's three thirty-three. My thoughts race around and around in my head. I hate the noise of the quiet. I'm forced to listen to the loud sound of my heart beating. Its beat and rhythm echoes in my ears, as loudly as a train speeding down a track. I notice Freida has left my side. She's probably snuggled between Mum and Dad. All I can do is lie there, staring through my open bedroom doorway, into the darkness of the upstairs hall. I see something. Something that I've seen before. Pink neon lights flicker and flare in different directions. I slowly pull myself up and swing my legs over the side of my bed. The pink lines jig in the air and I purposely walk straight into them, causing an instant explosion of pink lights that multiply and shoot horizontally in both directions of the hallway. I stand in the middle of it all, soaking up the magic. How it doesn't wake my parents up, I have no idea, it's so bright.

The truth dawns on me. It was real. All of it was real. Intelligent elementals are here on earth. Not everyone can see them, but I most certainly can. After all, imagine if everyone could! I bask in the wondrous pink flare till they fizzle out and the hallway is left in darkness once more. Happy in the knowledge that it wasn't a dream, and dreams are not always just dreams. They can be a portal to somewhere else, magical.

Chapter 71: Surprise, Surprise

It has been a few weeks since I was allowed to return home. I'm desperate to find out if Lynk came back to earth or if he decided to stay with Mary. Mum finally agrees and insists on calling Lynk's Mum, to check if it's okay for me to visit for an hour. She then proceeds to give her copious instructions about what I can and can't do. How embarrassing!

'I won't overdo it,' I promise as she waves goodbye.

'Straight there and sit down. If you're not back in an hour, I'm coming to get you. Call me if walking is too much. Please be sensible Maya,' Mum begs.

She watches me walk down my street, the street that I've walked down hundreds of times. I haven't been out for so long. My legs feel wobbly as I move one in front of the other. It feels strange to be out. Out in the big world. Walking down a street. I don't get a chance to press the bell. Lynk's Mum is waiting to greet me.

'Maya, I'm so pleased to see you!'

She gives me a gentle hug on the doorstep, tears in her eyes. I wave to Mum, let her know everything is ok and go in.

'Where's Lynk?' I ask her.

She points into the living room and whispers quietly.

'I haven't told him that you're coming,' She offers me a drink and says to shout if we need anything, she'll be in the kitchen. He's sprawled on the sofa, tv on and playing on his phone. He looks like Lynk, and he sounds like Lynk.

'Maya, I'm so glad you're out of hospital, Mum wouldn't let me see you until you felt stronger.'

Something's not right. Something's different.

It's the way that Lynk is sitting. That's not how Lynk sits.

'Maya, it's me, Hort,' Lynk whispers to me.

'Wow, Hort! I wasn't expecting to see you again,'

'Thank goodness you're here now,' he says 'I haven't got a clue what I am doing with this human stuff. Lynk told me to constantly look at my phone and no one will suspect I'm not him,'

He holds up the mobile phone to show me. It's a dark, blank screen. He hasn't even got it switched on.

'I haven't got long, we need to start right away,' I tell him, 'And invite me around tomorrow when you get home from school, OK?'

Boy, have I got my work cut out!

Chapter 72: Keys to the Future…

We park in the shopping centre car park, so I don't have to walk very far. It's my first trip into town with Mum. She has an order that has arrived in store, so we need to go up a floor level to collect it. I step onto the escalator and hold on to the handrail. It's strange, the world looks different to me now and I see people differently too. I suppose that they don't annoy me so much. I'm more interested in them.

A lady with the most incredible red hair, can't help but catch my eye as she travels down the escalator. Red as rose petals it is, and I instantly recognise her. I've seen her before. As we pass each other, I'm compelled to speak.

'Hello,'

Will she recognise me? She smiles.

'Hello,' She pointedly looks at my necklace. 'You have all the keys you need now.'

Our escalator's transport us in opposite directions.

'Who's that?' Mum asks over her shoulder.

'Our school mealtime assistant,' I quickly improvise.

I can't tell her that the lady with bright red hair is called Tyra and she's the most powerful sorceress I've ever met.

Tyra turns as she reaches the floor below. She waves and I wave back. Mum interrupts.

'Look where you are going! I don't want any more trips to A and E.'

Is she wearing her sandals? I'm drawn to touch and feel my charm necklace. I put it on for the first time this morning. I play with it, pulling it out from underneath my shirt collar. Tyra gives me a quick thumbs up before walking away in the direction of the lower shops, and no, she isn't wearing her sandals. She's wearing flats. Whoever she is, she must live close by. I need to keep an eye out for her. I must speak with her, ask her more about the necklace and the keys. Our fates seem to be intertwined somehow. It seems we are on this mission together. For now, though, I must concentrate on getting stronger. There's no way I'm going to be allowed in town by myself for a while.

Thinking about the experience, I've learnt a lot. My most important lesson has been that it's not what happens to you that matters, but how you move forward from it. Reflecting on those lessons and choosing what you take with you on your onward journey through life. I am a warrior, and I will continue to rise; higher and higher. I have mysteries to solve. The first one being how on earth has Hort managed to swap places with Lynk and come all this way in his place? To me, it's obvious, but it appears his Mum hasn't noticed anything out of the ordinary, yet! I have a lot of work to do with Hort if we're going to pull this off long term. I have to give it to Hort, he is almost as brave as me. For now, though, we have some shopping to do.

I should have looked after my heart. When I look back, there were warning signs that I either thought weren't important or I chose to ignore. I now know how important it is to take great care of my heart and help it to stay strong. They can be easily broken and it's not always possible to tell until it is too late. As for me, I'm happy in the knowledge that it wasn't a dream, well, maybe some of it was. But dreams are not always just dreams. They can be a portal to somewhere else, magical.

Milton Keynes UK
Ingram Content Group UK Ltd.
UKHW020339160923
428761UK00012B/111

9 781912 358083